JORDON'S WAGER

JORDON'S WAGER

Frank C. Strunk

Walker and Company
New York

Jordon's Wager is a work of fiction. The people, places, and events are wholly
imaginary, excepting only the character Berkley Jordon who was inspired by
my grandfather, Isham M. Strunk. Buxton , King's Mill, Stanton County, and
the Middle Fork of the Cumberland River as portrayed in this story exist
only in my imagination. Any actual places are included by reference only.

First published in the United States of America in 1991
by Walker Publishing Company, Inc.
Published simultaneously in Canada by Thomas Allen & Son
Canada, Limited, Markham, Ontario

Library of Congress Cataloging-in-Publication Data
Strunk, Frank C.
Jordon's wager / Frank C. Strunk.
p. cm.
ISBN 0-8027-5771-5
I. Title.
PS3569.T743J67 1991
813'.54—dc20 90-12890
CIP

Printed in the United States of America

2 4 6 8 10 9 7 5 3 1

ACKNOWLEDGMENTS
With Deep Appreciation

To the memories of: Miss Besse Mahan Rose, who many years ago did her best to teach me the rudiments of the English language and to encourage me to write; my mother, Vessie Slaven Strunk, whose enthralling stories about the way it used to be in the mountains (where I was privileged to grow up) still power the movies in my mind; my grandfather, Isham M. Strunk (known to some, not entirely without justification, as "Bad Isham"), who surely would recognize more than a little of himself in Berkley Jordon; and Bill W.

To John S. Saia, M.D., Patrick C. Walsh, M.D., and F. Brantley Scott, M.D., fine, caring doctors without whose expertise, diligence, and intervention I probably wouldn't be here, or if I were, wouldn't much give a damn.

To my editor, Janet Hutchings, for valuable assistance and for helping to make the publishing of *Jordon's Wager* a pleasant and satisfying experience for me.

To Gary Provost, for generously sharing his abundant knowledge about the craft of writing and the making of books, for moral support, friendship, and . . . oh, yes, spiritual advice.

And finally to the people in my life who expressed optimism about my writing at times when I had begun to wonder: Al, Barbara, Bill, Charleen, Doug, Ernie, Gail, Glenda, Herbie, John, Julie, June, Keith, Lary, Linda, Nancy, Norman, Renn, Tom, Valerie, Virginia, the WRW gang, and probably others.

I thank you all.

JORDON'S WAGER

$\triangledown$

Chapter One

IT WAS JUST AFTER dark on Wednesday evening when Deputy Sheriff Berkley Jordon reached the Trotter place. He parked his Model A Ford at the gate and walked across the hard-packed dirt yard. The sound of women weeping came from somewhere back in the house.

Abel Trotter squeaked back and forth in the porch swing, smoking a cigarette in the orangey light from the front room window.

"Evening," Jordon said. "I'm looking for Chief Sewell."

"They're out there," Abel said, nodding toward a wooded ridge in back of the house. "I'll show you." He eased his skinny frame from the swing and hitched up the galluses of his bib overalls.

As Abel led the way with a flashlight along the narrow path into the underbrush, Jordon had the eerie feeling, so strong it was almost physical, that he was being drawn through a dark tunnel into an evil place. It was a feeling he'd experienced before, but he couldn't place exactly where or when. Trying to put it out of his mind, he asked Abel Trotter what had happened.

"Emma, that's my little girl, she found her."

"Found who?"

"Didn't they tell you?"

"Just that a girl was dead."

"It's Bitsy."

"Your daughter?" Jordon asked gently.

"Stepdaughter. Always been like one of my own, though. Never treated her no different."

Jordon thought he remembered seeing the girl around town. "I'm sorry for your loss," he said. After a moment, "What time did Emma find her?"

Abel glanced back over his shoulder. "A little bit after four."

In a small clearing up ahead of them, Jordon could now see silhouettes of two people standing in a dim pool of light from a lantern someone had hung on a tree. Jordon dreaded what he expected to find there.

At the clearing were Chief Ike Sewell and the county coroner, Homer Sprague. They greeted Jordon with nods. Abel Trotter moved quietly to one side as Jordon glanced around the scene, then hunkered down next to the body for a closer look.

Jordon had seen enough death in his time, he should have become used to the sight of it. But he hadn't. And he knew he never would.

The feeble light from the lantern cast monster shadows and did little to illuminate the details of the killing. Slaughter, maybe, was a better word for it.

Jordon shook his head and sighed. He slowly guided the powerful beam of his shiny, long-barreled flashlight over the dead girl's body and the area around it.

She was on her back, legs slightly apart, arms lying neatly along her sides, palms turned upward as though pleading. It was almost as if the gruesome scene had been arranged for viewing.

Blood soaked the front of her dress, covering most of the floral pattern. More than the sight of it, the smell of blood was what had always bothered Jordon, nearly made him gag.

The girl's throat had been cut, a gaping obscenity. Stab wounds ranged from her breasts to her abdomen—Jordon didn't try to count them—and several slashes marred her neck and face.

In spite of the blood and the face of death on her, it was easy to see the girl had been very pretty. She was small, a little less than medium height, and the close-fitting dress she wore made it clear she was well-built. She couldn't be more than nineteen or twenty, Jordon guessed.

"Messed her up real good, huh?" Ike Sewell said.

Abel Trotter looked away. He lifted a lean, stringy arm and with nervous fingers fussed with the strands of oily black hair that dangled in his eyes.

Jordon stared up at Ike. Why couldn't the bastard show a little feeling? Jordon had known him for years. And he wished to God he never had to work with him. Ike's head and body were like a slab of muscle and bone, and his manner fit his looks. He was Chief of Security for the Buxton Corporation, with law enforcement authority that extended to all the company's holdings, including its half-dozen coal camps in the county as well as the town of Buxton. He used his authority like a blunt instrument in the service of HR Buxton and his corporate hierarchy. Ike had been called since the girl's body was found on Buxton property. Jordon was here because custom and the law required that the sheriff's office be notified at once of any serious crime.

Jordon looked back at the girl's body.

Below her left ear he noticed a purple splotch, irregular in shape, about the size of a quarter. Her reddish blond hair covered some of it. It did not look like a bruise.

Jordon glanced up at Abel Trotter. "Birthmark?"

Abel nodded.

Homer Sprague spoke to Jordon. "They're bringing a truck to take her to Doc Klein for an autopsy. Unless somebody wants me for something else, I'm going on home." He started to leave.

"Looks like we got a murder on our hands," Ike Sewell said.

"You figured that out, huh?" Homer said, apparently trying to lighten things up a little.

Ike fixed Homer with an icy stare. "I was just remarking," Ike said. "No cause to show your ass."

Homer's eyes met Ike's for a moment, then flitted away. He said to Jordon, "You need me for anything?"

"I'll call you later if I do," Jordon said.

Homer turned and walked away, his flashlight aimed at the ground as he found his way through the undergrowth.

A half-hour later, sitting alone at the kitchen table in the Trotter home, Jordon watched as Abel carried a large blue-and-white speckled enamel pot from the cast iron kitchen stove and poured coffee for the two of them. Jordon glanced around the small room, wondering if some kind of fracas might have taken place there today. The place seemed abnormally neat.

From another room came a woman's shuddering sobs.

Jordon's eyes scanned the wooden table, straight-backed cane-bottom chairs, the stove. Kindling box and coal bucket. Fly-specked bare bulb dangling from the end of a cord in the middle of the ceiling, casting a sickly light. In the corner, a sink with a single faucet, a luxury not found in a lot of coal camp houses. Jordon saw no sign that would suggest anything unusual. A coal camp kitchen. Just neater.

Abel pulled a chair out from the table and sat down. "Sugar and cream," he said, nodding toward the covered bowl and small can of Carnation condensed milk in the middle of the table.

"Black's fine," Jordon said, sipping his coffee.

"You said you wanted to ask me some questions," Abel said finally.

"I'd like to find out anything you might know about Bitsy's death."

"What do you mean?"

Jordon took a little notebook and a pencil from the pocket of his coat and placed them on the table. "What I mean is, what do you know about it?"

"Nothing. Just that she's dead is all. What are you saying?"

"I thought maybe you might have some notion who killed her. Or why."

"It sounded like you think I know something about it."

"Do you?"

"I told you, nothing."

From the bib pocket of his faded overalls Abel took a bag of Bull Durham and began to roll himself a cigarette, spilling some of the flakes of dry tobacco on the table, then sweeping them away. He extended the bag toward Jordon, who shook his head. "Don't use them," he said. "Look, why don't you just tell me what you do know. Whatever that is."

"Like what?"

"When was the last time you saw her?"

Abel scraped a kitchen match across the bottom of the table, waited until the sulphur flash had died down, and lit his cigarette. He took a deep drag and blew the match out. "A few minutes ago. When they carried her out and put her in that truck."

Jordon wondered why he was being so difficult. Or was he just dumb? "I mean alive," Jordon said drily.

"This morning when I left to go to town."

"What time was that?"

"Maybe about nine-thirty or ten."

"Bitsy was here then?"

"Right here in the kitchen." Abel sucked hard at his cigarette and inhaled the smoke deep into his lungs.

"What time did you get back?"

"About three o'clock, it was."

Jordon made a note in his little book. "Where was Bitsy then?"

"How would I know? She wasn't here, I know that."

"What about her mother? Does she know when Bitsy left?

And where she went?"

"Whyn't you ask her stead of me?"

"I plan to," Jordon said quietly, "but I thought maybe you and me could get some of the details out of the way first."

"I'd just as soon go get her."

Jordon nodded and took another sip of his coffee as Abel went into the next room. In a moment he returned with his wife and a little girl, saying, "This here's Myrt. And Emma."

Myrt Trotter was a heavyset woman somewhere past forty, wearing a shapeless faded dress with an indistinct striped pattern. She dabbed at the red puffiness of her eyes with a wet washrag and pushed a loose strand of graying hair back out of her face. High on her left cheek was a bruise, not too old, Jordon figured from the color.

Close behind the woman, holding onto her dress, trailed Emma, very blonde and very thin and frail-looking. Her bright blue eyes were wide with wariness. Jordon stood and tried a smile on the woman and child as they entered the kitchen. The woman said, "Abel got you some coffee?"

"Yes, I'm fine. I hate to bother you right now, Mrs. Trotter, but I need to ask you all just a few questions."

Mrs. Trotter pulled out a chair and sat. Emma huddled close to her.

Jordon again tried smiling. "Don't you be scared, Emma. I just need to find out what you all know about Bitsy's . . . uh, whereabouts today."

"You know my name?" Emma was surprised.

"Your daddy mentioned it a while ago." Jordon smiled again. He reached into his coat pocket and pulled out a few roasted-in-the-shell peanuts. Field rations, he'd begun to think of them lately. He offered them to the child.

She looked at her mother, got a nod of approval, then accepted the gift and mumbled a thank you.

"How old are you, Emma?" Jordon asked.

"Nine." She cracked open a shell, put the nut in her mouth and began to chew it.

Jordon watched her for a moment. She looked younger than nine, smaller. He'd have guessed not more than six or seven. Her eyes showed she'd been crying, too, but now she was preoccupied with the peanuts.

"You know who I am, Emma?" Jordon said.

Emma shook her head from side to side, not looking at him.

"I'm Deputy Sheriff Jordon. I need to ask you all some questions."

Emma again looked at her mother, who nodded.

"Your daddy said you found Bitsy out there in the woods this afternoon," Jordon said in a gentle voice. "Will you tell me about it?"

The little girl was silent for a moment, then she started to cry.

Her mother said, "She can't talk about it right now." She put her arms around the child and patted her shoulder.

Jordon felt terrible, wishing he did not have to put them through this. Still he knew it could not be avoided. He sipped at his coffee and waited.

At last Myrt Trotter spoke. "Let me tell you."

Jordon nodded.

Mrs. Trotter made another pass at her eyes with the washrag, then wiped Emma's face and started talking, so low that Jordon had to lean forward to hear her clearly.

"It was right after four o'clock when I sent Emma out to the end of the ridge to fetch Bitsy." Mrs. Trotter patted the child on the head. "She's feeling puny and I been keeping her out of school. Anyway, when she hollered and hollered and didn't get no answer, she went on out to the clearing and that's when she found her. Emma run all the way back here and told me. And then we all lit out for the clearing and there was Bitsy, laying there . . . dead." She wiped her eyes again.

Jordon waited a moment before he spoke. "Right after four, you said. You sure about the time?"

"I'm sure," the woman said. "The four o'clock whistle at

the lumber yard reminded me. It just finished blowing."

"How did you know she was out there in the woods?" Jordon asked.

"That's where she went."

"What time was that? When she went?"

"It must have been about two or a little after."

"Why did she go out there, did she say?"

"Didn't have to," Abel Trotter said. "She done it all the time."

"What for?"

"To be by herself," Mrs. Trotter said. "That was her place, out there in that clearing. Been going there I don't know how long. For years."

"What did she do back there?"

"Just read and think, I reckon," Mrs. Trotter said. "Used to go there to study when she was in school. Had herself a little bench-like made out of a log. It's cool and quiet back there, and when she had time, she just liked to go off and be by herself. That's the way she was." Mrs. Trotter began to sob again.

"Did anybody ever go there with her?" Jordon asked softly.

"Oh, no," Mrs. Trotter said between sobs. "Bitsy said it was her private place, and she made us all promise we'd let her keep it that way. She took me out there once, just to show me, but that's the only time. And Abel, I reckon she took you out there once, too, didn't she?"

"Just that one time is all." Abel stared at the table. "We all respected her wish and let that be her little hideaway. A girl, or anybody else, needs time to be by herself once in a while." He looked around the kitchen. "And there ain't that much room in this house, or any other coal camp house, for that matter."

"How old was Bitsy?" Jordon asked.

"Eighteen," her mother said. "Last May."

"Was Bitsy her real name?"

"It was Lizabeth," she said, pronouncing it with the

emphasis on the end. "We started out calling her Betsy, then we changed it to Bitsy cause she was always so little."

"Either of you have any idea who might have done this? Anybody who'd have any reason to want to?"

Abel and Mrs. Trotter shook their heads as Emma busied herself with the last of her peanuts.

"What did Bitsy do?" Jordon asked. "Did she have a job?"

"She was working part time for the Buxton company."

"Doing what?"

Mrs. Trotter answered, "At the telephone switchboard. And sometimes in the office for Mr. Graham." After a moment she added proudly, "Bitsy graduated from high school a year ago."

Jordon made another note in his little book.

"Tell me," he said, "did Bitsy have a boyfriend?"

"Well," Mrs. Trotter said. "Not really."

"Exactly what does that mean?"

"He was more like just a friend. You know?"

"What's his name?"

"Farrell Nilson. Lives with his folks on the road to Little Horse Creek. Him and Bitsy went to school together, till he quit. They used to go places some, but he ain't been here for a while now."

"Something happen that caused him to stop coming?"

"Not that I know of," Mrs. Trotter said. Abel shook his head.

"You know the Nilson boy's folks?"

Abel Trotter spoke. "His daddy's dead. Name was Zack."

Jordon studied the red and green flowered pattern on the table's oilcloth cover for a moment before looking up. He remembered Zack Nilson from many years ago. And not fondly.

"Anybody else Bitsy went out with?" he asked.

Mrs. Trotter furrowed her forehead as she searched her memory. "There's a Three-C boy. But she ain't seen him for a while neither."

"His name?"

"It's a funny name. Manochio," she said. "Sal Manochio. He's a Eyetalian, Bitsy said."

"You know how to spell it?" Jordon asked.

"Eyetalian?"

"No, ma'am. Manochio."

She shook her head, and Jordon wrote it down the way it sounded to him, below Farrell Nilson's name. "She have any arguments with either one of them that you know anything about?"

Mrs. Trotter said no. Abel got up and poured himself another cup of coffee, extending the pot toward Jordon, who shook his head.

"How about girl friends? She have any?"

"Lenarue Wooten was her best friend. She was about the only girl Bitsy ever run around with very much."

Jordon made a note of Lenarue's name, asked for and got the name of her father and where the family lived. It was a mile or so from the Trotter place. Jordon took a sip of the strong black coffee, getting some of it into his mustache. Brushing it away, he asked, "Is there anything else you can think of that might help me in any way to find out who . . . did this thing to Bitsy? Anything at all?"

Mrs. Trotter shook her head and started to sob again. Emma joined her, hugging her mother's leg and burying her head in her lap.

Jordon stood up and said, "I won't bother you folks anymore tonight. I'm sorry I had to trouble you and for what's happened. I'll do everything I can to find out who did it." After a moment, he added, "And see that they pay for it."

Abel Trotter stood up too and followed Jordon out onto the little front porch.

From the top of a ridge somewhere off in the woods came the frantic whoops of a dog, a series of full-throated bugle calls. Jordon cocked his ear. A spirited Walker hound hot on the trail of a fox, it sounded like.

"How's the election going?" Abel Trotter asked. "You going to be our next high sheriff?" Abel was standing so close Jordon could smell the sweetness of moonshine on his breath.

"Hard to say." Jordon took a peanut from his pocket and cracked it. He held it for a moment, then tossed it away. "Everybody figures it's going to be close. I reckon they're right."

"For whatever it's worth, me and mine'll be voting for you."

Jordon gave him a little nod. "Right now my mind's not much on politics. Yours neither, I know."

"I just wanted you to know."

"Yeah." Jordon stepped down off the porch and walked across the yard.

Before starting his car, he sat behind the wheel for a moment, letting some of the tension drain from him.

He could hear the hound in the distance more clearly now, baying frantically as he closed on the fox. Jordon couldn't remember how long it was since he'd been in the woods on a fox hunt. As much as he enjoyed it, he wondered why he didn't go more.

He imagined he was there on the ridge now, sitting by the fire with a few buddies, sipping good moonshine and enjoying the chase. Maybe playing a little poker.

He listened some more. If the fox was cunning enough, soon it would circle and double back across its own trail, then go to ground, leaving the dog to wear himself out trying to figure out which path was the right one.

If the ruse worked, it was all over for the night. On the other hand, sometimes none of the fox's maneuvers succeeded. Sometimes a dog with heart and brains, staying with the hunt until the end, took his prize.

Reluctantly pulling his attention away from foxes and hounds, Jordon considered returning to where Bitsy's body was found and looking around some more. He decided he'd do better if he came back in the morning.

He started the car and headed for Cassie's. He hadn't
called her as he'd meant to. But he was tired. He needed to
see her, just to be near her and feel her life and warmth. Most
of all, he needed for at least a little while to blot out the
picture of Bitsy Trotter and her pleading hands lying there
in the woods in her blood-soaked dress.

$\triangledown$

Chapter Two

JORDON HELD THE FORD near the center of the narrow ribbon of blacktop as he wheeled around the steep curves of the mountain road to where Cassie lived.

He gripped the steering wheel with his left hand, reached into his coat pocket, and took out a handful of peanuts. He hadn't eaten since breakfast.

Cracking one of the nuts, he deposited the shell on the seat next to him and popped the kernels into his mouth. He began to munch as he shelled another. He'd loved the damn things since he was a kid, and he'd never been without them since. Well, hardly ever.

The peanuts often came in handy these days. For Jordon, missing meals had become routine. Running for high sheriff himself as well as being chief deputy for a retiring sheriff who was laid up with rheumatism was no small challenge for a man now on the far side of fifty.

It was harder than being high sheriff himself, Jordon thought. And it paid a lot less. But the biggest difference was, a deputy was basically a hired hand. And that's all he'd ever been. As high sheriff, he'd be elected to public office by the people of the county. He'd like that, just once in his life. For a lot of reasons. He'd like to show his son and daughter, and Cassie—and himself, too, damn it—that his life amounted somehow to more than just drifting and gambling and being some sheriff's hired hand. Unless it happened in this election, though, Jordon knew it never would. Not at his age. This was his first, and last, time to run for public office.

He took the wheel with both hands again and concentrated on his driving. He tromped down on the accelerator, anxious now to get to Cassie's. Underneath his hunger for her, he felt a prickle of resentment at his growing need for this woman. He didn't like needing anybody.

Jordon relaxed on the sofa and watched Cassie pour the sparkling clear moonshine from a quart fruit jar into their glasses, then come around the little table and ease herself down beside him.

"A bad day," she said. It wasn't really a question.

"A bloody day. Took Luke Purcell in for stealing and slaughtering a hog. Then had to go look at a poor butchered girl. A lot more blood than I wanted to see."

"Isn't it awful about Bitsy Trotter?"

"You heard already?"

"The party line. Three more people have called to try to tell me since I first heard it."

"The damned telephone," he said, shaking his head.

"What about it?"

"I think sometimes we were better off before Buxton put it in. At least bad news didn't spread so fast."

"How could you do your job without it?"

"Seems to me we did just fine," he said. "And had more peace. Anyhow, like a lot of other things, we got it, good and bad alike."

He massaged his eyelids with his fingertips. "Days like this make me think I'm in the wrong line of work." His voice was heavy with weariness.

"Somebody forcing you to stay in it?"

He glanced at her, then lifted his glass and took a long swallow of the whiskey. He shook the glass and watched the

bead quickly disappear. "Ransom Creech still makes the best
straight corn in three counties." He set the glass down and
looked directly at her. "Nobody forces me to stay in it," he
said evenly. "Or do anything else."

"Whose fault is it, then, when you have days like this?"
A sharp edge had crept into her voice.

Jordon heaved a weary sigh and stared at his drink. "Is
this going to be one of those times?"

"What times?" She moved away a little and turned to face
him directly.

"Shit, Cass. What is it makes us quarrel and fuss when
we ought to be getting along?"

"Are we quarreling and fussing? I thought we were talking.
Do you want to quarrel?"

He held up his hand. "Oh, no. No. What I really wanted
was to come over here and have a drink of this confiscated
whiskey with you. Maybe sit here and hold you a little bit.
Listen to a couple of your Victrola records." He sipped his
whiskey. "Quarreling was the last thing on my mind."

"You know what time it is?" she said, looking at her
watch. "You didn't call."

"I know. It's late. Nothing I could do about it."

"Your buddy Willis called, said you'd be getting in touch
with me. I killed a chicken. Cooked shucky beans with
boiled potatoes. And now it's nearly eleven."

Jordon took a sip of whiskey. "I know it."

Cassie wasn't finished with it. She nodded toward the wall
by the door. "There's the telephone. The way we left it
yesterday, you were going to be here for supper at six-thirty
or seven at the latest. Don't you think I have feelings, Berk?"

He smiled and reached for her hand. Maybe he could
charm her out of it. "You're the only person in the world
calls me Berk."

"A smile won't do it. Don't you think I have feelings?"
she repeated, pulling back.

He looked into her glistening brown eyes. Eyes that reminded him for the world of the eyes of a doe. He could stand almost anything except to see a woman cry. He knew they sometimes did it for that very reason, to get to a man. But it didn't make any difference, he still couldn't stand it. One thing about Cassie, she didn't do it a lot. "Are you going to start crying? Because if you are, I better go. I mean, I've already had about all the trouble I need for one day."

She looked at him with defiance. "I'm not going to cry. I know you don't like it. I don't either. But, damn it, Berk, it's more than six months we've been going together. What's going to happen to us? I never know what to expect." She swept a bit of moisture from underneath her eye.

Jordon almost wished now that he'd gone home and read himself to sleep. "Can we talk about this later? It's not the best time in the world for me right now."

"Will there ever be a good time?"

"I've told you there will be."

"Yes, but when? When, damn it?"

"After the election. Whatever happens, win or lose, we'll get straightened out. We will." He squinted his eyes shut, rubbed the lids with a thumb and finger, squeezed the bridge of his nose.

She looked at him for a long time. The expression on her face began to soften. She pushed a strand of hair out of her eyes and seemed to relax a little. Then she set her glass on the table and, a moment later, leaned forward and kissed him on the cheek. Finally she said, "I know you've had a rough day. You didn't come here to listen to me bitch. It's just that I worry so about you. About us."

He took her hand and squeezed it.

"I'm not trying to run your life," she said. "I just know what you do for a living, and I get so damned scared. I lost one man six years ago, and I thought they'd have to bury me, too. I don't believe I could go through something like that again."

"You're not going to have to go through it again. I know

how to take care of myself. Been doing it long enough."

She rose and took him by the hand. "Come on in here and I'll feed you. You've got to be starved."

He started to say something, but she interrupted. "I know, I know. Your peanuts. But once in a while you need a decent meal. The chicken and beans are cold, but I reckon they won't kill you." She led him into her spotless little kitchen. As she put the food before him, she flashed a devilish smile. "I may even be able to find you something special for dessert after while."

As Jordon ate, he told her what little he knew about Bitsy Trotter, leaving out the more gruesome details.

When he'd finished and they were on the sofa again, he leaned back and stretched out his legs. She turned off the lights except for a dim table lamp across the room.

"Let me take off your shoes," she said. "It's the least I can do after climbing all over you when you got here."

"I've got no objection to you climbing all over me, if nothing else will satisfy you," he said with a grin. "Just don't talk so much when you do it."

She moved closer and began to undress him, ever so slowly. "You know, mister, I might not put up with your bullheadedness if you weren't so good-looking."

It pleased him that she found him attractive, though it was hard for him to imagine why. His thick shock of straight black hair was beginning to turn gray, no longer just at the temples. And there was a hardness in his face, a network of lines left by the years and the life he'd lived that neither his mustache nor anything else could do much to soften. At least his body was still in pretty good shape. At five-eleven and a hundred-seventy-five pounds there was little fat on him. But good-looking? Only a woman with her vision clouded by love would think so. "You ever thought about having the doctor check your eyes?" he said with a grin.

"My eyes are fine," Cassie said, fumbling with a button on his shirt. "What I need, I can't get from a doctor."

He slipped his arm around her, pulled her close. "You're a shameless hussy," he said. "You know that, don't you?"

"Of course."

He kissed her roughly. For a moment, he thought he might try to tell her about his growing feeling for her, but he just was not able to say the words. He wasn't sure why.

She had stripped off the loose black coat he wore with his badge pinned over the left pocket. Now she was working at the skinny black tie and white shirt. "Stand up," she ordered, and he complied. She quickly removed his gun, belt, trousers, and the rest.

"You don't leave a man a hell of a lot of armor, lady."

"You think you need armor around me?" she said. Then, "On second thought. . . ." She flashed her wicked smile once more. He loved the way her front teeth were a little bit out of alignment, all the more pleasing to him for their imperfection.

His undressing of her was done faster, with less patience. When she was completely naked, he held her at arm's length, put his hands on her shoulders and slowly turned her full circle, bringing her to face him again, admiring every part of her. At forty, her body was no longer that of a girl, but of a pretty, mature woman in her prime. His eyes feasted on the fullness of her breasts, the slight mound of her belly, the graceful sweep of her hips. How beautiful she was. "By God," he said, pulling her to him, "you are some woman."

"Are you planning on looking and talking all night. Or did you have something else in mind?" she whispered.

He picked her up, stepped through the pile of clothes on the floor and carried her into the bedroom.

"You love to do this, don't you?" she said.

"Carry you to bed? I do love it."

He placed her on the bed, her head on a pillow, and lay on his side looking at her. In the half-light from a dim table lamp, he could see her watching him. As gently as if he were touching the edge of a butterfly's wing, he brushed back a wisp of her dark hair and kissed her forehead, her eyes, the tip of her nose, then at last her lips, searching with his tongue, finding his way inside. He pulled back and studied her face. She meant more to him than he had thought any woman ever could again after so many years. He kissed her once more and drew her to him.

"Wait," she whispered, pulling away. "Here." She eased him over on his back, kissed him on the chest, nuzzled her face against the mat of graying hair. "A man who's had a day like you've had shouldn't have to work at night, too."

"I haven't yet reached the point where I consider it work."

"Hush."

The time for talk had passed. Her hands found familiar places and brought responses that held no surprise, only delight.

Soon she straddled him and took him inside. When her slow, measured strokes had become too urgent, he turned her on her back and drove them with a steady rhythm to the top and over the edge.

Later, as she lay with her head cradled on his shoulder, he wondered why he had not been able to say the things to her that he felt in his heart. Why he couldn't tell her he felt himself slipping ever more deeply under the spell of her. Before he could think it through, his mind went on its own to the woods behind the Trotter house, and he saw again the tiny body in the bloody dress. He tried to pass from it, but the picture lingered.

Finally, as he drifted away, he felt Cassie's hand on his cheek, heard her mumble, "Bullheaded."

At breakfast Jordon was groggy, unable to shake off the drug of sleep. Cassie had arisen early, before he was awake, in the manner of mountain women. She built a fire with newspapers, pine kindling, and coal in the kitchen stove, made biscuits, eggs, coffee, then called him.

After he'd eaten and was sipping on a second cup of her strong black coffee, she said, "You were restless during the night. Was it the white mare?"

He nodded, knowing she had waited to mention it. A bad dream will come true if you tell it before breakfast, old folks said. And whether you believed it or not, it was impolite to bring it up.

She reached for the pot and topped off his cup. "It's only a dream."

So it was. But not just any dream. It was that big white mare again. Like always she was lazily grazing in a rich rolling field, far away toward the horizon. He stood there watching her, so at peace.

Then the white mare raised her head and looked his way, started walking slowly toward him. He saw her come, knew what was about to happen. He wanted to turn and run, but was held spellbound by her beauty, the rhythm and grace of her movements, despite her massive size. Sixteen or seventeen hands tall, she seemed to be.

She started to trot, coming straight at him, then broke into a gallop. Now he was turning, but it was like being in a river up to his chest, so he could only move slowly and with great effort.

He tried to run, to escape the white mare, but he knew it was useless. Looking over his shoulder now. Seeing her coming closer, closer, nostrils flared, mane flying in the wind. Now right on him, rearing up on her hind legs, her front hooves slashing like knives through the air above his head. Snorting, whinnying, her face full of fury, striking, striking at him with those sharp flailing hooves. He trying to run, to scream for help, but unable to do either.

He realized he was dreaming, but that did nothing to ease the sickening, mortifying fear he felt. If he could scream loud enough, he knew he could wake himself. Escape once more.

He remembered waking last night, as he always did, just before the mare struck him.

And then he remembered Cassie, cradling him in her arms, stroking his head, lulling him back to sleep.

Now Cassie stood next to him, still holding the coffee pot. "It was just a dream," she said quietly. "Don't let it bother you." She set the pot down, put her hand on his shoulder.

"It always seems so damned real," he said. He'd told Cassie about it once before, when they were talking about whether dreams really meant anything. Told her about how he'd had the same one from time to time since he was a young man. Not recently, but often in the past. And always it seemed to come just when something awful was about to happen.

He'd had it before he went into that battle in Cuba in 1898. When he got pinned down by Spanish rifle fire and thought it was all over. Again before that bloody hand-to-hand encounter in the Philippines when they'd come unexpectedly upon a village full of insurrectionists, when he'd been slashed on the arm and it got infected and some of the doctors wanted to cut it off.

And that time at Stateline, when the two men, just for the goddamn sport of it, had pistol-whipped him, beaten him nearly to death before he got away from them. He went home and got his guns, came back and killed them. He'd seen the white mare two nights before that.

And he'd dreamed about the mare in France, before going into battle at Belleau Wood, where so many of his buddies died in the muddy trenches, as he'd thought he surely would too.

Other times, too, he'd dreamed about the white mare. When he was in prison, the mare was there, three days before he received the news that Vera was dead. Sweet, gentle Vera who would have been better off if she'd never heard his name, much less married him and borne two children for him.

That goddamned white mare, always coming across the field for him, following him around all his life, trying to kill him in his dreams, and predicting the worst things that had ever happened to him.

Cassie squeezed his shoulder. "It's only a dream," she said once more.

"Yeah," he said. "A dream." He stood up to go, gave her a hug and a lingering kiss. "Thanks for taking me in last night. I'm glad I didn't have to go to Danny's and maybe wake them up in the middle of the night." He walked into the front room and put on his coat. "I'm still not sure I did the right thing moving my stuff in with him and his family. The boy's got enough responsibilities without being bothered by his no-account daddy."

"I'm sure he and Mary Helen are glad to have you," she said as she straightened his tie. "I know I am. And you're not no-account." Then she smiled. "Even if you do thrash around in bed all night."

"Look," he said. "I'm going back over to the Trotter place and poke around some more this morning. Then I've got a dozen other things to try to get done. *But*," and he held up his right hand, "I, Berkley Jordon, do solemnly swear that I *will* call you this evening before it gets too late. Okay?"

She shook her head. "Not this evening. Not here," she said. "Tonight I work. Tomorrow night, too. Della called yesterday and asked me to work more hours, more nights."

"How come?"

"Business is picking up. This depression sure hasn't kept men from finding money to spend at Della's."

"Most folks find a way to do what they really want to," he said.

"Especially men folks."

He ignored it. "Things still going all right for you out at Della's? Any trouble?"

Her smile was all sweet innocence. "Now who do you know who'd risk his life by giving me trouble? When everybody knows Deputy Sheriff Berk Jordon's courting me?"

"Some of Della's customers get a little bit more moonshine than food in them sometimes and it interferes with their judgment. Just be sure you stay out of their reach."

"Drinking around Della's? Why, Deputy Jordon, how could you even think such a thing? It's a plain old simple restaurant. Have you forgot about Prohibition?"

"Don't devil me, lady. I've got serious business to tend to today. Maybe I'll come by and see you at Della's this evening and have a bite to eat."

"And get a look at Della, too, huh?"

"After what you did to me last night? The only thing I'm interested in today is work."

"Then go," she said, pulling his head down for a final peck.

As he got in his car and headed for the Trotter place, Jordon's mind was a jumble of things competing for attention. He needed to do some campaigning, had to if he was going to have any chance to pull this election off. But even if he gave it his best shot, could he win? He wanted to believe he could. Wanted it a lot more than he'd have been willing to admit to anybody, maybe even to himself. But could it be done?

And then there was that damned white mare after him again. What was it going to be this time? Or was the whole thing just his imagination? A damned superstition. Something to do with the pressure he was feeling.

Casting its shadow over everything else, though, was the matter of the dead girl.

$\triangledown$

Chapter Three

THE MORNING SKY WAS clear but the sun's anemic autumn rays delivered little warmth as Jordon drove up the last leg of the road to the Trotter place.

He parked the Model A in front of the gate and walked across the barren yard to the small frame house. Dirty blisters of white paint were peeling from the weatherboard walls, and the green-framed windows needed washing. The yard itself, however, was free of junk. A swing made from an automobile tire hung from the limb of a hickory tree near the fence.

Though this one could have used some tending to, Buxton houses generally looked a cut better than most Jordon had seen in mining towns around the Eastern Kentucky coal fields. Of course, the town of Buxton wasn't actually a mining camp, but rather the commercial hub old man Buxton had built to serve his half-dozen outlying mining communities.

Abel Trotter sat rolling a cigarette in a rocking chair on the front porch. Jordon paused in the yard just long enough to tell Abel he was going back out on the ridge and look around some more.

"You want me to come?" Abel asked.

Jordon told him no and headed around the house and

along the path to Bitsy's retreat.

It was a little clearing, no more than twenty feet across, but it looked like a small park the way she kept it. Except for the footprints of those who were there last night, the place was neat.

It was too bad Ike had not kept the scene closed off to everyone. Footprints or something might have been left by Bitsy's murderer. Jordon looked around carefully anyway, but found nothing. There was very little blood or evidence of struggle.

He was inching his way around the outside rim of the clearing, about ready to leave, when he noticed what he thought was another path. Not well-defined, or well-used, but it led off through the woods, in the opposite direction from which he'd entered the clearing.

Jordon followed it as well as he could, not always sure which way it turned since the undergrowth was so dense. Working his way through the woods and brush along the ridge for upwards of a quarter of a mile, he came upon another clearing, smaller than the one where Bitsy's body had been found. He stood at its edge, slowly and carefully scanning it, trying to register everything he saw. It was a sort of natural nest in the woods, surrounded by large boulders, near the foot of a huge cliff.

Jordon could see signs that people had been there. No distinct footprints, but scuffled dirt and pine needles. In a large crevice between two of the rocks, he found an area filled with leaves, indented as though someone had lain there.

Stooping down to examine it more closely, he saw a splatter of something dark on the nearby ground, near one of the huge stones. It looked like blood. He moved some of the leaves and saw more of the same. It was blood, he was sure now.

He pushed the leaves away and could see where a lot of blood had soaked into the ground. Someone had covered it with leaves, intending no doubt to hide it completely.

In the silence of the woods, Jordon could hear his own
heart beating, pumping life through his body, the way Bitsy's
heart had done until its final throb here where he knelt.

Now he knew why there was so little blood in the other
clearing. She must have been stabbed here, have died here,
then been carried through the woods to the other place. Why,
he wondered, had her killer felt it important to move the
body? What difference did it make?

He searched the area very carefully now, particularly
around the nest of leaves. He discovered a little mound of
fresh dirt, no larger than his hand. Digging it away with his
fingers, he found four cigarette butts. Somebody had
smoked, then buried the butts, not an uncommon thing for
smokers in the woods to do. Jordon examined the butts. Two
were Camels, two Avalons.

He searched the area some more, methodically working
back and forth across it so he would not miss any part. On
the other side of the clearing from where he'd found the
blood, he spotted another cigarette butt, not covered up, this
one a roll-your-own, containing some kind of dry, flaky
tobacco. He tore a sheet of paper from his notebook and
folded it into a small envelope, then placed the butts inside.

He was about to leave when a slight gust of wind caught
something white on the ground just outside the clearing and
moved it a little. It was stuck at the base of a mountain laurel
bush. He walked over to it, bent down and looked. It was a
crumpled piece of paper. He unfolded it and saw it was a
page from a small notebook, with pale blue lines for writing.

On the paper, written with a pencil in a fine, delicate
script were the following lines:

> *Soon, Oh soon, I'll fly away, but not to Glory Land,*
> *A place where fate directs me, to sea, to sun, to sand,*
> *I bide my time a little more,*
> *I'll walk with him along the shore,*
> *My heart awaits its destiny, the time is soon at hand.*

The writer had marked through the last line, then scrawled a dozen back-and-forth slashes through the rest of it before wadding it up and throwing it aside.

Jordon sat down on one of the rocks. He studied the paper and the place. He tried to imagine who might have come here, smoked cigarettes with Bitsy, and stabbed her to death. He wondered who she might have dreamed of walking with along the shore. Wondered if it might be the one who had killed her.

Looking further, circling the area carefully, Jordon found another path leading off between two of the huge stones, into the woods. He followed it, wondering where it came out, trying to reconstruct the nearby geography in his mind from what he remembered about it.

He had gone only a little way, maybe an eighth of a mile, when the path turned over the hill and descended steeply to the bottom of the ridge.

There Jordon found a flat sandy area with a dirt lane leading away from it. In the sand were tire tracks.

He bent down and studied them carefully. He could see there was a notch in one of the tracks, like a crescent had been cut in the rubber of the tire by something sharp, maybe a broken bottle. The squiggly treads were similar to those on his own car. Probably made by a Ford, he figured.

Jordon took out his notebook and carefully made a sketch of the tire print, including the cut and where it was located on the tread.

For a moment he let himself think about what his life might have been like if he had made more effort to develop his natural ability to draw and sketch. It had always been just a hobby, something he could use to amuse himself and others, but he had never stopped wondering what more it could have become had he pursued it. Like a lot of other things in his life, it was a question without an answer.

Folding the drawing and putting it into his pocket, Jordon made a careful search of the area. Several used condoms, liquor bottles, and cigarette butts littered the ground. Jordon followed the lane through the woods for a short distance until it came out on a dirt road.

Jordon thought he knew this road, but to be certain, he walked along it for a little way toward a bend just up ahead. When he rounded it, he saw a ramshackle old frame house, unpainted and in general disrepair.

He recognized the place, had driven by it before. An old woman named Rachel Blackwell, must be in her seventies, maybe older, lived there. She made and sold herb remedies. And some folks said she was a witch. Jordon hadn't believed in witches since he was a boy, but he knew lots of folks who did. And having seen Rachel out in town a few times, Jordon had to admit the old woman was right strange looking.

The yard was littered with junk; old tires, tin cans. A dominecker hen was scrunched up on top of the rusting remains of a Model T Ford. And by the fence was a one-horse wagon with the two back wheels missing.

Jordon decided to get back to his car. He'd drive around and talk to Rachel later, find out if she'd seen anything or anybody out of the ordinary on the road recently.

He retraced his steps down the road and along the path, up the hill to the clearing where he'd found the cigarette butts and blood, and the hopeful little verse. He backtracked to where Bitsy's body was found, then finally returned to the Trotter home.

Along the entire route, he scanned the bushes and ground for anything that might have been left by the murderer, but saw nothing.

Jordon looked at his watch. It was a little after ten-thirty. Abel Trotter was still sitting on the porch. Jordon said, "I'd like to talk to you and your wife a little more now if you're not too busy."

Abel nodded and hollered, "Myrt!" A moment later she appeared at the door, drying her hands on her apron.

Jordon stepped up on the porch and half-sat on the

handrail while Mrs. Trotter came out and took a seat in the swing.

Jordon pulled the piece of paper with the verse on it out of his pocket and handed it to Mrs. Trotter. "Did Bitsy have a notebook like this?" he asked. "And is that her writing?"

Mrs. Trotter studied it a long time before nodding. Then she said, "Yes, it's in her hand. It come out of her notebook."

"You have any idea who she might have been talking about? Who the man might be she dreamed of walking along the shore with?"

Mrs. Trotter shook her head.

A gray-striped short-haired cat slunk onto the porch from the yard, eyed Jordon for a bit, then arched its back and rubbed against his leg.

"How about you?" Jordon asked, looking at Abel.

Abel stared out into the yard and said, "I don't have no idea."

Looking back at Mrs. Trotter, Jordon asked, "You know where Bitsy's notebook might be?"

"She had more than one," Mrs. Trotter said. "But she never left them around where anybody could see them. I don't know where she kept them."

"What did she write in them?"

"She never let nobody see. Once she said she was trying to write songs, but she wouldn't let us see them." Mrs. Trotter looked as though she might be about to start crying again this morning. "You know the Carter Family on the radio? She thought they might buy some of her songs."

"Did she ever send any of them in?"

"I don't think so," Mrs. Trotter said. "But I don't know for sure." She looked down at the porch. "Bitsy kept a lot of things to herself. Ever since she was a little girl, she never would talk much about what she was feeling or thinking."

Jordon felt he could understand a little about Bitsy Trotter. He was that way himself.

The cat was tracing a continuous figure-eight in front of

Jordon's feet, sweeping against his shins with each pass. It was beginning to distract Jordon, who gently nudged it away with his toe.

"Did Bitsy smoke?" he asked.

Mrs. Trotter nodded. "Sometimes."

"You know what kind?"

"Avalons mostly."

"One other thing," Jordon said. "Did Bitsy have a purse?"

Again Mrs. Trotter nodded. "It was about this big," she said, holding her hands about eight inches apart. "Blue. Leatherette."

"You have any idea where it might be?"

Abel and Myrt Trotter both shook their heads.

"I didn't find it out there on the ridge. You think it might be around here someplace?"

"No," Mrs. Trotter said. "She kept it with her all the time. Had it when she went out there yesterday. I remember."

Jordon thought about asking them if they knew about the second clearing, but decided against it. If he did, they'd either go there themselves or maybe tell somebody else about it, or both. And he didn't want anybody tromping around there. Or even to know he'd found where Bitsy was actually killed.

He took the paper from Mrs. Trotter and said, "If you will, ma'am, I wish you'd look every place you can think of where you might find any of Bitsy's notebooks. Or anything else of hers that might be of any help to me. Anything at all. However little it might seem to you. Let me be the judge of it. Will you do that?"

Mrs. Trotter nodded gravely.

"And if you find anything, call me at the sheriff's office." He stepped off the porch, then turned back to face them. "When's the funeral going to be?"

"Tomorrow," Abel said. "They're bringing the body home this evening. We'll set up with her tonight. And then bury her at the Maple Grove cemetery at two tomorrow."

Jordon nodded and said, "I'll be talking to you all later."

As he started to drive away he glanced back at the two of them sitting in silence, each staring off in a different direction. The little girl, Emma, had come out onto the porch and huddled next to her mother, looking up into her face.

In the yard, the gray cat stalked a bird at peril of paying a high price for not having flown south.

Jordon stopped at a crossroads general store not far from the Trotter place. The proprietor, Othel Marcum, was one of Jordon's supporters in his campaign for sheriff.

One of the large posters Jordon had had printed up was in the front window of the store, just underneath a sign that said, "Bruton's Snuff—Sweet and Mild," along with posters of a couple of candidates for other county offices, and a sign advertising Lydia Pinkham's remedy for unspecified female complaints.

Jordon paused a moment to look at his poster and the photo he'd had made for the campaign. He wished he hadn't looked so damned solemn. He smiled enough when he was with friends. He just found it hard to do, somehow, when he knew he was posing. Shit.

Anyway, he guessed most folks would figure he looked tough enough to be sheriff. Underneath the picture it said, "Vote for JORDON for SHERIFF." And under that, "Reliable. Experienced. Sober." He smiled. What the hell, he thought. Close enough for politics.

Inside, Othel was putting canned goods from open cartons up on the shelves running along the walls below the pots and pans, horse collars, garden tools and nine thousand other things Othel stocked and displayed.

Jordon always loved the smell of a general store. The aromas of cheese, tobacco, bacon, spices, leather, coal oil and a multitude of unidentified substances melded into something that was homey and pleasing.

Jordon greeted Othel and the half-dozen loafers who comprised his court, then asked to use the phone. He cranked the handle and when the operator came on said, "Sheriff's office." While he waited for the call to go through, he asked Othel to get him a dozen eggs, some flour, salt and coffee, stuff he'd drop off at Cassie's later.

When Willis came on the line, Jordon said, "Just checking in."

"Nothing much happening here this morning," Willis said. Jordon felt sorry for Willis having to spend all day, every day, in the office, passing along messages, being a go-between, talking to disgruntled citizens, some with real problems, others just born complainers. Jordon remembered how much pleasure he and Willis used to have before Willis lost his leg. Hunting together, chasing women, dancing. Back then, Willis could do a buck dance that would stop everybody else on the floor. They'd just all stand back and watch his feet fly. But a man who went into the mines to make a living often ended up trading more for his wages than he ever would have bargained for.

Suddenly Jordon remembered when he'd first had the feeling he'd experienced last night going through the woods to where Bitsy Trotter's body lay. That feeling of being drawn through a dark tunnel into a dreadful place. It was when he was just a boy and his Uncle Cal had taken him back into a coal mine so he could see what it was like. Uncle Cal had to walk all stooped over because of the low top. The farther they went into the tunnel of damp, cold darkness, the worse Jordon had felt, until finally Uncle Cal had said, "This here's fur enough, I reckon. You can see what it's like, can't you boy?" Then Uncle Cal had pointed a finger to a spot right before them, and said, "A cousin of mine was killed right here, crushed to death in a rock fall." Jordon had felt like running out, but had resisted it and stayed next to Uncle Cal. Jordon was only nine or ten at the time. But that must have been one of the reasons he'd never felt comfortable in the mines. Maybe that's why Uncle Cal had taken him back there in the first place.

Willis was saying through the receiver, "Are you there? Or have you gone to sleep?"

"I'm here," Jordon said. "I was just thinking about something."

"Well, as I was saying, Noble called a while ago. Wants you to check in with him at home."

"I was planning on doing that," Jordon said.

"Only other thing I know is Doc Klein's office called. Said he'd have a report on that dead girl ready for you before the end of the day. You can go by his office and pick it up. What happened out there yesterday, anyhow?"

Jordon could see that the men in the store were watching him, listening to everything he said. He told Willis, "I don't have time to fill you in right now, but I'll be in later today and give you the details."

"Everybody in the county probably knows more about it than I do," Willis complained. "Hell, I'll probably end up having to beg one of the operators at the switchboard to tell me what's going on," he said. "And me a deputy." He hung up.

Jordon looked at his watch. It was nearly noon. He bought a Coke and waited for Othel to get his stuff ready.

"Bad about the Trotter girl, huh?" one of the loafers said.

Jordon nodded. "Bad."

When he said nothing else, they didn't press him further.

"How's the election going?" one man asked. "Folks say it'll be close."

"I expect so," Jordon said. He'd never learned the right way to pretend it was already in the bag for him. He understood it was a good tactic, and he knew pretense was one of a successful politician's most useful skills. It just didn't come naturally to him. "I hope you all are going to vote for me."

A couple of them nodded, and the others glanced away. No one said anything.

Jordon finished his drink, then cranked the handle of the

phone again and got the sheriff on the line.

"Come on out to the house," Noble told him. "I'd like to
go over some things with you." Jordon said he'd be there
shortly, thanked Othel for the use of the phone, and paid for
his groceries.

"I could use some more of your cards to hand out," Othel
said. "I'm just about shet of the ones you give me. I think it
looks pretty good for you in this precinct."

Jordon promised to bring Othel some more campaign
material in the next day or two. He said so long to the
bench-warmers and left.

Fifteen minutes later, Jordon pulled into the driveway of
Sheriff Noble Treadway's home and parked in a gravel lot
that was large enough for a dozen cars. He walked along the
flagstone path to the front door of the large, two-story red
brick home.

Noble's shiny Packard sedan rested in the garage, alongside a new tan Model A roadster. Taking it all in, Jordon
reflected, as he had many times before, that being high
sheriff wasn't the worst way to make a living in the mountains. At least the way Noble did it.

Of course, over the years Noble had never been far from
the center of the political life of the county, often serving in
one office or another. A career politician.

While holding public office had never been a high priority
for Jordon before, this time he wanted it. He wanted the
financial security, the freedom to make his own decisions
about how to do his job, and yes, he wanted a sense of
acceptance, or respectability or whatever it was called.
Maybe some of this, most of it even, had come as a result of
his involvement with Cassie. But whatever its name, or
wherever it arose from, Jordon knew it was important to him.
And he wasn't sure he liked that very much. Things got too
important to you, you became a slave to them.

Jordon's knock on Noble's front door brought an almost

immediate response. Standing there holding the door open
was Noble's wife, Bonnie, her brown eyes sparkling, a smile
playing at her full lips. "Come in, Jordon. The sheriff's
expecting you." The way she said "the sheriff" sounded like
she was referring to someone other than her husband.
Maybe that's the way she thought of him.

"Thanks," Jordon said, and stepped inside. He knew
Bonnie from way back, long before she'd married Noble. She
was a handsome woman with chestnut hair who couldn't
have been much more than forty now. She wore a pretty blue
dress which was tight enough to reveal that she was still
well-built, a little on the juicy side. A woman who radiated
an unmistakable sexual energy. Jordon didn't know if it was
intentional, but it was definitely there. Until he'd gone to
work for Noble, Jordon hadn't seen her for years. But Jordon
still remembered with pleasure some of the evenings he'd
spent with her in those days, the way she hadn't been
fettered the way a lot of women were with ideas about what
was proper when she was alone with a man. He still felt a
little tingle just standing so close to her.

"Were you about to say something?" she asked, smiling
at him with a twinkle in her eyes.

He shook his head.

"Well, then, the sheriff's back here." She led him into a
large beautifully furnished living room with a fire smoldering
in the open stone fireplace.

Noble sprawled in an overstuffed chair facing the heat. He
twisted around to look at Jordon as they entered the room.
"Come set," he said, extending his hand but making no
effort to get up. "Damn rheumatiz just about got me on my
last legs." Noble had to be somewhere past seventy now,
Jordon figured.

Jordon shook his hand and took a seat near him.

Noble looked at his watch. "Almost noon. Ain't had
dinner yet have you?"

Jordon shook his head.

"Good." The sheriff glanced up at his wife who still stood nearby, waiting. "Bonnie'll fix us up something, won't you, darlin'?"

Bonnie said of course and left the room. A wisp of sweet perfume haunted the place where she'd stood.

"Fine woman, Bonnie," Noble said. "Been a hell of a comfort to me since my first wife died. Must be what? Ten years and better. Hell of a comfort."

"I'm sure she is," said Jordon.

"How is it you never decided to get married again?" Noble asked.

Jordon shrugged. "Rolling stone, I guess."

"Well, after the election, you get to be high sheriff, you can get yourself a couple of good deputies and relax a little bit. Find time to get married again even." Noble glanced toward the fire. "Throw another log on there and poke it up a little, will you?"

Jordon selected a large piece of oak and laid it on the fire, pushing it into place with the poker. What a comfortable life Noble had provided for himself, Jordon thought, by practicing the art of politics with shrewdness and patience.

Jordon finished fixing the fire and returned to his seat. "You wanted to see me?"

"Tell me about the Trotter girl."

Jordon told him most of what he'd found out, including the cigarette butts and the poem fragment. For some reason, he wasn't sure why, he didn't mention the tire tracks. Maybe they weren't significant anyway. Noble didn't interrupt him with any questions.

When he'd finished, Jordon waited. Noble digested it. "That's it, huh?"

Jordon nodded. "Not a hell of a lot at this point."

"Most of the killings I've ever seen—and I've seen a few—hell, we knowed right away who it was done it. Somebody in the family usually, or somebody there'd been a quarrel with, or a jealous husband or boyfriend. No big mystery. But once in a while something like this comes along."

They sat in silence for a few minutes. Finally Noble spoke again. "It's a terrible thing about that young girl. It surely is. But it'll get you elected sheriff for sure if you can find out before the election who it was done it."

Jordon had not thought about this aspect of the murder before, but he realized what Noble said was probably true. He felt uncomfortable with the idea, but he pushed the feeling back and said, "The election's less than two weeks away."

Noble stared into the fire and nodded, his eyelids drooping, reminding Jordon of a lizard sunning itself on a warm rock.

Jordon waited. When Noble said nothing, Jordon finally spoke. "Helluva way to get elected, huh? Ride in on the back of a dead girl."

Noble sighed. "That's the way things go sometimes. In politics, you learn to take advantage of whatever comes your way. And not ask yourself too many questions about it."

Jordon studied Noble, who continued to study the fire. Noble never seemed to twist and turn much over the fine points of questions involving ethics. It was as though, to Noble, this was a world he had nothing to do with designing. He was only passing through, and he tried to make the trip as pleasant as possible, looking out for himself within the wide boundaries of his own beliefs about the way things are, not how they ought to be. It was a neat trick, Jordon knew, if a man could do it. Sometimes, though, Noble cut it a little too close for Jordon's taste.

"Before the election or not," Jordon said, "I'm going to do my damnedest to get to the bottom of this thing. That girl was butchered up something awful. I'm glad I'm not Doc Klein having to examine her. It looked like the work of some kind of animal."

"There's some animals around, all right," Noble said.

"Speaking of which, what's this about Luke Purcell and a hog being stole?"

Jordon didn't mind changing the subject. "Judge Payton called me into his office yesterday. Old man Hacker was with him, madder'n hell. Said he heard one of his hogs squealing, just before dark the day before yesterday, and went to the door in time to see Luke and somebody else, maybe one of Luke's boys, running through the woods with his hog in a coffee sack. He swore out a warrant, insisting that it had to be served at once, before Luke and his house full of kids could eat up the evidence, he said."

"So you picked Luke up?"

"The judge said go do it, right then."

"You don't work for the judge, do you?" Noble was eyeing him coldly.

"I work for you. But I thought you were trying to get along with the judge. The election and all especially."

"I do try to get along with him. Up to a point. I've got friends running, including you, even if I ain't running myself. But if you'd have called me, maybe we could have put off taking Luke in for a while. Could have maybe saved you a few lost votes." Noble looked directly at Jordon and added, "Which I expect you'll be needing."

"I expect you're right." Jordon felt a little foolish. Damn it, he thought, he should have called Noble. It was just that his mind didn't work like that, like a politician's ought to.

"Luke give you any trouble?"

"Not really. I drove out near his place and parked in the woods. Then cut through the back way, and there in the woods, maybe a quarter of a mile from the house, was sign of where he'd butchered the hog. Or somebody had. Blood on the ground. A few shovelfuls of fresh dirt scattered around. But not enough to really cover it."

"Folks in bad shape," Noble said. "Steal a hog, bring it home and butcher it, then wait for the law to come. Stealing's a serious offense in the eyes of the law, even if some folks don't act like it." He heaved a sigh. "Unless something's done pretty soon about this damned depression, though, hog stealing's liable to look like the least of our problems."

Jordon nodded, but said nothing.

"You probably don't pay much attention to such things," Noble said, "but did you know that more folks voted Democrat last fall than any time in history? Things are that bad."

"Looked to me like somebody sure needed to do something. And I reckon Roosevelt's trying to."

"But hell fire, man, the Democrats damn near carried this county. For the first time ever. That's going a little too goddamn far. I mean, we don't need no New Deal here in Stanton County. I kind of like the Old Deal, considering I'm part of it."

"I see they're sending in a little food for the relief."

"It's going to take more than grapefruit and Red Cross flour. Anyway, most people around here are ashamed to go pick it up and carry it home. It's not exactly something to make a man proud. Folks need work."

"There's the WPA. They're putting a few men to work. And some of the young fellows going into the Three-C's."

Noble nodded, but looked doubtful. "Some name. Civilian Conservation Corps. You been out to the new camp?"

"Drove by a couple of weeks ago. But I'm planning to stop in out there later today."

"How come?"

"The Trotter girl had been going out with a Three-C boy."

Before they could discuss it further, Bonnie Treadway appeared in the doorway. "I've scared up a little something for you boys to eat if you're ready."

Jordon stood up and Noble reached for his hand to pull himself to his feet. Standing upright, he looked down at Jordon. Noble stood six feet four and weighed more than two hundred and fifty pounds. Nobody gave him a lot of shit when he was in his prime. Or even now, for that matter. The

two men followed Bonnie into the dining room where she'd
scared up more than a little something for them. Consider-
ably more than grapefruit and Red Cross flour.

It was mid-afternoon by the time Jordon got to the CCC
camp.

The neat wooden sign at the entrance read, "U. S. Government, Civilian Conservation Corps." CCC—or as the
local people called it, "Three-C's." One of the cards in FDR's
New Deal that had fallen in Stanton County.

Jordon drove inside and down the wide gravel street flanked
on both sides by half a dozen long, low wooden barracks
painted light tan. The area was deserted except for two young
men in olive drab uniforms raking leaves. At the end of the
street stood a flat one-story frame building with a flag flying
on a tall pole and a sign that said "Headquarters."

"I'd like to speak to the man in charge," Jordon said to the
skinny young clerk with fine blond hair who fussed with a
stack of papers at a desk just inside the door.

"Anything I can help you with?" the boy said, barely
glancing up. He looked like he couldn't have been shaving
for more than a year or two.

"Not unless you're in charge here." The tone of Jordon's
voice snapped the clerk's head up. For the first time the
youth noticed the badge on Jordon's coat, the gun on his hip.

The boy stood up, hitched up the wool olive drab pants
that were too big for him, adjusted his glasses and said, "Just
a minute."

He crossed the room, knocked on a door marked "Private"
and entered without waiting. In a few seconds he was back
and said, "Captain Sweeney can see you."

Jordon nodded and went into Captain Sweeney's office.

Sweeney stood up and reached across his desk to shake
hands. His grip was firm. He, too, was dressed in CCC OD's,
but he was beginning to run to fat and the uniform fit snugly
on his short, powerful body. He wore round, steel-rim glasses

like the clerk's. "Sit down," he said. "What can I do for you, sheriff?"

"I'm a deputy," Jordon said. "My name's Jordon. I understand you've got a fellow here named Sal Manochio. I'd like to talk to him."

"About what?"

"About a murder."

"What! Sal Manochio?"

"That's right. I have information he's been involved with a girl that was murdered yesterday."

"What on earth are you talking about, man? I know Sal Manochio as well as any of the boys here. He's no murderer."

Jordon looked at him evenly. "I didn't say he was, captain. I said I wanted to talk to him about a murder. See what he might know."

The captain calmed down a little. "A girl was killed you say?"

Jordon nodded. "Lizabeth Trotter. Called Bitsy. According to her folks, she'd been going out some with this Manochio fellow. I'd like to talk to him. Is he around somewhere?"

"This is a federal reservation. You know that, don't you? Your jurisdiction ends at the gate, unless you're requested to come in."

Jordon stood up. When he spoke his voice was cold and hard. "I'm investigating a murder, captain. I can send to the federal court in London and get a warrant for us to come in and take your Sal Manochio. Or I can bring in a U.S. marshal to do it for us, if that's the way you'd rather go." He'd need a lot more reason than he had now if he tried to do it that way, Jordon knew. But Sweeney probably didn't.

Sweeney stood up too. "Hold on a minute, will you? Give me a little time to let this sink in. Sit back down."

Jordon sat. "Is there some reason you think Manochio needs protecting from routine questioning? Something you want to tell me about?"

"Nothing. No reason at all. I was just surprised. I don't mind if you talk to him. I just mentioned this is a federal

reservation, that's all." Sweeney fussed with some papers on
his desk, evidently trying to save face.

Jordon leaned forward in his chair and looked straight at
Sweeney. "Where can I find the boy?"

"You'll have to come back later. He's out with a crew in
the Kady's Knob area, working on a fire road."

"You know where he was yesterday afternoon?"

Sweeney took a deep breath and sighed. "Same as today.
Kady's Knob. They've been working out that way for a week."

Jordon's mind quickly reviewed the geography involved.
Kady's Knob was something like two miles through the
woods to where Bitsy's body was found. "Any way Sal could
have slipped away from his crew for a while and not be
noticed?" he asked the captain.

"No. I mean, I don't think so. They work in the woods,
but usually at least two of them go together."

"What time will the crew be back in camp?"

"About five o'clock this evening. You could see Sal then."

Jordon made a couple of notes in his book. "What kind of
fellow is he?"

"What do you mean?"

"Is he easygoing? Rough? Rowdy? A drinker? What can
you tell me about him?" Jordon leaned back in his chair and
stretched out his legs, ready to listen.

"He's a clean-cut Italian kid from New Jersey. Minds his
own business mostly. Kind of high-tempered, but cools
down quick, too. Writes to his folks regular. Gets along with
the other boys okay. Likes girls well enough, I gather. A hard
worker. He'd never kill anybody."

"You notice anything unusual about him yesterday evening when they got back in?" Jordon was watching Captain
Sweeney carefully.

"I don't even recall seeing him . . . " Sweeney was looking
at the ceiling, seeming to search his memory. "Yes, I did,
too. He was in the mess hall when I went through there,
talking with a couple of his buddies."

"You notice anything at all?"

Sweeney shook his head. "Nothing. I'm sure he's the wrong person to think might do something like this."

"If that's so, he's got nothing to worry about." Jordon stood again and started for the door. "I'll get back over here sometime this evening, maybe about six. Tell Sal to stick around, but don't say what it's about. Okay?"

Sweeney came around the desk, stuck out his hand. "Sure. Sorry we got off on the wrong foot. I want to cooperate with the local authorities to the fullest extent possible. We've got lots of work to do here in this county. And we need all the help we can get." Sweeney seemed sincere. "You come on back tonight."

They shook hands and Jordon left. On the way out, he checked his watch. He decided to head for the sheriff's office in King's Mill. After that he'd go to Buxton, stop at the company office and talk to the people Bitsy had worked with. Then he'd still have time to go by Doc Klein's office and pick up the autopsy report.

Another day on the run. At least today he'd had a decent dinner at Bonnie Treadway's table. And last night chicken at Cassie's. Becoming downright domesticated.

Crossing the courthouse lawn in King's Mill, Jordon had a chance to shake a few hands and ask for some votes. But his heart wasn't in politicking today. He was preoccupied with Bitsy's death.

In the sheriff's office Willis Dobbs was puffing on a Camel and talking on the phone. Jordon and Willis were the only two full-time deputies Sheriff Noble Treadway had. Both men reported directly to Noble. The two of them had known one another since they were boys. They worked well as a team, a fact Jordon was grateful for. Had there been friction between them, his job would have been infinitely more difficult.

"Yes, ma'am," Willis was saying into the telephone, "I

know bootlegging's against the law. And we're doing all we can to stop it." He listened for a minute, then said, "Yes, ma'am, I know the good Lord frowns on drinking and them that approves of it. Believe me, we'll get somebody on it right away. You can count on it."

Jordon shook his head in wonderment as he thought about the conversation he and Cassie had had last night about the telephone, the part the thing played in their lives today.

Willis hung up the receiver and rolled his eyes. He ran a hand through his short, cinnamon colored hair and gave Jordon a sour look. "You finally find time to stop by, did you? That was old lady Cross from out Slater's Creek way. Says Rufus Tinch is bootlegging moonshine right off of his front porch out there. Wants something done to stop it. Now. Jesus!"

"Upset, is she?"

"Upset?" Willis turned his hands palm up. "Hear her talk, you'd think somebody take a drink of whiskey the Lord's gonna come right down here and shake his finger in the fellow's face and tell him to stop it, by God, or go straight to hell. And if the Lord don't do it, old lady Cross'll do it for Him. Whew, that old woman gets going, she can burn up a telephone wire." Willis blew on his hand and shook it.

"Sounds to me like you got it under control," Jordon said.

"Well, by God, you heard me promise her somebody'd be out there. And there's just me and you. Who do you think's going to go?" Willis pressed the palms of his hands flat on the desk and pushed himself up. He reached for the crutches leaning against the wall behind him and swung his short muscular body expertly around the desk, where he rested on his one leg.

"I don't have time to go sneaking around to try to catch Rufus Tinch selling whiskey," Jordon said. "How about Burrhead Dillon? He's the constable in that district. Give it to him."

The tone of Willis's voice was like that of an impatient teacher to a slow third grader. "It's Burrhead's first cousin Johnny makes the whiskey Rufus sells. You forgot about that? Burrhead ain't about to arrest Rufus and put Johnny out of business."

"Give it to him, anyhow. It'll get old lady Cross off our backs for a day or two. I can't go out there now." Jordon shook his head in disgust. "Why the hell do we spend our time chasing people for making and selling and drinking whiskey? Don't we have enough serious problems to keep us busy? Why?"

"You mean to say you don't know?" Willis asked with feigned concern. "And you wanting to be high sheriff of this county? Trafficking in whiskey is against the law. Federal law, at that. Have you forgot? And it's our job to enforce the law. You forgot that, too? Oh my, you are forgetful for a man who's been deputying long as you have."

"Quit riding my ass, Willis. What I mean is, why is it folks get their bowels in such an uproar about a little whiskey drinking, when they just step over all the other crap like it wasn't even there? That's what I want to know."

"Figure that one out, you ought to be running for governor instead of sheriff. Or maybe even president." Willis lit another cigarette off the butt of the one he was finishing and took a deep drag. "And now, unless it's too much strain on you, would you mind filling me in on this dead Trotter girl? I'm a deputy, too, even if all I do is hop around this goddamn office like a crippled rabbit and listen to old ladies complain about the work of the devil."

Jordon liked Willis. A lot. And trusted him. Owed him. They'd served together in the army in France during the last war. Willis came through it without getting a scratch, and then a few years later lost his leg in a slate fall in one of Buxton's mines. Because he was a cousin of Sheriff Noble Treadway's first wife, Noble had seen to it that Willis always had a job of some kind around the courthouse, the most recent of which was this one as office deputy. Jordon believed it was Willis who'd saved his life in the Argonne Forest by killing a German rifleman who was just about to dispatch him to eternity. Willis sloughed it off, saying it must have been somebody else shot the German. But Jordon was pretty sure he was lying. Willis just didn't want the responsibility of having saved somebody's life, Jordon figured.

Now he sat down and told Willis all he knew about the Trotter girl's death, his search of the area, and his talk with Noble.

"He's right, you know," Willis said. "You figure out who killed that girl, and John Bill Trumble ain't got a chance to beat you. You'll look like a hero. And John Bill's going to keep right on looking like the droopy-faced dog turd he is."

"Whether I'll ever look like a hero or not, you're right about John Bill Trumble. He'll always be a dog turd. All the lies his people are spreading around the county about me, it'll be a wonder if I get any votes at all. I wouldn't if folks believed half of it."

"That's one of your biggest problems right now," Willis said.

"Seems that way." Jordon looked at his watch and stood up. "I've got to go. A lot more tracks to make before this day's over."

"Wish I could get out of here and help you," Willis said.

"Hang in here by the phone and fend off the old ladies. That'll help me more than anything right now."

Willis looked disgusted. "Sure."

On the way to his car Jordon was stopped by Lonnie Hoskins, one of his campaign workers who insisted that they had to talk some about the campaign in the South Flatstone precinct if Jordon was to have any hope of carrying it in the election.

"I been hangin around here all day, hopin I'd catch ye," Hoskins said. "They're spreadin all kinds of stuff about you down in my part of the woods."

Lonnie was a split rail of a man, long and thin, all keen

edges and angles. He wore clean faded bib overalls and a starched blue work shirt. Jordon had known him for years, knew he was well liked in his community, knew he was honest and forthright. Also, he had a multitude of kinfolks and was sharp as a snake's tooth when it came to politics. Jordon considered himself lucky that Lonnie was with him.

"Exactly what are they saying?" Jordon asked.

"For one thing, they say you got a bad reputation for crackin fellers heads open if they give ye any back-talk when you arrest them."

"That's a damned lie," Jordon said angrily. "I've never laid a hand on a man didn't force me to do it. And I've never in my life hit a man with a blackjack or a pistol. Never had to."

The two men strolled toward Jordon's car, talking as they went.

"I know you don't abuse people," Lonnie said. "But you know how it is with a lie. Once it gets on its feet and starts a runnin, the truth has an awful hard time catching up with it."

Jordon thought about it for a moment. "What else are they telling?"

"They's folks sayin Buxton's agin ye."

This was a surprise. Jordon didn't know HR Buxton had taken a position either for or against him. Because Noble had always seemed to have peaceful relations with the old man, Jordon had figured Buxton was more or less neutral in the sheriff's race this time.

"Maybe he is against me," Jordon said. "But I haven't heard anything either way. Have you?"

Lonnie shook his head. "Nothin 'cept hearsay is all. But the word's goin around. And somebody's spreadin it. Only one place it could be comin from. John Bill Trumble's people."

Jordon said, "Well, maybe having Buxton against me will help more than hurt. Lots of folks are not that fond of the company."

Lonnie Hoskins shook his head. "But lots of others is. A

lot of paydays in this county come out of his pocket. Even now, with his mines runnin no more than two or three days a week most of the time, ain't nobody much would want to talk up agin Buxton. If he comes out strong agin ye, he can make it awful hard for ye to win."

"What about the union men? They don't follow Buxton."

"Most don't, that's true," Lonnie said. "But they ain't enough of them to turn it, I don't believe."

Jordon kicked at a rock. "Damn it. The man owns nearly everything around here, anyhow. Half the stores in the county, the theater, the newspaper, right on down to the barber shop and pool room." He rammed his hand into his pocket and pulled out a handful of metal tokens and stared at them. "Even the money we spend's not real money at all. Most of it's his damn scrip."

"I know all that," Lonnie said quietly.

Jordon put his hand on the man's shoulder. "I know you do. I just get mad thinking about it sometimes. You'd think he'd be satisfied to leave the election alone."

Hoskins waited a moment before he spoke. "Maybe he is leavin it alone up to now. I just heard what folks been sayin. Maybe you can learn more about it yourself."

"Yeah, maybe I can. The question is, what can we do to get things going our way right now?"

"You could come down to South Flatstone and spend some time with me, go around to see folks, set'm straight about some of the lies been told. Let'm see what you look like in person, shake their hands, look'm in the eye. All that'd help, Jordon. More than you know, maybe."

Jordon looked squarely at him. "I appreciate all you're doing, Lonnie. I want you to know that. Any way I can ever repay you, I'll do it. And I'll try my best to find time to get down there and go around some with you."

Lonnie grinned. "We all got the same amount of time. Twenty-four hours a day. It's a question of how we decide to use it, ain't it?"

Jordon grinned back at him. "I reckon you're right."

The two men shook hands and Jordon got into his car and thought about what to do next. The afternoon was gone. It was almost five, too late now, he knew, to get to Buxton and talk to the people in the office where Bitsy Trotter had worked; or to pick up the autopsy report at Doc Klein's. But Jordon figured he still had time to drive over to Della's, grab a bite to eat, and see Cassie before going back to the CCC camp to talk with the Manochio boy.

Della's Place was a long, low, flat frame building, wearing a coat of battleship gray paint and hidden back in a grove of tall yellow pines maybe a quarter of a mile off the main road, about four miles out of Buxton. Not the kind of building or location you'd ordinarily figure for a restaurant, but then Della's was no ordinary restaurant. And Della was no ordinary restaurant operator.

Half a dozen cars, Model A's and Model T's except for a Chevy coupe and a beat-up Plymouth, sat in the parking lot. Three horses were tethered to nearby trees.

Everyone in the place turned to look at him when Jordon stepped inside. Whatever conversations had been in progress stopped, and the only thing to be heard was a record on Della's Victrola. It sounded like the Carter Family.

Jordon's eyes scanned the room. Two men and two women sat at a table in the back. At another, two women sat alone. Across the room, three shaggy-haired men wearing rough dirty clothes huddled together.

At a table near the front door, away from the others, Della and Doc Klein sat drinking coffee.

Behind the counter a girl in a white apron was setting sandwiches in front of a man and woman.

The customers resumed their muffled conversations and Jordon walked over to where Della and Doc sat.

Della smiled and said to Doc, "Looks like the law's finally found you." She was a beautiful young woman, about thirty,

Jordon figured. Dark eyes, black hair, and lovely skin. A body so well organized that it brought you to a dead stop the first time you saw her. She'd been born in the mountains, in the backwoods over near Little Horse Creek, and had run off somewhere up north and got married when she was just a girl. A year or so ago she'd come back, with money of her own evidently, had the building put up, and opened the restaurant. Sheriff Treadway had made it clear when he hired Jordon that Della's Place was off limits when it came to enforcing the Volstead Act. "You won't see any open drinking out there," the sheriff had said. "And there's no call to sniff anybody's glass." Which suited Jordon fine.

Doc Klein gave an elaborate sigh and shrug and said to Della in mock seriousness, "I suppose a bloodhound like Jordon had to catch up with me sooner or later. Might as well be now."

Jordon pulled out a chair and sat down with them. "Matter of fact," he said to Doc, "I was hoping to see you earlier. But I didn't expect to find you here."

"What kind of crack is that?" Della demanded. "This place not high-tone enough for a respectable man like Doc?" She pretended anger, then smiled at Jordon, a brilliant flash of even white teeth. The bright red lipstick she wore made her creamy complexion even more radiant.

"Anywhere you are is high-tone, darling," Jordon said.

"I almost forgot, you're running for high sheriff," she responded. "You've already got my vote. You don't have to butter me up."

"So you're looking for me," Doc said. "I wonder why." His hands fluttered upward to pat his short-cropped salt-and-pepper hair, then back to the table, where they kept up a constant motion, tapping, drumming, rubbing.

Jordon had noticed Doc was always like this. It seemed to be an excess of energy, not nervousness, that kept him from being still. Now he smoothed his neatly trimmed mustache, adjusted his silver-rimmed glasses, and fussed with his tie.

Doc had come to the mountains from someplace in the North, right after the war. Jordon figured he was somewhere around forty, a man loved and respected by everyone in the county. Whatever the reason he had chosen Stanton County, Doc was now a vital part of it. He'd married a local girl, one of the Buxton company officials' daughters, and he practiced medicine with a passion for healing and relieving suffering.

"Actually," Jordon said to Doc, "I came by to see Cassie. But finding you here is a welcome surprise."

"Cassie's in back doing some paper work for me right now," Della said. "She'll help out here in front when the crowd starts coming in—if they come in."

"Don't they always?" Jordon said.

Della smiled. "Most always." Then, "I can get Cassie for you if you like."

"If it's okay with Doc, and if you'll excuse us, maybe him and me can talk a little first." He looked at Doc and said, "Outside okay?"

The two of them stepped out into the cooling evening air.

Doc lit a Philip Morris, offering one to Jordon, who said, "No thanks."

"You never smoked?" Doc asked.

Jordon shook his head. "I have other vices."

"Don't we all?" Doc took a long drag and inhaled deeply. After he blew the smoke out he said, "About the Trotter girl."

Jordon nodded.

Doc reached into his inside coat pocket, pulled out a folded paper and handed it to Jordon, who glanced at it and said, "Can you give me a quick summary of this?"

Doc's spoke in a flat voice, without emotion. "Throat cut. Stabbed seventeen times, chest and abdomen. Knife with a long slender blade. Some slashing. Face, neck. You saw those, didn't you?"

Jordon nodded again. "Anything else?"

"Like?"

"Rape, for instance."

"No indication of rape." Doc took a long drag on his cigarette and raised his eyebrows as he blew out a plume of smoke.

Jordon watched him. "But?"

"But—she had sexual relations with somebody not long before she was killed."

Jordon thought about it for a minute. "You mean somebody made love to this girl, with her consent, and then butchered her up like that?"

"It could be the way it happened."

"What kind of creature could do something like that? Hold her in his arms, make love to her, then . . . ?"

"God only knows. I remember reading somewhere that a fellow considered by everyone to be a good and gentle man was once asked if he had any idea what goes on in the mind of an evil man. You know what he said?"

Jordon shook his head slowly.

"He said, 'I don't know what goes on in the mind of an evil man. But I can tell you what goes on in the mind of a good man. It's horrible.'" Doc paused, took a long drag of his Philip Morris, then added, "Or words to that effect."

Again Jordon was silent for awhile before he spoke. "You're saying, since we all have evil thoughts, it could have been most anybody?"

"Under the right set of circumstances, most anybody could do most anything, I reckon."

"That's not much help to me, Doc. And you realize it's not too flattering to the human race generally."

"Maybe not, but then you're not looking for sugar with your turpentine, are you?"

"How'd you get so smart?"

"Not doing autopsies," Doc said. "Or jawing with deputy sheriffs."

Jordon grinned. "Thanks for the report. If it wasn't for

Prohibition, and me being an officer of the law and all, I'd buy you a drink."

"If you'll excuse me while I go to my car, I'll buy myself one," Doc said. "Sure I can't tempt you? I mean, Prohibition will be over in a month or so. Just a technicality or two left."

Jordon put on a serious expression as though carefully weighing the matter. "You're right," he said. "What's a technicality or two."

They strolled over to Doc's car where he reached into his doctor's bag and produced two small silver cups and handed them both to Jordon. Then Doc brought out what looked like a large medicine bottle filled with clear liquid. He unscrewed the cap and with great ceremony filled each of the cups almost to the top, put the cap back on the bottle and returned it to the bag. He took one of the cups from Jordon and said, "For medicinal purposes only, you understand."

"I couldn't accept it for any other reason," Jordon said, taking a sip. He looked at Doc. "Ransom Creech?"

"He makes the best," Doc said, sipping and savoring his drink.

Both men sipped again, then finished their cups.

"Thanks again," Jordon said. "What the doctor ordered was exactly what I needed. Come inside and I'll buy you something to eat."

Doc shook his head, put the cups away and got into his car. "Another time. Mrs. Klein is holding supper for me at home. And she's not a woman to be trifled with." He started the car and wheeled it around to face the road. He rolled down the window and said, "If you have any questions on that report, call me. And good luck. I expect you're going to need it."

Jordon turned to go inside when Doc said, "Oh, by the way, another thing."

Jordon faced him again.

Doc's hand patted his hair, adjusted his glasses. "You'll

find this in the report when you read it, but I'll tell you now."

Jordon waited, then when Doc just looked at him, said, "Christ's sake, Doc, what is it?"

"Bitsy Trotter was going to have a baby."

"Pregnant?"

Doc nodded. "They always are when they're going to have a baby."

"Pregnant," Jordon said again, his voice hardly more than a whisper.

"Between two and three months gone, I'd say."

Jordon stared at him, then said quietly, "You saved the best for last, did you?"

"Thought I'd put a little drama into your life."

"Drama," Jordon muttered. "Just what I needed." Then, after a moment, "Can we keep this just between the two of us for the time being?"

"I'm ethically bound not to discuss such things as a matter of practice," Doc said. He gave a little wave as he headed out to the main road.

Jordon went inside, his mind straining to find the right place to fit this new piece of information into the jigsaw puzzle of facts he was beginning to accumulate about Bitsy Trotter's murder.

As he stepped through the door, Cassie spotted him from across the room. She came to him smiling and said, "Find a seat. I'll get you something to eat." Then she added, "While you were with Doc, Willis phoned. You're supposed to call him back for sure before you leave here."

The telephone again. Use it or not, like it or not, it had become critical to getting his job done.

"Thanks, Cass," Jordon said, "Bring me some coffee, will you? And whatever you've got back there to eat." He walked across to the wall where the telephone was.

When Willis answered, Jordon said, "What is it?"

Willis said, "I'm glad I caught you. The Manochio boy? The one you're supposed to go talk to?"

"What about him?" Jordon said.

"Save yourself a trip. He went over the hill today."

"What?"

"That's right. Disappeared."

It was a moment before Jordon said, "How'd you find out?"

"Captain Sweeney called for you a little bit ago. Says this Manochio didn't come back in to camp with his crew today."

"That's it?"

"All he knows. Said he'll call when he finds out something. What the hell's going on anyway?"

"Not on the phone. Tell you when I see you."

"I hear that a lot lately." But Willis's tone of voice said he understood. Jordon and he had talked enough about the switchboard. They both knew that, with its network of party lines, the phone system was as leaky as a barrel full of auger holes.

Jordon went to the table where Cassie had set his supper. A piece of fresh roast pork, boiled potatoes, pinto beans, corn bread. It was more than he wanted after the lunch Bonnie Treadway has laid on, but he figured he'd better eat it since Cassie had brought it out.

He glanced up to see Della strolling toward his table. "Company?" she asked.

"Sure," he said, half rising.

She watched him eat for a little while before asking, "Are you going to find out who killed the Trotter girl?"

"I'll find out," he said. "Sooner or later."

She studied him as he ate. He looked up and saw her watching him. "What are you thinking about?" he asked.

"I'm wondering how far I ought to go with you."

"Meaning what?"

"Meaning I don't know you all that well. What is it now, nine or ten months you've been back around here?"

"Eight."

"Eight months. And I haven't had reason to talk to you

that much. But I know how Cassie feels about you. And
she's got a good head on her shoulders."

Jordon nodded. "No argument there." He watched Della
closely, wondering where this was going.

"If I told you something, and you promised never to let on
where you heard it, could I believe you?"

"What do you think?"

She stared at him, and a little smile started to form on her
lips. "I think if you promised something—anything—that'd
be all there was to it."

He grinned at her. "Della, you know enough about me to
know I'm a rambler and a gambler. I've been known to take
a drink of whiskey on occasion. I've never amounted to a hill
of beans when it comes to accumulating money. On top of
all that, I'm still young enough to appreciate a pretty woman.
None of these things speaks very well for me with a lot of
the 'better' people around here." He took a sip of his coffee
and looked her straight in the eye. "But if I promise you
something, you can hang your girdle on it."

"I don't own one," she said with a giggle. "But since I'm
not one of the better people you mentioned, what they think
don't mean a damn thing to me. Most of them don't think
much of me, either." Now she gave him an impish smile.
"The women, that is. Of course when it comes to the men
it's another thing entirely. Specially at night when they're
less likely to be seen coming and going."

Jordon finished his food and wiped his mouth and mustache with a napkin. "You were thinking about telling me
something?"

"Never to go any farther."

He nodded.

She leaned close to him and whispered, "Did you know
that Young Harry Buxton had been going out with the girl
that was killed?"

He shook his head slightly. Young Harry, as everyone
called him, was HR Buxton's only son. Jordon knew him

only by sight and reputation. The young man was said to
spend most of his time drinking and womanizing.

Della went on. "The two of them, Young Harry and the
Trotter girl, came here several times together. First time I
happened to be standing near the door when he drove up
and parked in the dark. He came in for a few minutes by
himself. Left her in the car."

"Maybe we ought to step outside to talk about this."

They stood and started for the door. Jordon noticed Cassie
sitting near the cash register, doing some paperwork. She
glanced up as he and Della went outside.

Other cars were beginning to arrive now, so Jordon and
Della walked to the edge of the parking area where they could
not be heard and stood in the shadows.

"So you saw her in Young Harry's car?"

"While he came inside."

Jordon didn't ask what Young Harry came in for. He was
sure it was to find a bottle. "And they were here several
times?"

She nodded. "After the first time, I made a point to glance
outside when he would come in. At least twice I knew for
certain it was her in the car with him. Another time or two
I couldn't tell for sure."

"Anything else?"

She nodded. "Once when it was late, in the middle of the
week and nobody else was here, he came inside and saw the
place was empty. Then he went back out and brought her
in and they sat over in the corner where it was dark. Asked
me to put on some music so they could dance."

Jordon thought it over for a while. "Thanks," he said.

"I see a lot out here," Della said. "Some things a lot of
folks wouldn't believe. And I make a practice of keeping my
mouth shut. I hate gossip." It was a moment before she
added, "But I also hate cold-blooded murder."

"What you told me wasn't gossip."

"I know. I also know that if it got out that I talked about

my customers out of school, it could kill my business." After
a moment she said, "Maybe me, too."

Jordon nodded. "It could be a problem."

"The last thing I'd want is to get old man Buxton really
mad at me. It may not be anything at all, but . . ."

"Don't worry about it, darling. I appreciate what you've
told me." He took her by the arm and walked her to the door.

Chapter Four

Back inside the restaurant, Jordon saw the evening crowd had begun to grow, and Cassie stood at a table talking to some customers.

Jordon said to Della, "Mind if I use your phone again?"

"Help yourself." She gave him that dazzling smile of hers. "I have to get to work. Come see me again."

"Real soon," he said.

Jordon cranked the phone and told the operator to get him the residence of Clyde Wooten. He wanted to go out and talk to Wooten's daughter, Lenarue, the girl Mrs. Trotter had said was Bitsy's best friend.

Jordon told Clyde Wooten who he was and what he wanted and learned that Lenarue was at the Trotters' home, sitting up with Bitsy's body along with other friends and neighbors. "Her mother's there with her," Clyde Wooten said. "They won't be home till after midnight at the earliest. Said they might stay all night if they're needed."

Jordon decided he did not want to intrude on the ritual that preceded the funeral. He would talk to Lenarue later. He stood thinking for a minute, then cranked the phone again and asked the operator for Captain Sweeney at the CCC camp.

"Captain Sweeney," the voice came over the line.

"This is Jordon. Any news on the Manochio boy? I understand he's disappeared."

"He didn't come in with his crew. He somehow got separated from his buddy in the woods today, and never came back."

"Any reason to think he might be hurt?"

"None. He seemed fine, according to his buddy. Just drifted over the top of a ridge and disappeared. We've got a team out looking for him tonight, but there's no sign of him so far."

"Did somebody tell him about the Trotter girl's murder?"

"That's what I understand. One of the boys heard about it somewhere last night, then told Manochio today. He knew Manochio had dated the girl."

"Did anybody say how Manochio took it?"

"I talked to his buddy about it. He said Manochio was very disturbed. Almost fainted. I just don't know what to think."

"I'd like to come over in the morning and talk to Manochio's buddy. What's his name?"

"Jack Bailey. I'll keep him in camp tomorrow."

They hung up and Jordon took a deep breath and sighed. His watch said nearly seven thirty. He felt like calling it a day. But he was just getting into the investigation.

He picked up the phone and asked for the home of Milton Graham, the man Bitsy Trotter's mother said she worked for at the Buxton Corporation. He'd see if Graham could shed any light on Bitsy's activities and friends.

"Hello," Graham said.

Jordon identified himself and asked if he might drive over and talk with Graham.

"Is it important?" Graham asked. "My wife and I are listening to the radio." The man had a speech impediment. He couldn't pronounce his "l's" and "r's," said them as "w's." "Wistening" for "listening." "Wadio" for "radio."

"It's important," Jordon said. "I want to talk to you about

Bitsy Trotter. I understand she worked for you."

"That's right, she did. What an awful tragedy," Graham said. Twagedy. Jordon felt sorry for him. How much that must cost him in dealing with other men. "I don't know how I can help you, but if I can I'll be more than happy to."

"I can be there in a few minutes," Jordon said.

"You know where we live?"

"Not exactly."

"Buxton Avenue. Where the other company executives live."

Jordon said, "Just tell me which house."

"Fifth one down on the left past Mr. Buxton's," Graham said.

Half an hour later Jordon sat in the Grahams' comfortable living room and waited.

When he'd arrived, a chuckling Milton Graham had let him in and said, "Lum and Abner is just about to go off. Claudia wants to hear the last of it. You don't mind, do you?"

Jordon said of course not. He was glad to sit and rest.

He watched the Grahams as they cocked their heads to catch every word coming from the big round speaker which sat on top of the Atwater-Kent radio in the large dark wooden cabinet which occupied a prominent place in their living room. Though Jordon hadn't bought one yet, lots of families in the county now had radios and listened to them every night after supper. One notable exception was old man Obadiah Honeycutt, a deacon in Kady Creek Primitive Baptist Church, who'd returned the radio he'd bought and explained to the storekeeper, "Durned thing handles some talk I don't want my chillern to get aholt of."

Milton Graham smiled as Abner elaborated on some finer point of human nature to Lum.

Jordon slid his back down in the easy chair and stretched his tired legs out straight in front of him. He massaged his thighs, pleased with the hardness of them. It had a been a long day, one of many such days he'd lived through recently. And there would be more before it got any easier. He studied the Grahams while they concentrated on the radio, watching it as if somehow that gave added substance to Spider Weehunt and Squire Skimp and the rest of the characters who, with Lum Edwards and Abner Peabody, populated the world behind the lighted dial of the radio.

Milton Graham was a soft-looking man carrying a lot more weight than his frame was built for. A lot of people considered this a sign of success and prosperity, Jordon knew, but he couldn't help thinking it might not be good for them. Graham's rear end strained his trousers as he leaned forward in his chair. He looked to be no more than his mid-forties, but he was bald except for a fringe of sandy hair around the sides and back of his head. He wore gold-rimmed glasses, house slippers and a robe with red and black stripes.

His wife was a thin wisp of a woman, probably about the same age as Milton, but with a drawn, tight look about her. She sat forward in her easy chair, tense, like a sparrow ready to spring into flight. Some women get that way in their middle years, Jordon had noticed.

The program ended and Graham got up and turned the radio off.

Mrs. Graham said, "I'm going to bed. I have a terrible headache." Her voice sounded as tense as she looked.

Jordon stood up and said, "I'm sorry you're not feeling well. I hope you're better tomorrow."

"We'll see," she said, but the tone of her voice said she doubted it. As she walked in front of Jordon on the way out of the room he noticed she faltered a little. He detected the faint smell of alcohol.

As his wife left, Milton Graham pulled his chair around to face Jordon. "Tell me now, how can I help you?"

"The Trotter girl, what exactly did she do for you?"

"She was a part-time employee. We try to spread the work

around so as many deserving people as possible get a chance at it. These are tough times."

Not quite so tough for those who lived on Buxton Avenue, Jordon thought. "And what did she do?"

"Worked on the switchboard and did some of my personal secretarial work. She was an intelligent and well-trained young lady." He shook his head. "I still can't believe she's dead."

"When did you first hear about her murder?" Jordon asked.

"My wife told me when I got back in town yesterday evening. I was away on a business trip."

"Tell me, can you think of anybody who might have had a reason to kill Bitsy Trotter?"

Graham shook his head. "No. Sometimes I would hear her and some of the other girls in the office talking about going out on dates. Some of them went out with these CCC boys, I understand. But I never heard her talk about any problems with any of them."

"Anything in her life, anything at all, that she might have talked about at work that might explain any of this?"

Graham thought about it for a moment. "I don't think she was very happy at home. She talked to me a few times about how she wished she could go to college, get an education and move away from here."

"Anything specific she said about her problems at home?"

"Not in so many words." Graham hesitated, then said, "Her father was dead, you know. Abel Trotter was her stepfather." Graham shrugged. "I don't know how well they got along. I gathered not too well, though she never was specific."

Jordon could hear someone, Mrs. Graham he assumed, moving around somewhere back in the house. Then he heard water running.

"Excuse me a moment," Milton Graham said. "Let me go see if Claudia is all right." He hurried through the house.

While he was gone, Jordon stood up and walked around the room, admiring the dark walnut furniture, the filled bookcases, the slightly worn but expensive looking rugs.

In one corner of the room, mounted high on the wall, was the stuffed head of a mountain lion, and nearby were other stuffed specimens of small game, a bobcat, a raccoon, a red fox, a pheasant, and a couple of gray squirrels.

"You a hunter?" Graham asked when he came back.

"Not really," Jordon said. "Used to like to fox hunt. I enjoyed the socializing. But I can see you like the sport."

The two men sat back down and relaxed.

"When I have the time," Graham said, adding, "which is not too often anymore."

"Where'd you get these stuffed?" Jordon asked, nodding toward the trophies. It felt good to sit back and just talk a little.

"Did them myself, all except the mountain lion," Graham replied. He was obviously proud. "Shot it out west several years ago and had it mounted and shipped to me. After that, I decided to learn taxidermy, sent away for a correspondence course, and started mounting the small game around here myself. Something to keep my mind occupied. A hobby." Graham walked over and studied the bobcat. "I've given most of the stuff I've done to friends here and there."

"You travel around a lot?"

"Quite a bit. We try to go on vacations out of the mountains when we can. And then I have to go away on business from time to time."

"Your accent," Jordon said. "It's not local."

Graham smiled. "I'm originally from Delaware."

Jordon slid down in his chair and crossed his legs. "Exactly what do you do for the company?" Jordon had never really taken much interest in what went on at the Buxton Corporation. He'd never worked for it himself, and had little interest in how it operated.

"Mainly internal administrative work. I'm over the telephone system, the power plant, the water system."

"That doesn't take you out of town very often does it?"

"No. My business trips mostly have to do with sales."

"You handle that, too?"

"Just a few things. I happened to meet a man once in Cincinnati who was a lumber broker and got him to give us a try. He eventually became one of our good customers. And he's always wanted to continue to do business with our company through me. So I do it as a courtesy to him."

Jordon smiled. "A good account?"

"All steady accounts are good in times like these," said Graham, smiling too. He looked at his watch. "Is there something else that I can help you with on the business about Bitsy Trotter? To tell the truth, I'm getting tired."

"Nothing else. Thank you for seeing me at this hour," Jordon said.

"Not at all. If you think of something more, let me know." Graham reached out his hand. "I hope you catch whoever it was did it. I thought a lot of that girl. What an awful way to die."

Jordon shook hands with Milton Graham and left. He drove straight to Cassie's, let himself in with the key on the ledge over the door, and called her at Della's.

"This is Deputy Sheriff Berk Jordon, ma'am," he said when she came on the line. "I thought you might like to know there's a man in your house."

Cassie's voice sounded cool as she said, "You planning on staying over again tonight?"

Jordon wasn't sure what was wrong, but he said, "Only if you want me to."

"Tell the truth, I'm kind of tired," she said. "I don't think I'd be very good company."

"You sick or anything?"

"I'm not sick."

"I'll go home then. Talk to you later." Jordon wondered what it was with Cassie, but not for long. He'd given up years ago trying to understand women's moods.

He started to leave, then remembered the groceries he'd picked up. He brought them into the house, locked up and left the key where he'd found it, then headed for his son Danny's home in Buxton.

As he drove through the darkness, Jordon felt the dead weight of his rootless ways. For whatever reason, Cassie did not want to see him tonight. And he did not want to go to Danny's. Yet he had no place else to go.

He wished he had not let himself be persuaded to move in with his son and daughter-in-law and their two children. The house was plenty big enough, but he had little real privacy, something he'd grown to value and protect more and more through the years. And he hated to disturb the family with his coming and going at odd hours.

He'd only been there for little more than a month now, and he was almost ready to move back to the boarding house where he'd lived before.

Danny had a company house in one of the best parts of Buxton, not far from the center of town, an area where the second and third echelon company workers lived. It was deliberately distant from the coal miners' and mill workers' homes. A reward for dedicated service to the Buxton Corporation.

The house was dark as Jordon let himself in. He eased in the door and toward his bedroom, feeling his way along past the furniture.

"That you, dad?" Danny said from the bedroom where he and Mary Helen slept.

"Yeah. Sorry I woke you."

"It's okay. We weren't asleep."

"Goodnight, son."

"You be here for breakfast? I'd like to see you."

"I'll be here," Jordon said.

"Goodnight, dad."

Chapter Five

IT WAS A LITTLE before eight on Friday morning when Jordon arrived at the CCC camp. "Jack Bailey's waiting in his barracks," Captain Sweeney said. "Building Four, whenever you're ready."

"Before I go over there, tell me a little about him."

"He's from here in Kentucky. Clinton County, outside of Albany. He and Manochio hit it off from the start. Wanted to work together. They're both good workers, so we let them."

"How about off duty? They run around together?"

"That's my understanding."

"Exactly what did Bailey say to you yesterday evening?"

"He said some of the other boys had heard about the murder and got to talking about it on the way out to the woods. Later in the day, when they'd split up and were working in teams, Manochio just up and cut out when nobody was looking."

Jordon thanked the captain and walked across the compound. Jordon's breakfast sat heavy in his gut. Danny had hinted strongly this morning, and not for the first time, that maybe Jordon would find life better if he had a "regular" job. Somehow it had reminded Jordon of the down-and-out men he'd seen in a Louisville skid row mission once who, along with their food and shelter, got a strenuous sermon on sin and redemption. Salvation and eggs made a heavy breakfast.

Inside Building Four, looking at the long rows of bunks and foot lockers, Jordon felt a wave of nostalgia. He'd been in two wars, and, like many other men, he had found that military life appealed to him in many ways. He liked the adventure, the camaraderie, the field training. Even the discipline, except for the arrogance sometimes displayed by stupid officers and non-coms.

At the far end of the room a man lay on one of the bunks staring at the ceiling. Jordon was about halfway down the row when the young man sat up and looked at him.

"Jack Bailey?"

The young man snapped Jordon a "Yes, sir." He jumped up and stood at attention.

"Sit down, son," Jordon said, sticking his hand out to the boy. Bailey was a slim, wiry youth, with an open baby face. Nineteen or twenty Jordon figured. His thick brown hair was carefully combed and pushed into a cowlick in front. His handshake was firm, but Jordon could feel the nervousness in him, the dampness of his palms.

Jordon took a seat on the next bunk. "I'm Deputy Sheriff Jordon. Captain Sweeney tells me you and Sal Manochio are buddies." Jordon swung his legs up on the bunk, stretched out and leaned back.

"That's right," Bailey said, swallowing and looking uncomfortable. "We work together."

"Run around together outside, too?"

"Some."

"Tell me what Sal said to you yesterday. Before he left."

"Nothing much." Bailey was swallowing hard now.

"You're his buddy. Surely he must have said something."

"Just that he didn't know if he could stand it."

"Stand what?"

The boy looked at the floor. "Bitsy being dead."

"Were the two of them that close?"

"Sal was, I know."

"But?"

Bailey was hesitant, fumbling for thoughts and the words to fit them, it seemed to Jordon. "But I don't think Bitsy was too . . . serious, you know?"

Jordon prompted him. "Sal was serious, but Bitsy . . . ?"

"She didn't want to go steady, talk about getting married, anything like that."

"Do you know when was the last time Sal saw her?" Jordon watched Bailey shift his position on the bunk, swallow, then clear his throat.

Bailey didn't say anything.

"Son," Jordon said quietly, "if you know anything about this, it'd be a lot better for everybody concerned, your friend Sal included, if you'd just tell me what it is."

Bailey's voice became a plea. "Sal didn't kill her, Mr. Jordon. He was crazy about her."

"Why did he run off? You have any idea?"

Bailey stared at the floor and said nothing.

"What's the matter?" Jordon asked.

"I don't want to get Sal in trouble."

"He's in trouble already. Taking off like that makes him look pretty bad. If you know something, it might help him if he had nothing to do with Bitsy's murder."

"He didn't."

"Then why did he run away?"

Bailey looked at Jordon, then back down at the floor. "He was scared. That's all."

"Scared of what?"

Still staring at the floor Bailey finally said, almost in a whisper, "Sal saw Bitsy a little while before she was killed. And he was scared maybe somebody would think he done it."

"How long before she was killed was it when he saw her?"

"I don't know exactly. Maybe an hour or two."

Jordon tried to digest this. "I thought you boys were working over on Kady's Knob day before yesterday when she was killed."

"Yes, sir, we were. But we go off in separate groups a lot of the time, cut brush and trees in an area by ourselves. And right after we had dinner that day, about one o'clock, Sal took off through the woods."

"You know for sure he went to see Bitsy?"

Bailey nodded. "We saw her and another girl the night before that. At the confectionery in Buxton. She said she'd wait for him the next day someplace in the woods, I don't know exactly where."

"He'd met her there before?"

"I think so."

"Wasn't he afraid he'd be caught sneaking away from the work crew that way?"

"Yes, sir. He was scared, all right. But he said he had to see her."

"You know why?"

"Why he had to see her? He didn't tell me. Just that he had to go. And I know he wouldn't have done anything to hurt her."

"I hope that's true, son. I truly do. But somebody hurt her. As bad as anybody can be hurt."

"It wasn't Sal."

"How long did he stay gone the day he went to meet her?"

Bailey thought for a moment before saying, "About two and a half hours, I guess. He left about one, got back about three thirty. We regroup to head into camp at four, and he was back in plenty of time."

"How did he seem when he got back from seeing Bitsy?"

"Okay."

"Happy? Sad?"

"Just usual. Not sad, not happy."

"Or nervous?"

"Nothing like that."

"Why didn't you tell this to Captain Sweeney, son?"

Bailey was staring at the floor again. "Scared, I reckon. I don't know. Didn't want to get Sal into trouble."

Jordon stood up and put his hand on the boy's shoulder. "If you think of anything else, call me at the sheriff's office, will you?"

Bailey nodded uncertainly, then lay back on his bunk. Jordon couldn't remember when he'd ever seen a boy look more miserable.

"First time away from home, son?" Jordon asked him.

Bailey looked up at him and nodded.

"I remember my first time away from home," Jordon said. "In the army. I was just about your age. Don't worry too much, boy. It gets easier."

"I sure hope so," Jack Bailey said.

Jordon sat in a chair outside one of the offices in the Buxton Corporation's main office building. He was waiting to see Harrison Randolph Buxton, Jr.—"Young Harry."

Jordon looked at his watch. Ten thirty-five. His visit to the CCC camp and his talk with Jack Bailey hadn't taken that long. He'd decided to stop on his way to the sheriff's office and have a talk with Young Harry Buxton. The secretary outside Young Harry's office had told him to wait. She'd gone inside and had not come out.

Jordon stepped over to the large plate-glass window and stared down at the town square of Buxton. Town street would have more accurately described it. Jordon knew well the history of the town. Everybody in several counties did.

Harrison Randolph Buxton, Sr.—HR—had launched his coal and timber empire in the mountains along the Middle Fork of the Cumberland River nearly twenty years earlier, long after the first speculators and coal operators had followed the railroad into the mountains.

He had built a short broad street perpendicular to the railroad, had paved the street with brick, and erected buildings for stores and shops along both sides.

On the hill in back of one row of stores he placed the building for his bank and his corporate offices.

This cluster of commerce adjacent to the railroad was the hub of the Buxton Corporation's operations. It owned the businesses as well as the buildings they occupied: grocery, clothing and hardware stores, confectionery, pharmacy, theater, barber shop, pool room, whatever a miner or his family might need or be persuaded to spend money on.

For employees who had pay coming, the corporation would issue between paydays, on request, coin-like metal tokens in denominations equivalent to cash—"scrip"— which could be spent like money at any of the company's businesses. Soon everyone in the county came to accept and use the scrip as cash.

The corporation's actual mining and timber operations were strung out along the Buxton-owned local railroad line like knots in a rope. Flatcars hauling logs and gondolas loaded with coal were pulled out of the hollers to Buxton every day to increase the wealth of the Buxton Corporation— which was wholly owned by HR Buxton.

"Mr. Buxton Junior will see you now, sir," the secretary said behind Jordon.

Jordon left his place at the window and stepped inside Young Harry's office.

The younger Buxton sat behind a dark wood desk on which a few papers were stacked. The office was well furnished and neat.

Jordon didn't really know Harry, though he had seen him enough times around the county. Harry was only in his late twenties, but his body was already beginning to reflect his easy life. Extra weight showed around his belly as well as on his face and neck. He ran his hand through his loose brown hair and slumped in his swivel chair. He made no move to get up or offer his hand.

"You wanted to see me?" His voice was cool. Condescending.

"Mind if I sit down?" Jordon asked.

Harry waved indolently toward a chair. "Be my guest."

"Thank you." Jordon sat down and got out his little note-book and pen. He took his time, leafing through several pages and appearing to study his notes. Let the bastard wonder.

Finally Harry spoke, with a sneer. "Would you mind getting to the point of your business? I do have work to do."

Jordon looked up from his notes and fixed him with an icy stare. "How well did you know Bitsy Trotter?"

Jordon watched as Harry's eyes widened and he stiffened visibly. Then the younger man's complexion began to redden. "Just what do you mean by that?"

"Seems to me it's plain enough. How well did you know her?"

"What makes you so sure I knew her at all?"

"Are you saying you didn't know her?"

Harry was beginning to look flustered. He twisted in his chair. He looked out the window, then back at Jordon. "Yes. I mean, no. I'm not saying I didn't. I knew her. Everybody in the office did. She worked here."

"So I understand. She ever work for you personally?"

"No. Why would you think that?"

"She worked for Milton Graham. I thought maybe she also did some work for you."

"I have a secretary I'm very satisfied with. She does everything I need."

Jordon gave him a hard cold look. "In the office."

"What's that?"

"Your secretary does everything you need in the office. You didn't need Bitsy to do anything for you here."

"What the hell's that supposed to mean?" Harry's voice took on a strong, tough tone. The authority of the heir to the Buxton throne. "Look," he said, standing up, "I think I've spent enough time with you. I've got other things to do."

Jordon didn't move. He fixed Young Harry with a stare and said quietly, "Why don't you sit back down." After a moment, Harry did so. Jordon went on. "I happen to know that you and Bitsy were more than just fellow workers in the office.

And more than just casual acquaintances on the outside."

"Now wait a minute! I don't know where you're getting this sleazy stuff, but. . . ."

Jordon held up his hand to quiet him. "I'm investigating a murder, Mr. Buxton," Jordon said. He made "Mr. Buxton" sound slightly nasty. "I have knowledge that you knew the girl. You were seen with her by more than one witness, more than one time." Not exactly the truth, but not necessarily false, either.

"What witnesses? Who are you talking about?"

"You deny it, then? You didn't go out with the girl? You want to stand on that?"

"Goddamn you, I don't have to stand or not stand on anything. Who the hell do you think you are coming in here and accusing me of having something to do with Bitsy's death?"

"I haven't accused you of anything. I'm just asking you some questions." Jordon's tone was easy.

"Not any more you're not." Harry was on his feet again now. "Get out!"

Jordon made no move to go. "I could arrest you as a suspect."

"Like hell you could. I was working the day she was killed."

"Where?"

"I went out to look over some timber land we're thinking about acquiring."

Jordon made a note in his book. "Alone?"

"Yes, alone. But there are people who know where I was."

"Where?"

"Other end of the county."

Jordon scribbled some more. "Were these people with you all the time?"

"I don't have to discuss this kind of shit with you any more. This is over."

Jordon got to his feet and stared into Harry's eyes. "It's

not over, boy. Not until whoever butchered that girl pays for it. You understand me?"

Young Harry's voice was shaking. "Get out, goddamn you."

Jordon took his time. Closed his notebook, screwed the top on his pen and put them both in his inside coat pocket. He gave Harry a last hard look, then a thin smile. "See you soon."

Harry was trembling. Fear or rage, or maybe both, Jordon figured.

"If you've got any sense, which I seriously doubt," Harry said, "you'll take your investigation in some other direction. I had nothing to do with Bitsy's death."

"We'll know for sure before I'm through," Jordon said. "Count on it." He left the office and closed the door.

The secretary at the desk outside gave Jordon a wide-eyed look. He figured she must have heard at least part of what went on between him and Harry. She quickly turned her attention back to her typewriter, and Jordon strode down the hallway toward the exit.

Outside, on the wide stairway leading down to the street, Jordon passed Milton Graham, who smiled and spoke. "Hard at work, I see."

"Just gathering information," Jordon said. "Wherever I can find it."

"Good wuck."

"I need all I can get."

Jordon got in his car and headed for King's Mill. He wanted to go over a couple of things with Willis, try to get his thinking clear. Much as he hated to admit it, he didn't have a hell of a lot on Bitsy's murder so far except suspicions.

The funeral was this afternoon. If he attended it, maybe he could catch the Wooten girl, Bitsy's friend, and talk with her. Also, the boy, Farrell Nilson, another of her friends.

In the sheriff's office, Willis sat puffing on a cigarette and looking at some old warrants that had not been served. Most men, when they heard through the grapevine that a warrant had been issued for them, scouted out in the woods and avoided arrest as long as they could, sometimes for months.

"Any calls I need to hear about?" Jordon asked.

Willis nodded. "The boss."

Jordon pulled a straight-backed chair to him, turned it around, straddled it and sat down, resting his arms on the back and his chin on his arms. It was one of his habitual ways of sitting when he was with friends. "What's Noble want? Did he say?"

"Wants you to call him. He sounded madder than a wet hen. Something about you must be trying to lose the election." Willis was looking down at the warrants as he talked. Without moving his head, he arched his eyebrows and cut his eyes toward Jordon. "That what you're trying to do?"

"At this point, I'm not too damn sure just what I'm doing. I need an election campaign right now about as much as a hog needs a sidesaddle." Jordon took off his hat and tossed it toward a hook on the wall. It missed and fell to the floor. He picked it up and said, "That's just about how I feel my campaign is going."

"Think you're slipping?"

"I'm not sure. But there's nothing to make me feel like I'm winning. I don't know anything about politics, Willis. Sometimes I wonder why I ever got into this thing."

Willis studied him for a while. "You'd be a good sheriff. Maybe that's why."

Jordon stared out the window at the people strolling across the courthouse lawn. "Thanks. I believe I could make a good sheriff. And I'd like the chance to give it a shot, just once, on my own." He looked at Willis and grinned, "I take it I've got your vote, then?"

"Me?" Willis said, looking as the papers. "I never vote."

Jordon knew, of course, that Willis was a tireless political worker, that he and every relative he could round up voted in every election. Some more than once, depending on who was working the polls. And Jordon also knew they'd all be supporting him.

"So, you think I better call the sheriff and see what's on his mind?"

"I strongly recommend it."

Jordon cranked the phone and told the operator to ring Sheriff Treadway's home. When Bonnie answered, Jordon identified himself and asked to speak to the sheriff.

Noble didn't waste any time with preliminaries. "What the hell are you trying to do? Lose the election?"

"What's this about?"

"You going to Young Harry Buxton's office and giving him a ration of shit, that's what."

"You know about that?"

"What makes you think I wouldn't?"

"I just left there."

"And Young Harry just walked down the hall to his daddy's office and said you were threatening him. And HR just picked up the phone and called me. And I picked up the phone and called you. How goddamn long you think it takes to make a couple of phone calls?"

"Obviously not very long."

"You got that right, anyway."

Jordon felt his anger rising. He didn't take chastisement well under any circumstances, and especially not when it was delivered the way Noble was doing it now.

"You think we could discuss this later, maybe face-to-face?" Jordon said quietly.

"Face-to-face is exactly what I had in mind. But not a hell of a lot later. I want to talk to you before you do something else." For a moment, Jordon thought Noble was going to add the word "stupid", but he didn't.

"When did you have in mind?"

"Today."

"I'd planned to go by the Trotter girl's funeral this afternoon, try to talk to a couple of her friends who I expect will be there. How about I drive on over to your place right after that?"

"I'm not going anywhere." The sheriff hung up.

Willis said, "I take it you and the sheriff have some disagreement?"

"He has some disagreement with me. I didn't know anything about it until just now."

"What the hell did you do?"

"Told Young Harry Buxton where the bear shits in the buckwheat. And he ran to his daddy. And HR called Noble."

"What's Young Harry into that you need to be giving him trouble?"

Jordon got up, turned his chair around and leaned back in it. He took out a handful of peanuts and started to munch on them as he filled Willis in on everything that had happened since he'd talked with him last: the Manochio boy's visit with Bitsy the afternoon she was killed, what he'd learned from Milton Graham and Manochio's Three-C buddy Jack Bailey, Young Harry Buxton's relationship with Bitsy and Jordon's interview with him.

"Where'd you learn about Young Harry and Bitsy?"

"Confidential sources."

Willis said, "You got any idea who might have killed her?"

"Not so far. It looks bad for Sal Manochio. Being with her that afternoon, he could have done it. Then taking off the way he has. But the question is, if he loved her, like Bailey says he did, why would he want to kill her?"

Willis shrugged. "What about Young Harry Buxton? You think he could have done it?"

"It looks like he could have. He'd certainly been out with her. More than once, if my sources are right. He's so easy to despise, it's natural to want to suspect him. But I've got to try to keep my personal feelings about him out of it."

"What about the other boy Bitsy went out with, the one you said you're going to talk to this afternoon?"

"Nilson. I got no idea yet. Have to wait and see." Jordon swept the pile of peanut shells from the desk into his hand and carried them to a waste can. "Anything else I need to know about right now?"

"Nothing I can't handle with the help of a couple of constables and my silver tongue." Willis grinned at him.

"Some would say line of bull."

"Not to my face."

"Of course not." Jordon left for the Maple Grove cemetery where Bitsy Trotter was being buried, hoping he'd find both Lenarue Wooten and Farrell Nilson there.

Jordon parked far back from the gravesite and walked close enough to hear, then leaned against a large old oak tree and waited.

A quartet sang "Precious Memories" and "I'll Have a New Body, Praise the Lord, I'll Have a New Life." The preacher said the words as women wept and men stared into space. The casket was lowered into the grave and the gathering came undone. Jordon spotted the Trotter family, approached them, extended his sympathies and asked Abel to point out Lenarue Wooten and Farrell Nilson.

"There's her," Abel said, pointing. "With her mother and that little girl, her sister. But I ain't seen Farrell. I don't believe he come."

Jordon thanked him and angled across the cemetery to a path where he intercepted Lenarue. He introduced himself to her and her mother. "I need to talk to you for a minute," he told Lenarue.

Lenarue's mother said, in a high, whiny voice, "You won't be needin her for long, will you? We've got to be gettin on back home soon."

Jordon assured her he wouldn't take long. The mother and little sister went to wait at a horse-drawn wagon. A tall slim boy in clean, faded overalls sat holding the reins.

Jordon walked Lenarue to the bench where they couldn't be heard by the others.

"The boy who's holding the reins over there, he your brother?"

"No. A neighbor. Just came with us to help."

Jordon looked at his notes for a moment, then said, "Tell me, Lenarue, do you have any idea who might have killed Bitsy?"

Lenarue took a handkerchief out of her little clutch purse and put it to her eyes, which were already red and puffy from crying. She was a pretty girl. Fair complected. Buxom. A sprinkling of freckles to go with her straw blonde hair.

"I don't know who could've done something like that. Lord have mercy. I heard they cut her to pieces. Is that so? They didn't even open the coffin." She was about to start crying again, Jordon could tell.

"Whoever it was stabbed her several times," Jordon said. "But you oughtn't to dwell on that, Lenarue. Just try to think of anything you can that might help me catch whoever did it."

"I don't know what to tell you."

"You were her closest friend, according to her mother. Tell me about Sal Manochio."

"He and Bitsy dated a lot."

"How did she feel about him?"

"She liked him." Lenarue glanced at her mother, who was watching the two of them as she twisted her handkerchief. The boy with the reins stared away toward the woods.

"Just liked him?"

"What do you mean?"

"She didn't love him?"

"I'm not too sure I know what you mean by 'love.' "

Jordon wasn't too sure he knew what he meant, either. The word meant something different to every person who used it. "Did she ever talk about marrying him, maybe? Or going away from here with him?"

Lenarue stared at Jordon. "What you need to understand about Bitsy is, she wouldn't marry anybody as poor as Sal. She'd made up her mind she was going to leave Stanton County, get away from the mountains. She had a dream of having another kind of life."

"What kind of life?"

"Not the kind of life she had. Jammed up in a little company house with her mother and sister and stepdaddy. She'd been inside better homes, read magazines, seen how other people live. That's what she wanted for herself."

"She have any plans for how she might go about getting it?"

"Some."

"Tell me about them."

Across the church yard, Lenarue's mother was pacing back and forth beside the wagon, continuing to watch Jordon and Lenarue.

"Momma's getting fidgety," Lenarue said. "I'm going to have to go pretty soon."

"I need to talk to you some more. I've got to try to learn as much as I can about Bitsy's life. What she was thinking, what she might have been doing or fixing to do that could have caused somebody to kill her." Jordon stared at the girl. "You understand this, don't you? You want to help me catch who did it?"

Lenarue nodded. "I do. But right now, Momma's going to be awful mad at me if I don't come on."

"I'll talk to her," Jordon said, starting to rise.

"Won't do any good for me when we get home. She'll still be mad."

"Then why don't I come out to your house later today, maybe this evening, and we can talk some more?"

"That would be all right. I won't be going anywhere." She got up and started walking toward the wagon. "You know about what time you'll be there?"

Jordon looked at his watch. It was a little after three. "Say about six-thirty? That okay?"

She said it was and went to join her mother and the others at the wagon. They all climbed aboard, and the tall boy clucked the horse into motion.

Jordon got into his Model A and headed for Sheriff Treadway's home. If it weren't for the honor of the thing, he thought, I'd just as soon skip this ride.

▽

Chapter Six

THE SUN HAD ALREADY dropped below the top of the
mountain to the west by the time Jordon got to Sheriff
Treadway's. Bonnie let him in and walked with him to
Noble's place before the fire.

Noble was wearing a frown. He waved Jordon to a seat and
wasted no time getting to what was bothering him. As soon
as Bonnie had left the room the sheriff said, "In a lot of ways,
you're a good peace officer, Jordon. Loyal. Reliable. Not
scared of anything living or dead far as I've been able to tell.
Trouble is you've never realized that being a good officer just
plain ain't enough."

Jordon knew the sheriff was just getting started, so he kept
quiet and waited.

"Being sheriff is two-thirds politics." Noble said. "Matter
of fact, most things in life are." He hesitated a moment, then
shot Jordon a cold, hard look. "And, boy, you don't know
shit about politics. Not shit."

"Is that what you wanted me to come out here for?" Jordon
asked. "To tell me that?" Jordon felt he was a little long in
the tooth to be called on the carpet like a schoolboy who'd
been caught pulling some little girl's pigtail.

"Partly."

"What else?" Jordon's words were clipped.

"Are you going to sit here and sass me? Or are you going to pay attention and try to learn something?"

Jordon tried to relax a little. "I guess I'm just upset about this dead girl."

"Why's that? She something special? Folks of yours or something?"

"Nothing special. Not folks. It just almost made me sick to look at her, that's all."

"You've seen dead people before. Put a few in that condition yourself, as I recall. What is it about this Trotter girl?"

"It's the first time I ever saw a girl cut up like that. And . . . I don't exactly know. She was just a little girl. Whoever killed her didn't have to do what he did. Seventeen stab wounds, other stuff."

"It's bad, that's so," the sheriff said. "But the way you feel about it don't give you the right to jump astraddle of Young Harry Buxton like you did. HR was fit to be tied."

Jordon was silent.

Noble heaved a mighty sigh. "You ain't a boy, Jordon. I figured when you decided to run for sheriff, you'd made up your mind that getting elected to public office takes some compromising. I reckon I might a been wrong."

"I didn't think I was that hard on Young Harry."

"With him, you don't have to be very hard to get him riled up. Everybody knows that. His daddy's rich, and he does pretty much what he wants to around here. His old man's been cleaning up his messes ever since he was a boy."

"Even when it comes to murder?"

"Murder?" Noble exploded. "What makes you think he did it? You got any evidence that he did?"

"He knew the Trotter girl. Had been out with her more than once."

"Hell fire, man, that's not murder! What kind of leap in your imagination did you make to get to murder?"

Jordon sat staring into the fire. "Maybe I was too rough on him."

"No maybe about it. You come down on him like a wagon load of horse turds, according to what HR said. Threatened to arrest him and I don't know what all." Noble shook his head in disgust. "Shit, man, that ain't no way to treat HR Buxton's boy."

"I guess I might have been too blunt, or something." It was as much as Jordon could bring himself to say. He knew much of it grew out of his general feeling toward the Buxton Corporation and everything connected with it.

"You ever heard the word 'finesse'?"

"I've heard it."

"Well, by God, I strongly suggest you start trying to use some of it if you expect to have any chance to get elected sheriff of Stanton County."

"I probably don't have much chance anyway."

Noble watched the fire for a moment before replying. "You might as well know this. I thought about it a long time before I decided to back you. Almost decided against it. You're a good deputy. Always have been, what I hear. But you're so goddamn stubborn. Bullheaded, a lot of folks say."

Jordon nodded. He'd heard that before.

"Frankly, it wouldn't matter to me more'n a fart in a whirlwind whether you get elected or not at this point, except for this: my reputation is on the line behind you. What happens to you will make a difference in the way people think about me. And the way people think about a man is everything in politics. You understand that?"

Jordon said, "You're retiring, aren't you? It couldn't make a hell of a lot of difference to you one way or the other now."

Noble shook his head. "Shows how much you understand about it. I can't succeed myself as sheriff, that's true. And I decided not to run for any other office this time, either. But I'm not ready yet to retire from living. I've got friends and relatives running, and will be running long after I'm gone. My reputation means something to them. And it means a hell of lot to me. You understand now?"

"I'm sorry for being a burden to you, Noble," Jordon said
drily. Then added, "I'll try to blunder on through this thing
without doing so much damage."

"You'd best, if you expect to win this election. Or do you
even give a damn, one way or the other?"

"I give a damn, Noble. I want to win. But I've got a job to
do."

"Your job is to do what I tell you to do," Noble said quietly.
"It's my job to decide what needs doing. You see the difference?"

Jordon nodded. "But if it turns out Young Harry had
anything—"

Noble held up his hand. "Ain't that Italian Three-C boy
the Trotter girl was running around with done took off some
place? That's what I heard."

"You hear things almost before I do."

"That's another part of my job."

Jordon grinned a little. "Yeah. Manochio's over the hill,
scouting some place, looks like."

"When they find him, if they do, I wouldn't waste any
time before I arrested him."

"For murder?"

"Suspicion. Arrest him on suspicion and hold him for
questioning. Till we find out more about this thing."

"I'll think about that."

"Don't think about it. Do it." Noble's voice was firm.
"That boy's got some explaining to do. If we get ahold of him
I don't want him running off again. Understand?"

Jordon nodded. "Anything else?"

"Not right now, I reckon."

Jordon stood up to leave. He arched his back, put his
hands on his hips and stretched.

"Keep me posted," Noble said. "I want to know everything
that's going on with this thing."

Jordon nodded. "Sure."

Noble gave him a straight look. "You can still win this election."

"I'd sure like to think that's possible," Jordon said.

"Oh, it's possible, all right. You can be the next sheriff of Stanton County, you play your cards right. For a gambler like you, seems to me that ought to be easy enough."

"If this is easy," Jordon said, "don't show me hard."

On the way to King's Mill, Jordon thought over the thrust of what Noble had said to him. The pressure was on. It looked like HR Buxton was calling in markers from Noble. Jordon hoped he could avoid further confrontation with Noble on this thing. But that depended on which way the trail led as Jordon pursued Bitsy's murderer.

Jordon's train of thought was interrupted when he realized one of his back tires had gone flat. He felt the flop-flop-flop and pulled off the side of the road. He got out the jack and spare and changed the flat, then drove to Buford Crenchaw's gas station to get it patched.

Buford was deep into the innards of a Model T. "I'll get to it soon as I finish with old Lizzie here," Buford said. He had grease all over his hands, face and coveralls. "Unless you want to leave it and pick it up later."

Jordon said he'd wait. He didn't like the thought of being caught out somewhere without a spare.

As he worked, Buford asked, "What about the Trotter girl? You arrested anybody?"

"Not yet," Jordon said. He really didn't want to talk about it with Buford.

"They say a Three-C boy done it," Buford said hopefully.

"Whoever 'they' are, they seem to know a lot more about it than the rest of us, Buford," Jordon said. He reached into the front seat of his car on the passenger side and took a book from it. It was a large book with heavy blue covers, a book Jordon had spent a lot of time with over the past few years.

He walked off to the side of the building and found himself

a seat on a wooden crate. He looked at the title imprinted on the cover of the book. *The Story of Philosophy* by Will Durant. It was one of the dozen or so books Jordon owned and thought of as his library, which of course it was, though he knew library was too much word for it.

Jordon had come across the volume by Durant as he browsed in a Louisville bookstore a few years back after losing in a cut-throat poker game there. He'd been reading in the book ever since, marking special passages, trying to comprehend the ideas of men like Plato and Aristotle, Schopenhauer and Santayana.

Jordon regretted that he didn't have the background to understand it all, or even most of it. His formal education, in tiny one-room mountain schoolhouses, had been spotty at best. The majority of what he knew had come not from classrooms but from his wanderings and the books he'd bought and read along the way.

His fascination with the minds of great men had sharpened through the years as he'd learned more about the wider world beyond the steep mountain walls that bounded Eastern Kentucky. Walls behind which his people had lived and died for generations.

Nothing Jordon knew, however, was more important than what he'd learned about the ways of men under pressure as he'd gambled and enforced the law and fought in two wars and done his hard time in the penitentiary.

He'd learned that desperate men behave in unpredictable ways. Some will buckle. Some will run. Some will stare death in the face and never flinch. And some will destroy whoever or whatever stands between them and what they lust for.

It had to have been such a man who murdered Bitsy Trotter.

Jordon sat idly turning the pages of Durant's book until he came to a place where he'd marked something for further study. Durant was writing about a man named Immanuel Kant.

It is the categorical imperative in us, the uncondi-
tional command of our conscience, to "act as if the
maxim of our action were to become by our will a
universal law of nature."

Jordon wondered about his own curiosity over such
things, why he bothered to try to understand them. Nobody
else he knew would have been interested, with the single
exception of Cassie. Sometimes the two of them would make
a game of it, exploring ideas they came across in books. He
knew it was one of the things that attracted them to one
another, this common interest in ideas.

A little while back, Jordon had copied the passage from
Kant in his notebook and read it to Cassie one evening when
they were sitting on her sofa.

"Let me look at it," Cassie had said, reaching for the
notebook. After a little bit she'd asked, "What do you think
he means?"

"I'm not real sure," Jordon said. "But I think he's saying
that we ought to behave so that if we could turn the rules
we live by into law, they'd be good for everybody, everywhere,
all the time. Something like that."

Cassie studied it some more. "Isn't that kind of like the
golden rule?"

Jordon thought about it a while. "I guess maybe it is. It
just sounded like more when I read it."

He remembered clearly, now, what Cassie had said
then. She'd laid her hand on his arm and told him, "More
or not, Berk, you read it and thought about it. That's what
matters."

Buford Crenchaw stepped around the corner of the building, wiping his hands on a wad of excelsior. "She's all done,"
he said. "Good as new—almost." He added, "Anyhow, it was
only flat on one side." He laughed.

Jordon closed the book and asked, "How much do I owe
you?"

"Two bits," Buford said. "Dime for the patch and the rest for me."

Jordon paid him and started for his car.

Buford eyed the book. "Whatcha reading?"

"A book by Will Durant."

"Is he the feller wrote *Riders of the Purple Sage*?"

"That was Zane Grey, I think."

"Oh yeah," Buford said.

$\triangledown$

Chapter Seven

"THE GIRL WAS A whore," Ike Sewell said. "That's the long and short of it."

Jordon looked at him with distaste. On his way to King's Mill, Jordon had stopped at the drugstore in Buxton to pick up a newspaper. When he had a chance, he liked to read the Louisville *Courier-Journal*. Ike, who as Buxton's Chief of Security spent most of his days strolling up and down the one broad street, had cornered Jordon to talk about the murder.

"A whore," Ike repeated.

"Why do you say that?" Jordon asked. "The girl had a job. She worked all she could."

"Well, then, if you want to split hairs, not a whore. A slut. Or a trollop, if it makes you feel better. Whatever name you put on it, she didn't have no objection to spreadin that wooly-booger around."

Jordon stared at him, then turned to go.

Ike pressed on. "You don't think so? Listen, you ain't been around here much the last few years. I've watched that girl since she was little. Ten or eleven, maybe. Coming here to the picture show at night, hanging around the soda fountain, twistin and shakin it when she seen men looking at her."

Jordon had a good idea who had been among the chief
lookers. "That didn't make her a slut."

"Other things I know about her did."

"Such as?"

"She done plenty of friggin. Plenty. I know that."

"With who?" Jordon asked.

"You want me to help you out on this case? Is that what
you're asking?"

Jordon did not reply. The last thing he was going to do
was let Ike Sewell worm his way into this investigation.
Aside from being rude and crude beyond redemption, Ike was
a direct pipeline back to whoever in the Buxton Corporation
hierarchy might have an interest in knowing what was
happening.

Ike said it again. "You want me to work with you or not?"

"I'll let you know if I need any help," Jordon replied. It was
as much as he could bring himself to say. "But tell me, who
was it you were referring to that was going out with Bitsy
Trotter?"

"I didn't say going out with. I said friggin."

"All right, frigging. Screwing. Whatever you want to call
it. Who was it?"

Ike gave Jordon a grin that was mostly a leer. "I'll let you
know if I remember who it was."

With no further word, Jordon turned and went to the
drugstore telephone. He called Willis and asked for any
messages.

"Just one you need to know about," Willis said. "Your
boy's back."

"Who?"

"Manochio. Captain Sweeney called from the Three-C
camp and said the boy walked back in a while ago. Said you
can come talk to him anytime you want."

It was late afternoon when Jordon took Sal Manochio into
custody at the CCC camp. "I want you to come with me to

the courthouse at King's Mill and answer some questions,"
Jordon told the young man. Manochio looked at Captain
Sweeney, who nodded.

"Am I under arrest?" Manochio asked, his eyes wide.

"Right now I want to question you. Then we'll decide
what comes next."

"I didn't do anything to hurt Bitsy."

Jordon took him by the arm and said, "We'd better go."

On the way to the courthouse, Jordon tried making conversation with Manochio. "How old are you?"

"Nineteen."

"Your full name?"

"Salvatore Manochio."

"I understand you're from New Jersey."

The boy said yes. "This is the first time I've ever been away
from New Jersey." He smiled, showing a mouthful of strong
white teeth. "I kinda like it here in the mountains." His smile
quickly faded. "Anyway, I did until Bitsy got killed."

Jordon looked at him. He was a handsome young man. A
thick shock of black wavy hair, even features, a small but
athletic-looking body. Jordon could see how he'd be attractive to girls.

"Exactly how were things between you and Bitsy?" Jordon
asked.

"What do you mean?"

"Were you all in love?"

"I was," Manochio said quietly.

"And Bitsy?"

"I don't know. She wanted more out of life than just a
man. She wanted a future, somewhere away from here."

"But not with you, is that it?"

"She said she wanted to live like people she'd read about
in books and magazines. In a nice house, with pretty furniture. And money to buy things."

"And she didn't think you could give her those things?"

Manochio stared glumly out the window of the car. "I

guess not. She said she wouldn't marry me."

"But you kept on seeing each another."

"Some. But a lot of the time she wouldn't go out with me."

"She went out with other boys?"

Manochio's face was set in a hard mask. "I guess so."

"Her folks thought she'd stopped seeing you a few weeks ago."

"Well, she hadn't."

"Did you know Bitsy was going to have a baby?" Jordon watched him closely as he asked the question.

It was a long time before Manochio nodded. "She told me she was. About a week ago."

"Did it belong to you? The baby?"

"Yes! Goddamn you!" Manochio said. "What do you think she was?"

"Take it easy, boy. You need to learn to put a leash on your temper. I'm just trying to get to the bottom of this thing."

When he spoke, Manochio's voice was low and strained. "It was my baby. And I didn't kill her. Or it. Why can't you see that?"

"Why'd you run away?"

"I thought people would know I'd been with her, then think I'd killed her."

"And why'd you come back?"

"I got to thinking. I didn't kill her. And I didn't want to spend my life running." He thought for a moment, then added, "I damn near froze my ass off last night in the woods."

"Where'd you sleep?"

"Didn't sleep much. Built a little fire under a cliff and sat there by it all night, just going over it all in my head. I figured if I came back in, I could tell the truth and maybe folks would believe me." After a moment, he said, "You think they will?"

"We'll have to wait and see, won't we?"

Manochio thought about it for a minute. "Do you? Believe me?"

Now it was Jordon's time to think about it. After a while, he said, "I'm not sure yet." After a moment he added, "Anyway, what I think or don't think is not what counts right now."

"What do you mean?"

"I'm going to have to hold you until this thing is cleared up one way or the other." They had arrived at the courthouse and Jordon pulled into his usual parking space.

"Does that mean I'm under arrest?"

Jordon nodded.

"You're going to put me in jail?"

It was a long moment before Jordon replied. "I've got no choice, son." He took Manochio by the arm and led him to the red brick jailhouse.

Inside, Pete Creekwood, the jailer, glanced up from the desk where he sat. Reluctantly he put aside his "Rangeland Adventures" magazine. He rubbed his hand across the rough gray stubble of beard on his sagging jaws and scowled at Jordon.

Jordon handed over his prisoner. "Take care of this boy, will you? He's liable to be with us for a while."

The jailer's tobacco-stained grin was not a pretty sight. "Oh, we'll take good care of him, same as with ever'body," he said. "What you got him for?"

"The sheriff wants him charged with the Trotter girl's murder."

When he heard this, Manochio's body went slack.

The jailer took the young man by the arm. "Come on along, boy. I'll show you your room at this here hotel. You done missed supper, but you might like to put in your breakfast order before you ree-tire for the evening. Let's see, now, we've got bulldog gravy and baloney, or we've got baloney and bulldog gravy, or we can give you baloney without gravy, and we've got—"

Jordon interrupted. "Lay off, Pete. Just lock him up." Jordon glanced at the desk. "Then you can get back to your magazine and find out if the fellow in the black hat is really the one rustling Miz Cunningham's cattle."

"I wouldn't waste too much time making fun of somebody, I was you," Pete replied. "I'd get my ass out and do a little electioneering if I was you and wanted a job next year. Way I hear it, you ought to be making friends, not being a smart ass."

It was dark as Jordon walked across the yard to the sheriff's office, where Willis said, "Old lady Cross is still on my back about bootlegging out her way. You want to hear about that?"

Jordon dropped into a chair. He rolled his eyes and said, "I'm due to talk to Bitsy Trotter's best girlfriend in a little while. I got to get moving in about five minutes."

"What did the sheriff want with you this morning?"

"Mostly to tell me what a poor excuse for a politician I am," Jordon said. "And to make sure I'd bring in Sal Manochio and lock him up."

"You did that?"

"Just now."

"You think he killed her?"

"Hard to say."

"He did run away, didn't he?" Willis fired up a cigarette and blew a stream of blue smoke toward Jordon.

"And he came back and turned himself in."

"Maybe he knowed he'd be caught anyway. Or maybe he just got cold sleeping out in the woods."

"Whatever it is, he'll sleep in jail tonight. And maybe for a while to come." Jordon heaved himself to his feet and started for the door. "Any calls for me?" he asked.

"You mean like from Cassie?"

Jordon hated to admit it, but that's what he had meant. "Anybody."

Willis grinned. "She didn't call. Nobody else either."

On the way to see Lenarue Wooten Jordon went over in his mind what he'd learned so far. It didn't seem like a lot, for all the questions he'd asked. Maybe his visit with Lenarue would be more fruitful. At least, he figured, it wouldn't get his tail in a crack with the sheriff. And it might, just might, get him on the path to figuring out who killed that poor girl.

Jordon sighed, took a peanut out of his pocket, cracked it and popped the kernels into his mouth. At least, he reflected, he'd had a couple of decent meals yesterday. And some breakfast at Danny's this morning.

The dirt road to Clyde Wooten's house was badly rutted and the driving was slow and jerky. It was a section of tiny hillside farms, within easy walking distance of where Bitsy Trotter had lived.

Jordon parked near the front gate and used his flashlight to pick his way across the yard. When he stepped up on the porch and knocked, he was surprised to see Lenarue dressed to go out, wearing a gray cloth coat and carrying a small purse.

His nose caught the aroma of cornbread and something with onions in it coming from the kitchen. He heard a little girl, Lenarue's sister he supposed, whining about something.

Lenarue didn't invite him inside. "Daddy's gone to a lodge meeting tonight," she explained. "And Momma said I could go to the picture show at Buxton if you would let me ride to town with you. We could talk on the way."

Jordon hadn't figured on this, but he liked the idea.

They walked to his car and he helped her in. When he had turned it around and they were jolting back along the rutted road, Lenarue said, "I can ride back home with daddy after his meeting. He'll stop by the drugstore for a few minutes when the show's over."

"I didn't really expect you'd be going out tonight," Jordon said.

"Truth is, I didn't want to sit at home and talk to you about Bitsy with my mother listening."

"Why's that?"

"I didn't want her to hear about Bitsy. And me. Momma's

so old-fashioned, she thinks girls and boys shouldn't . . . you know."

"Shouldn't what?"

"Well, court. Spark. Whatever you want to call it. The way momma acts about it, makes you wonder how kids ever got born when she was young. If she really knew what was going on, she'd have a calf—with a paper tail."

"I suppose folks don't change all that much from one generation to the other." Jordon couldn't be sure in the darkness, but he thought the girl might be smiling. "How old are you, Lenarue?"

"Same age as Bitsy. Eighteen."

"And you two were friends for how long?"

"Ever since we were little. Our family moved here when I was nine, so since then." She thought for a moment. "Nine years now."

"You've grown up together."

"In a lot of ways. Went through grade school and high school together. Worked together at the telephone office."

"Dated a lot together?"

"Some."

Jordon considered his next question for a moment, then asked, "How long ago did Bitsy tell you she was pregnant?"

Lenarue did not reply at once. Finally she said, "Mr. Jordon, is what I say to you just between us? You know, like they say, confidential?"

"If you want it to be."

"I do. There are some things I don't want to get back to my momma and daddy. Or anybody."

"They'll never hear them from me," Jordon said. By this time they had reached the hard-surface road, and Jordon turned the car toward Buxton.

Lenarue was quiet until Jordon finally asked, "What are these things you were mentioning you were going to tell me?"

"I wouldn't be talking to you about Bitsy except to maybe help you catch whoever killed her. When we were little, we crossed our hearts and hoped to die if we ever told each other's secrets."

Jordon smiled. He remembered doing the same thing himself. A long time ago. "I understand," he said.

Lenarue took a deep breath and said, "You asked how long I knew she was pregnant? She told me when she missed her first period."

"When was that?"

"A little over a month ago. Then last week she missed her second one. She was sure then."

"Do you know who the father was?"

Lenarue didn't reply.

Jordon said, "It could be a big help to me to know."

Another wait, then, "I don't know for sure."

"She didn't tell you?"

"She didn't know herself. For certain." Lenarue turned to him and said in a pleading voice, "Mr. Jordon, Bitsy wasn't a . . . a . . . slut. But sometimes she let herself get into things that ended up with her in trouble." She waited a moment, then added, "Like getting pregnant."

"And getting killed," Jordon said.

"Do you think that's why she got killed?"

"I don't know. But tell me, who did she think was the one got her pregnant?"

"It was one of two people."

"Who?"

"Sal Manochio, for one."

"And the other?"

She seemed to dread to say the words. "Young Harry Buxton." She quickly added, "Nobody'll ever know I told you, will they?"

"Nobody. Don't you worry about it."

"She knew it could have been either one. But it didn't really make any difference."

"Why?"

"She was going to get rid of it. The baby."

"An abortion?"

Lenarue nodded. "She said she'd never have a woods colt."

They had arrived in Buxton, and Jordon parked near the theater where they could see people buying tickets and going inside. *Dr. Jekyll and Mr. Hyde,* the sign outside the ticket booth said, starring Fredric March and Miriam Hopkins.

"Tell me about her abortion plans," Jordon said.

"The show's going to be starting soon."

Jordon looked at his watch. "You've got a little time. What about Bitsy's abortion?"

"She knew somebody who would help her do it."

"Who?"

"Does it matter?"

"It could."

"You know the old woman folks say is a witch? Lives on the Beaver Creek road?"

"Rachel Blackwell?"

"That's her."

"You're saying Bitsy had already talked to Rachel about it?"

Lenarue nodded. "More than once."

"And Rachel was going to help her?"

Another nod. "She liked Bitsy. They got along fine. Bitsy used to slip over to Rachel's when we were little and play. And as we got older, Bitsy still would stop and visit Rachel. I never could understand why Bitsy wanted to hang around an old woman like that, but she did. Maybe she wanted Rachel to teach her witching."

Jordon heard something in her voice he took to be jealousy. Sharing Bitsy's friendship with Rachel Blackwell evidently had not set well with Lenarue.

Suddenly Lenarue opened the door and jumped out of the car. "I've got to get my ticket. The show's about to start."

"One more thing," Jordon said. "What about this boy Farrell Nilson that Bitsy was seeing? What kind of fellow is he?"

Lenarue shook her head. "Plain old mean and nasty. I'm scared to be around him."

"Was Bitsy scared of him, too?"

"Bitsy wasn't dumb. She knew what kind of person he is."

Like his old man, Jordon thought. Farrell Nilson's father, Zack, had been a nasty sonofabitch, too. Jordon had had a run-in with him years ago in a poker game. And Zack had carried the grudge right up until he was killed in a drunken fracas just before Jordon went away to the last war.

Lenarue was backing away from the car. "Honest, Mr. Jordon, I can't talk any more right now. I'm gonna miss the start of the show."

"I need to ask you some more questions."

"Call me this weekend, why don't you?" Lenarue came back to the window and stuck her head inside. "I hope you find out who did it." All at once she looked like she might cry.

"You have any idea who that might be?"

She stared at him for a long moment. Finally, she shook her head. He could see tears glistening in her eyes before she turned and ran to the theater.

Jordon sat in the car at the edge of the light from the theater entrance, turning over in his mind what he'd just learned from Lenarue. He liked this girl. She had been helpful, more by far than anyone else. It was no surprise that Bitsy's baby could have belonged to Young Harry or Manochio. But Lenarue's claim that Bitsy had intended to get rid of it—that was something to think about.

The more he learned about the whole business, the more depressing it became to him. And the more determined he was to keep on peeling back the layers until he got to the core of it. Whatever it was that was driving him on, and he was by no means sure, he did know that he couldn't stop until he knew the truth.

Jordon went into the drugstore and called the home of Farrell Nilson. A woman answered who said she was his mother, and no, Farrell wasn't at home.

"You know where I might find him?" Jordon asked.

"Who wants to know?" She sounded suspicious, belligerent.

Jordon hesitated only a moment. "A friend of his," he lied. "Name's Decker."

"I ain't never heard him mention no Decker."

"That's all right, ma'am. I'll see him another time," Jordon said. "I was just down in this part of the county tonight and thought I might catch up with him. I owe him a little money and wanted to pay him."

"Decker, you say?"

"Yes, ma'am."

"Well, he did mention a place called Della's, then said he might be going to see some buddies of his'n at Stateline. A place name of Black Cory Holcomb's. That's all I know to tell you. He might be at either place. Or neither one for all I know. Hit's more than I can do to keep up with that one." Her voice had the bitter edge of a woman who had known more than her fair share of trouble.

Jordon thanked her, went back to his car and drove to Della's. He checked his watch as he pulled into the parking lot. Not yet eight, but there were plenty of cars. And horses tethered to nearby trees.

As he got out of his Model A, he could hear music and laughter. Friday night at Della's was just starting to build up a head of steam.

Inside, the place was alive. At one end of the room, on a little platform, stood four men with string instruments: a fiddle, guitar, mandolin and banjo. They were playing a fast fiddle tune. It sounded like "Billy in the Low Ground" to Jordon. He didn't have much of an ear for music, but he could recognize a few songs. This one he remembered because it sounded a little bit like bagpipe music he'd heard once during the war.

A tall, lean young man in faded overalls was on the floor doing a dangerous looking buck dance with a pretty, plump young girl in a bright flowered dress. Lots of knees and elbows flying.

People at several of the nearby tables clapped their hands to the beat of the music.

Jordon spotted Della at her usual place by the cash register. A lady who kept her priorities straight.

She saw him at about the same time and beckoned to him. When he approached her, she flashed her dazzling smile. "Come to have a little fun with us tonight, deputy?"

"Mainly to get a bite to eat," he said, glancing around the room. "I don't see Cassie. Is she here?"

"Somewhere. She stays busy in the evenings. Like me and the rest."

Jordon looked around for a table. Della said, "Sit here at the counter and talk to me."

Jordon sat down, ordered chicken and dumplings from a passing waitress, then took a moment to survey the room. He saw several people he knew, but nobody had paid much attention to him when he came in.

"Have you seen a young man named Farrell Nilson in here tonight?" Jordon asked Della.

"I don't think I know him, at least not by name," she said. "You might ask Tiny."

As he continued to look around the room, Jordon could see most people had glasses and coffee cups in front of them, along with soft drink bottles and ashtrays. Jordon knew Della never openly sold whiskey in the place. He also knew that pocket bootleggers with their coats full of bottles were always close by to supply the needs of customers.

Jordon wondered exactly how he would come to terms with the matter of illegal whiskey if he won the election. He'd drunk enough of it himself, it didn't seem like so bad a thing. Yet it was against the law, had been by local option in most of the mountain counties even before Prohibition, on the Kentucky side of the line, anyhow. He put it out of his mind. There was time enough to deal with that problem if and when he became sheriff.

In a soft voice, Della said, "How are you doing on the Trotter girl's death?"

"A little progress, I guess you could say."

"I heard you butted heads this morning with"—she whispered the words—"Young Harry."

"That's making the rounds, is it?"

"I guess somebody passing his office must have overheard you all, or something. Anyway, I heard it this evening."

"It didn't amount to much," he said. The waitress brought Jordon's supper and he began to eat, keeping his eyes on the food. Della dropped the subject, and Jordon resumed his scanning of the room.

Near the door, sitting quietly by himself at a small table half in the shadows, was Tiny Bob Dinwiddie, a massive young man in overalls and plaid shirt. He was the principal reason Della's place created so little trouble for the law.

Tiny had once killed a man in a bare-handed, no-holds-barred fight. Broke his neck. It was ruled accidental. Today he couldn't tell you the total number of arms, fingers, collar-bones and such that he'd fractured over the years for people of so little judgment as to have taken him on.

When Della opened her place, Tiny was her first employee. On the job he wore a belt and holster carrying a .44 Colt revolver with a six-inch barrel strapped around the outside of his overalls. This, in addition to Tiny's awesome size, made Della's one of the most orderly places in the county. Officially, Tiny was a deputy constable, appointed to assist the magistrate in the district. Unofficially, he did whatever Della required.

Jordon walked over to where Tiny sat. "Della said you might have seen a fellow named Farrell Nilson if he was in here tonight."

"Ain't seen him," Tiny said.

"You do know him, though?"

"Just to recognize him is about all. They tell me he's

supposed to be mean, or thinks he is. He ain't been in here more than two or three times all told."

"Didn't cause you any trouble?"

Tiny gave Jordon a big, friendly grin. "Shucks, he wouldn't do nothin like that, surely. They say he's kinda dumb as well as mean. But I doubt that he'd be that dumb. Della don't like trouble around here."

Jordon laughed and went back to his seat at the counter.

The band at the other end of the room finished the tune it had been playing and started another, slower, piece. It sounded like "The One Rose." Several couples took to the floor and swayed gently to the music.

Jordon was almost finished with his coffee when Della called out, "Cass? Can I see you for a minute?"

Cassie came across the room and Della told her to check in the kitchen and see if they'd baked enough cornbread. If not, she should make up another batch.

"I already did," Cassie said. "It's in the oven."

"You're on top of everything," Della said with a smile. Then, nodding toward Jordon, she added, "Look who's paying us a call tonight, Cass. Our favorite deputy."

Cassie looked at Jordon, apparently noticing him for the first time, but he couldn't be sure. "Hello, Berk," she said.

"Cass," he said quietly. "I see you're busy this evening."

"It's the weekend," she responded. She seemed distant. She turned to Della. "I'd better check on that bread."

When Cassie was gone, Della said, "Is something wrong between you all?"

Jordon took his time in replying. Finally he breathed a huge sigh and said, "If there is, it's news to me. But it seems to me like there's always something wrong, big or little, between men and women."

Della studied him for a long moment before she arched her eyebrows and cocked her head to one side. "My, my," she said. "A philosopher. And unsung, as they say."

Jordon grinned a little. "A prophet is not without honor—"

"... save in his own country." She turned the full intensity of her smile on him and added, "One of these days you and I are going to have to get together for a long discussion on philosophy. After the election, maybe."

"Talking philosophy with you gets a high place on my after-the-election list," he said, "though I expect you'd outclass me."

Jordon heard one of the musicians saying something about the band taking a short break. As the couples started leaving the dance floor, Jordon saw Cassie walk up and start talking to the tall, dark-complected young man who had been playing the guitar. Jordon knew the boy vaguely. Knew his folks, the Halls. One of Stanton County's oldest and best families. Hard-working, honest people.

Jordon saw Cassie standing close in front of the boy, smiling up at him. Jordon turned back to Della. He didn't want Cassie to see him watching her. Damn it, he thought, here I am acting like some love-struck schoolboy, sneaking looks at his girl talking to a rival and feeling the hot rush of blood to his face. Jordon didn't like what he felt, not one damn bit. But he couldn't deny that he felt it.

He finished the dregs of his coffee and wiped his mouth and mustache with his napkin. As he started to stand up, he saw someone approaching out of the corner of his eye. When he turned he saw the guitar player had finished talking to Cassie and had come over to Della. He stood at the register with his hands jammed into the back pockets of his jeans. Several strands of jet black hair dangled across his forehead, and his face broke into a smile that competed with Della's for brilliance. He couldn't be much past his early twenties. His dark eyes squinted almost shut when he smiled. Jordon thought he looked like he had Indian blood in him.

"The music sounded great," Della said to the young man. "We were so busy talking I didn't even notice you'd stopped for a break." Then to Jordon, "You two know each other?"

Jordon stood and extended his hand to the young man,

who took it and said, "I know who you are, Mr. Jordon. I'm John P Hall."

"Sure," Jordon said. "Ben Hall's boy."

"I live with him," John P said. "But he's really my uncle."

"I remember now," Jordon said. "Well, since we're already shaking hands, I might as well take advantage of the situation and ask you to vote for me for sheriff. And see if you can get Ben and your Aunt. . . ."

"Margie," John P said. "Don't have to worry about them. Ninety percent of the Halls in the county will be voting for you, me included. It's my first time to vote."

"I hope you'll tell them all I appreciate their support."

"You can count on it." John P turned Jordon's hand loose and moved to stand next to Della, slipping his arm around her shoulder. "So you liked my playing," he whispered, gazing into her face.

Della glanced at Jordon, then back at John P and said, "If you're not already, you're going to be the best guitar picker in fifty miles."

"Not a thousand?" he said, pretending to be offended. "Or at least a hundred?"

"Don't let over-confidence ruin you in the spring of your life," Della said. Turning to Jordon she said, "I've just hired John P and his buddies to play Friday and Saturday nights. It could be I made a mistake telling him how good he is."

"If a man's good at something, it doesn't hurt to hear it once in awhile. Right, Mr. Jordon?"

To Della, Jordon said, "I don't expect it'll do a fellow like John P too much damage." Behind his easy smile and banter, there seemed to lurk a quiet shyness in John P Hall that he was making a special effort to overcome. In spite of himself and the fact that Cassie had been a hell of a lot warmer to John P than she had to him tonight, Jordon couldn't help liking the young man. In fact, Jordon could hardly think of one of the Halls in Stanton County that he didn't like. It pleased him to know they were supporting him.

"I know you all will excuse me," Jordon said. "I need to be getting along."

Della gave Jordon a lingering look. "To be continued."

John P grinned again and stuck out his hand. "See you around." Jordon could see why Cassie was attracted to him.

As he turned, Jordon heard Della say to John P, "Let me get Cassie to watch the register, and we can go into my office and talk during your break."

Outside, Jordon noticed two men standing near the corner of the building. They stopped their conversation when they saw him. A bootlegger and his client, Jordon figured. Between Prohibition and the sheriff's special arrangements, buying and consuming a drink of whiskey in the mountains had become a damned complicated affair.

At least the Prohibition part would soon be over. Ought to make the rest a little simpler. Jordon felt like having a drink or two himself, but not in a public place like Della's, not with the election coming up. Another little layer of hypocrisy.

He got into his Model A and headed south toward Stateline on the main highway. Across the line, in Tennessee, he would take off his badge and gun, walk into Black Cory Holcomb's place and have himself a drink of whiskey, like any self-respecting thirsty man anywhere was likely to be doing tonight.

If Farrell Nilson's mother had been right about where he was headed, Jordon figured he might find this young man with a reputation for being mean and dumb and ask him a few questions about the death of Bitsy Trotter.

After he crossed the state line into Tennessee, Jordon drove the quarter of a mile or so until he reached a large frame building set back from the road. It was surrounded by cars and horses. Whether Nilson was there or not, Jordon looked forward to seeing his old friend, Black Cory Holcomb.

Here, as at Della's, no whiskey was sold on the premises,

but the nearby darkness was alive with bootleggers, operating their businesses out of automobiles, tree stumps and coat pockets.

Cory's own people worked the area near his place, and he kept a supply under the counter for himself and personal friends.

Local law enforcement was "friendly" to the places along the state line, where the whiskey-and-women trade had flourished for generations. And federal officers found reasons for not coming near the place without the support of local officials.

Black Cory's was full of men, and several women, drinking and laughing, some with their hands on each other in places likely to lead to sex or fights, or both, before the evening was much older.

Jordon smiled at Black Cory and greeted him with a handshake. Cory handed him a coffee mug with moonshine in it. Cory wasn't actually black, he was just very dark. Swarthy, whiplike, with skin all tight and shiny as old harness leather. Black hair. Black eyes. And most of the time, a black disposition. The designation Black Cory was a way of distinguishing him from his cousins and uncles also named Cory Holcomb, of whom there were several.

Jordon had known Cory for most of his life. They had served together in the Philippines. And Cory had been nearby the time Jordon had killed the two young men who'd pistol-whipped him. Seeing Cory always brought the memories sluicing back to Jordon.

"You know a young fellow named Farrell Nilson?" Jordon asked Cory.

"When I see him." Cory looked around the room. "He was here a while ago." Their eyes scanned the roomful of drinkers, at tables and booths and standing near the counter. "There," Cory said, indicating two muscular young men seated in the corner.

"Thanks," Jordon said.

Black Cory nodded. "Don't see enough of you these days, my friend."

"I know the feeling," Jordon said and made his way across the room to the corner table where two beefy young men sat drinking. They paid no attention to Jordon until he spoke. "One of you fellows Farrell Nilson?"

They both stared at him. "Who wants to know?" one of them said. He was dark and wore about a week's growth of black beard on his face.

"My name's Jordon. I'm a deputy sheriff. I need to ask you a few questions."

The other young man spoke up. "I don't see no badge on you." He was as light as his drinking buddy was dark. He ran his hands through his long, silky looking blond hair, and watched Jordon with pale unblinking eyes.

"I'm a Stanton County deputy. Across the line," Jordon said.

"Well, shit, we're in Tennessee now. Or didn't you know? Who the goddamn hell are you asking questions down here?" It was the dark one. He turned to his blond companion and said, "He look like the law to you, Herman?"

Jordon looked at him for a moment before he spoke. "Since he's Herman, I take it you're Nilson."

"It might be best you take your ass out of my face before I lose my temper. You got no authority to ask me anything here."

Jordon gave the young men a tight little smile. He stared at Nilson, then spoke quietly to him. "I'll talk to you when we're back on the Kentucky side. We can settle this then."

"Go on about your business, old man," Nilson said. "Whatever that might be." They both laughed and went back to their drinks.

Jordon walked across the room, found an empty table in the corner and sat down. He felt a little naked in here without his gun and badge. He caught the eye of the homely, middle-aged waitress and when she came over told her to get him a bottle.

She looked at Cory, who nodded.

When she brought his bottle, Jordon filled his mug and took a big hooker of the moonshine.

He sat sipping his whiskey, trying to figure why Nilson was so nasty. Was it because he saw Jordon as some kind of "fastest gun?" A figure to be brought down? Evidently the boy knew of Jordon, who he was. Maybe it had something to do with Nilson's dad, old Zack, and the trouble Jordon had had with him long ago. Or could it be that Nilson had something to hide, something to do with Bitsy Trotter? Maybe he was simply disagreeable, another member of that mean-spirited class of men who prefer trouble to peace. Jordon had come across more than his share of such men in his time.

Thinking about fractious men sent Jordon back in his mind to that night nearly thirty years ago, when, not a quarter of a mile from here, he had encountered the two mean drunks in an episode that ended in a gunfight, with both of the men dead.

Recently back from the Philippines, Jordon had walked into a whiskey joint to get a drink, and within ten minutes found himself being chivied by the two. Jordon was not yet twenty-five, and his tormentors were close to the same age. One of them was a swarthy youth with a vicious laugh. Jordon could almost see them still. The other, a fair-complected young man with cruel blue eyes, pulled a pearl-handled .38 Colt and began to jab Jordon in the ribs with it.

"Why?" Jordon had asked. "Why are you doing this? I don't even know you."

"Because you're here," the fair-skinned one said. "And we're here." He eyed Jordon for a moment, then added, "And because your goddamned nose is too long. Right, Vernon? Ain't his nose too long?"

Vernon had reached for Jordon's nose, but Jordon stepped aside and swung on him. That was when the fair-skinned one, Cephas his name turned out to be, split Jordon's head

open with the pistol barrel. Vernon then pulled his own gun
and the two of them worked Jordon over.

Now, Jordon's hand went unconsciously to his head,
fingers feeling for the scar he'd carried all these years from
one of their guns. He'd got away from them then, telling
them, "I'll be back. You'd better not be here."

They laughed at him and watched him jump on his horse
and race away. At home, Vera had pleaded with him to let
it go, to think about her and the children. He was so torn
apart that he went outside and fired his guns into the ground
until they were empty. But it didn't free him. He had to go
back—carrying a .38 special and a .44.

And when he'd found the two still there, he'd killed them
both. With no talk or argument. He just started shooting at
them as soon as they saw him.

Then he'd turned without a word and ridden home again,
blood still in his hair and dried on his face from the beating
they'd given him. Neither he nor anyone else would ever
know why they'd chosen him to bully. He'd never been able
to figure out any reason, other than their plain, overbearing
drunken meanness.

It reminded him of the streak he thought he'd just seen
in Nilson. Well, whatever it was that was eating Nilson,
Jordon had had enough blunt talk to do him this day.

He recalled the way Cassie had acted at Della's. He
wondered what was on her mind. Why was she so cool
toward him? And was all the warmth for John P Hall just
show, or did it mean something?

Jordon took another drink. He knew he should be someplace trying to get votes tonight, not making the rounds at
the local hangouts. But it was all more than he felt like
dealing with right now.

He poured himself another drink. Then another. He
couldn't seem to relax. His mind had a sharp edge on it that
the liquor couldn't reach. Underneath everything else, he
knew, he was becoming obsessed with the Bitsy Trotter

murder. He didn't seem to be accomplishing much except getting Young Harry and HR Buxton and Noble mad at him. Sure, the Three-C boy was in jail. Yet Jordon just couldn't believe it was all that simple. There was more to it, he felt in his bones. But it sure wasn't easy to figure what it might be.

Jordon hadn't been paying any attention to how many drinks he'd had or how much time had passed when he became aware of someone saying something to him.

"You going to hog that table all to yourself, old man, or are you going to move and let us set down?"

Jordon glanced up to see Nilson and his friend—what was his name? Herman?—towering over him. They'd go over two hundred pounds a piece, he guessed. And not fat, either.

A third man was now with them. He was older, maybe thirty-five, not as big, but tough looking. All three of them wore dirty overall pants and muddy boots.

"Well, by God, are you or ain't you? Men work in the log woods all day need a place to set down and drink." It was Nilson speaking.

Jordon continued to look at them, trying to get them in focus. He had not intended to drink so much.

"Maybe he's deef, Farrell," the older man said, laughing. "That's probably it. He can't hear you."

"He can hear, all right," Nilson said. "I know who he is."

"Who?" the older man asked, obviously enjoying his role.

"He's a deputy from across the line. Name of Jordon. Running for high sheriff of Stanton County. He's just a little bit out of his territory, that's all. And forgot his badge and gun," Nilson said. "How about it, Jordon, you going to get up and let us set down?"

Jordon watched as Nilson postured for his companions, watched as they smiled their approval. Around the room, other drinkers had stopped their conversations to see what was about to happen.

Nilson was saying, "Maybe he is deef after all. Cause if he ain't, then he's by God without a doubt the dumbest sonofabitch I ever seen. Deef or dumb, or both, he'd better move." Nilson paused for a moment, then grinned at Jordon and said, "Or maybe you'd druther I stomped your ass."

Jordon stood up slowly. He stepped from behind the table as if to leave, avoiding looking directly into Nilson's eyes.

Nilson continued to grin.

Then, without changing his expression or giving any other sign of warning, Jordon swung his right fist with every ounce of strength he had and connected with Nilson's nose. Blood squirted, and Nilson rocked backwards but did not go down. His two buddies stepped to one side, prepared to enjoy the slaughter as spectators.

Nilson gave his nose a swipe with his hand and looked at the blood. He shuffled his feet, moving into a fighting stance. He grinned and said, "What I was hoping you'd do, tough guy."

Jordon bounced a little on the balls of his feet and circled backwards, being careful to stay out of Nilson's reach. From the corner of his eyes, Jordon could see people sliding chairs out of the way.

Nilson feinted with his left hand, but he was slow, too heavy to move with any real speed or grace. As long as Jordon could stay out of his way he'd be okay.

But Jordon realized he'd had too much liquor, his reflexes were slowed. He knew he was no match for Nilson in this kind of situation.

Nilson tried to move in. He jabbed with his left a couple of times, then took a roundhouse swing at Jordon's head. When he missed, it threw him off balance.

Knowing he was done for if Nilson ever got close enough to him and connected, Jordon moved in tight and snap-kicked Nilson in the crotch.

Nilson let out a scream of agony and doubled over.

Jordon stepped back and kicked him again, this time a side-kick that caught Nilson in the head, just in front of the ear.

Nilson thudded to the floor and made no further movement or sound. A dark wetness started to spread on his pants in a widening pattern outward from his crotch, and a puddle of water began to form on the floor.

Jordon turned toward the other two men. His head was spinning. He could hear his heart pounding. Now he knew he'd drunk a lot more than even he had realized.

Nilson's companions took a step in his direction. The big blond said, "Kicking in the nuts. That ain't fair, is it?"

Before the other one could answer, Black Cory Holcomb pulled back both hammers of the double-barreled shotgun he'd laid up on the counter and pointed at the two men. "Closer to fair than three men jumping on one," Cory said.

At the other end of the bar, Cory's brother Horace stood with a long-barrel .38 Smith & Wesson special leveled at the men.

They looked at Cory. "Hold on, mister," the older one said. "Why don't we talk this over?" He sounded scared.

"The double-ought buckshot in this twelve-gauge talks for me," Cory said. Then he asked Jordon, "You all right?"

Jordon took a deep breath. Then he grinned and said, "Never laid a glove on me." He reeled unsteadily back to his table and sat down.

"You two fellers get your buddy up and get his sorry ass out of here," Cory said. "Where you all from, anyhow?"

"Stanton County," the older man said. "Same as Jordon."

"Except for the Nilson boy, I never seen you before," Cory said.

"No. We're cousins from up near the Laurel County line."

Cory's voice was quiet, but in the silence that hung over the room everybody heard it. "I'll take pity on your cousin there on the floor this once and have somebody clean up his mess. But don't ever show your faces around here again. There's a limit to my Christian charity, and you boys have done reached it."

The two of them lifted Nilson by the arms and dragged him out the door into the night.

Cory eased the hammers down on his shotgun and put it back under the bar. The other patrons resumed their drinking and talking.

Jordon lay on a cot in the back room of Black Cory's place and tried to bring the parallel lines formed by the ceiling boards into focus.

Black Cory was putting some coal in the big kitchen stove. "I knowed you was three sheets in the wind after you kicked that big sonofabitch in the nuts. Looked for a minute like you might fall right over on top of him. I reckon I ought to be thankful neither one of you puked on the floor. Even though he did piss his pants."

"I'm glad I didn't have to take on another one of them," Jordon said. "Whatever that stuff is you're selling kicks like a frigging mule. It's not straight corn, I know that."

"Plain old sugar whiskey. Cheaper and faster to make than straight corn. And most folks don't care one way or the other." Then Cory added, "But it's made in a clean copper still."

Jordon rubbed his hand over his face. "I believe you might have been right about me needing to lay down here and rest for a little bit. Can't handle it the way I used to."

"You want to sleep some?"

"Maybe just a little," Jordon said. The last thing he heard was Cory poking the fire in the stove, then walking back out front.

When Jordon opened his eyes, Cory was shaking his shoulder.

"You want to get up now, or stay here the rest of the night?" Cory asked. "You're welcome, you know that."

"I know." Jordon said. "What time is it?"

"A little after three. I closed up a while ago. Nobody here but me and you and Horse." Cory looked over toward a bunk at the other side of the room where his brother lay on his back snoring. "Sounds like Buxton's planing mill, don't he?"

As if in response, Horace—"Horse" everybody called him—snorted, then rolled over on his side facing the wall and let out a huge fart.

"Sweet Jesus," Cory said, shaking his head in disgust.

Jordon yawned and stood up, rubbing his eyes. He went to the sink in the corner of the room, dipped some water from the bucket into a pan and splashed it on his face. It was icy cold. "Any coffee?"

Cory, who had taken a chair at the small table in the middle of the room, nodded toward the stove where a large blue enamel pot sat on the edge. "Help yourself."

Jordon poured a cup and seated himself across from Cory, taking a large gulp. "My God!" he said, making a terrible face and staring at the cup.

"Only been going for three days," Cory said. "It's getting good."

"Three days?" Jordon looked at the cup with distaste.

"I start a fresh pot a couple of times a week," Cory said. "Then ever day I throw in some more coffee and water, and it gets better and better. Finally, a day or so after there ain't nobody but me can drink it, I break down and start another pot."

Jordon scowled and took another drink.

"What are you doing out getting drunk in Tennessee tonight, anyway?" Cory asked. "Don't running for sheriff in Stanton County keep you busy enough?"

Jordon stared at him for a moment, then said, "Tell me something, Cory. What ever made me think I ought to be running for sheriff in the first place?"

Cory looked serious. "Truth is, you never was too bright, Berk."

Jordon grinned a little. He'd forgotten that Cory called him Berk. Cory and Cassie. The only ones. "Remember that time in the Philippines? When I broke my hand fighting with that big bohunk from Wisconsin or wherever it was?"

"And Major Cheatham catched you at it." Cory laughed at the remembrance.

"That's the same thing the major said to me: 'You're not too bright, Corporal Jordon.' Next morning I was a private again."

"Ought to of took off your stripes before you fit the bohunk."

"I must have forgot."

"Or me and the major is right: you just ain't too bright."

"At least I was bright enough to learn to use my feet when I get into a fight with somebody bigger than me." Jordon grinned. "Remember that little Filipino? What was his name?"

"The one learned us to kick-fight? Delacruz. He'd be tickled to death if he could of seen you lay into that big old boy tonight." Cory got up and took a half-full gallon jug from the cabinet behind him. He uncapped it and poured himself a cupful. "Want some of this? Straight corn."

Jordon shook his head and said, "I've had enough for one night." Then he added, "Though the good Lord only knows whether moonshine or your coffee is more fearsome."

They sat in silence for a while, each working at his own cup. "Been a long time, Cory," Jordon said at last.

"What?"

"All of it. The stuff we've both seen and done. The railroad. The mines opening up. The war with Spain."

Cory nodded.

Jordon stared at nothing. His voice wandered. "Automobiles . . . airplanes . . . telephones . . . France . . . the flu . . . radio . . . Prohibition." After a while he said, "Jesus! How's a man supposed to keep up with it all?"

"Now this goddamn depression," Cory said. After a moment he added, "And I thought for a minute tonight there might be another chapter writ. One of us could of easy killed them fellers."

"I left my gun in the car."

"I had mine."

Jordon took a drink of coffee. "I appreciate it."

"No more than you've done for me. More than once, as I recollect." Cory took a long drink from his cup. "You know what I miss the most doing with you?"

"No."

"The poker games we used to have. That's what you ought to be doing."

"What?"

"Running a poker game instead of running for sheriff."

"If I lose this election, that's probably what I'll be doing."

"You can always do it here. You're better at it than anybody else I ever seen."

Jordon stared at the table. For the first time since he could remember, he felt like he might cry. And the worst thing was, he didn't know why. "Know something, Cory?"

"What?"

"In all these years, all the places I've been, all the things I've seen and done, I've never been able to forget about those two boys I killed up the road a piece."

"I remember."

Jordon went on, talking as much to himself as to Cory. "Hell, I was as young as they were." He shook his head. "Nothing in the world could've stopped me from coming back and killing them."

Cory sat quietly and listened. He took another pull from his cup. Then he spoke. "Long time ago, Berk. Thirty years almost."

"It still seems so clear to me." Jordon's voice was almost a whisper. "I've killed other men. In battle. In the line of duty. But none of them has bothered me like those two."

"They asked for it. Like them boys tonight."

Jordon drained the last of Cory's bitter brew from his cup and heaved a great sigh. "Yeah. But I still went to the penitentiary. Before I got out, Vera was dead. And my two little children got dragged around from pillar to post, from one relative to the other."

They sat in silence for a while. Then Cory said, "Will you win the election, you think?"

"Aah." Jordon waved his hand. "It could go either way."

"Don't you give a shit?"

"I give a shit. I'd like to be elected high sheriff, just once in my life. But I truly don't know if I can do it."

"What about the dead girl? You aiming to catch who it was killed her?"

"Oh, yes, Cory. I aim to catch him. Don't know who he is yet, and don't know exactly how I'm going to do it. But I aim to catch the sonofabitch."

"Some boys from up by Buxton in here early this evening," Cory said. "Talking like some dago Three-C boy done it."

"I got him locked up, but I don't much think he's the one."

"Them boys say if he gets out of jail, he won't live two days."

"Who was it said that?"

Cory looked at him without expression. "I'd rather not say." Then, after a moment, "But you might want to keep it in mind."

"I will," Jordon said. He stood up and passed his hand across his face. "I'm going to go."

Cory draped his arm around Jordon's shoulder and the two men walked to the door together. Cory, waiting to lock up behind Jordon, said, "Be careful, Berk."

"Yeah," Jordon said and stepped into the cold darkness outside.

$\triangledown$

Chapter Eight

SATURDAY MORNING DAWNED BRIGHT but cool.

When he first woke up and looked out the window, Jordon felt a little rocky from the previous night's moonshine at Black Cory's. But Mary Helen's biscuits and eggs with plenty of coffee brought him around.

After breakfast, Jordon's two grandchildren—Cindy, who was nine, and Dan Jr., seven—set up a clamor to go to a neighbor's house to play.

"It's okay if they can play outside, but I don't want you tracking dirt into the Duncan's house and pestering their mother. You understand?"

They agreed and rushed to get their coats and hats. Dan Jr. brought his to Jordon who helped him get his mackinaw on and buttoned up.

The boy had an aviator-style cap with goggles and ear flaps. "I want a hat like yours, grandpa," he said. "I want to look like you."

"You look mighty good in that pilot's cap," Jordon said. "I bet you'd make a fine aviator." He hugged the child and watched as Mary Helen finished buttoning Cindy up.

"Remember, now. No playing in the house," their mother said sternly as the children ran out of the house.

Jordon and Danny lingered at the table.

"More coffee, Dad?" Mary Helen approached with the pot. Jordon nodded. She'd always called him dad, always tried to make him feel welcome in her and Danny's home. Yet, somehow, he'd never been totally comfortable here. Maybe the place was a little too neat for him. He didn't want to mess anything up. In truth, it seemed he wasn't all that comfortable anywhere but by himself.

"Heard you and Young Harry had a run-in yesterday," Danny said. He didn't much favor Jordon's side of the family. He was handsome, had his mother's eyes and mouth. But he was built strong, like Jordon.

"I wouldn't exactly call it a run-in. More like a disagreement."

"It's all over town," Danny said.

Mary Helen busied herself cleaning up the breakfast dishes. As she worked in silence, her bright blue eyes cut back and forth from her husband to her father-in-law. She was a good match for Danny. Pretty and neat. And ambitious for her husband.

"Any little thing happens around here it's all over town before a day goes by," Jordon said.

"You really think Young Harry had something to do with the Trotter girl's murder?"

"I just wanted to talk to him, son. Never accused him of anything."

Mary Helen finished her cleaning in the kitchen. "I've got a thousand things to do," she said. "You all go ahead and talk."

Jordon looked at Danny. "Stretch our legs?"

They went outside. The sun was beginning to warm things up a little bit, but the aching cold of the coming winter was already foretold in the bite of the breeze.

"Seems like you're the topic of just about everybody's conversations these days," Danny said.

Jordon gave him a sidelong glance. Danny had always seemed to place a high value on tranquillity. Jordon could

understand that. When Danny and his sister Becky were
little, Jordon had been sent off to the pen. Then their mother
had died and they were shunted from one relative to another
until Jordon's sister Polly and her husband Grant had
eventually taken them and raised them. After he'd been
pardoned, Jordon had sent money regularly, but he knew
he'd been far from a good father. Now Becky was married
and living in Harlan. And Danny was a responsible young
man, a man who placed a high value on a predictable,
respectable life.

"I don't mean to shame you," Jordon said.

"It's not shame," Danny said, though Jordon was sure
much of it had to be. Danny added, "I guess I just wish you
were doing something else for a living. Being one of the law
keeps your life right on the edge most of the time."

"I'm not complaining."

"I know. But wouldn't you enjoy something else more?"

"Like what?"

"You could get a job with the Buxton company." After a
moment he added, "Maybe in one of the stores."

Jordon wanted to say, Me? A store clerk? But instead he
said, "I don't think I'm cut out for that kind of work,
Danny."

"You never tried it, did you? I didn't know if I'd like it
either, when I started. Next thing I knew, I was assistant
manager of the main store in Buxton. And I'm in line for
manager when Bill Jenkins retires. Or maybe manager someplace else before that. It's a good future for Mary Helen and
the kids."

"I know it is, son. I just don't think I'd be very good at it."

"Something else then. Another kind of work."

"Only other thing I know is gambling. A peace officer or
a gambler. That's about all I can do." Jordon glanced at the
row of well-tended houses they were strolling by, better
houses than any he'd ever lived in during his entire life. "I'm
proud of you, son. The kind of life you're making for yourself

and your family. I wish I could have done better for you and Becky and your mother, when you were growing up. But that's all gone. I can't live it over."

"It's not that, dad," Danny said. He sounded almost like he was a little boy again, not a man in his early thirties with a wife and two children and a regular place in the hierarchy of Buxton company employees. "I'm not blaming you for what happened a long time ago. But it's not too late to change. Become. . . ."

"Somebody?"

Danny turned on him. "Damn it, that's not what I meant and you know it." His face was tortured with frustration.

Jordon gripped his shoulder. "Stop worrying about me, will you, son? If I win this election, I'll get myself a couple of good deputies, then I'll strut around the county in a Stetson hat and a new blue serge suit with my badge pinned on the breast pocket. And be the respectable father of my respectable son and daughter." Jordon smiled and added, "I might even get married again. Settle down."

"Goddamn it," Danny said. "You twist it all around and make me sound like a narrow-minded piss-ant. I'm just concerned about you, that's all."

"And I appreciate it. Sorry if I rubbed you the wrong way. But the truth is, and we both know it, we're two different people. With two different lives. I guess we both just have to live them out the way they come."

As they headed back along the row of neat clean homes not far from the center of Buxton, Jordon remembered that a "speaking" was scheduled at the courthouse for two o'clock this afternoon. All the candidates for local office were expected to be there. Each would stand up and speak for a few minutes. There would be hundreds of voters, come to listen to the office-seekers.

Jordon hadn't thought much about what he'd say. In a way he dreaded it, but he knew it was part of the game he'd bought into.

Just before he and Danny got back to the house, Jordon said, "I've decided I'm going to move out next week."

"Why?" Danny asked. "Are you mad about what I said?"

"No, no, son," Jordon said, putting his hand on Danny's shoulder. "I've been thinking I'd like to live in one of those little company houses up on the hill above the mill pond. I heard somewhere that one just came empty, and I'm going by the office Monday and try to rent it."

"I wish you wouldn't. Mary Helen will be disappointed. And the kids." Danny hesitated. "Me too."

Jordon stopped and pulled his son to him and embraced him. "It's got nothing to do with you, Danny. It has to do with me. I just need me a place where I can come and go at odd hours and not bother anybody."

"It doesn't bother us. You ought to know that."

"It bothers me."

Danny stared at him for a moment, then said, "Have it your way." His voice was quiet as he added, "You always do," then turned and went into the house.

As Jordon started out the front gate, he saw his grandchildren come running down the road. He waited for them to reach him. "All through playing with your friends?"

"They had to go in," Dan Jr. said, his voice filled with disappointment. Suddenly his face brightened. "Hey, can I go with you, Grandpa?"

"You can't do that," Cindy said sharply. "You have to come in the house."

"Can I?" the boy begged Jordon. "I could help you be sheriff."

"Not this time, buddy," Jordon said.

Cindy said, "Bye, Grandpa," reached up to give him a hug and went running inside.

"When I grow up I want to be like you, Grandpa," Dan Jr. said. "I want to gamble and shoot bad men."

"Hey, now. You want to grow up and be like your dad. He's a fine man."

The boy crinkled up his nose. "Work in a store?"

Jordon heard himself in the child's voice. "You run inside now, son. I'll see you later."

The boy pulled a toy cap pistol out of his coat pocket, a present from last Christmas which he carried everywhere. He snapped it several times, then reached up to Jordon for a hug.

Jordon bent down and embraced him, then stood up and went to his car. As he drove away, he glanced back and saw Mary Helen come outside. She took Dan Jr. by the arm and led him into the house.

The fat black cat with white front paws stopped washing its face and gave Jordon a heavy-lidded but thorough inspection. Then it turned to Rachel Blackwell and uttered a plaintive meow.

"It's all right, darling," the old woman said, "he ain't staying." Looking at Jordon, she said, "Princess don't care for strangers. Specially menfolks." After a moment she added, "Can't say I do neither." Her voice was like the rustle of winter wind through a dead oak.

She led Jordon toward some chairs in front of the smoldering fireplace. "Not there," she said, "that's mine. Here. Set over here."

Jordon felt his way into the chair. His eyes had not yet adjusted to the darkness of the room. Rachel had all the window shades pulled down, and the only light in the room was what seeped in around them plus the glow from the fireplace.

After leaving Danny's, Jordon had checked his watch and decided he had enough time for a visit with Rachel before heading for the speaking at the courthouse in King's Mill.

Rachel threw some slack coal from a bucket into her fireplace and stirred it with a poker. Flames from the rescued fire cast a flickering light on her ancient face. What could have been a smile played at the shriveled and shrunken lips which covered the three or four snaggled teeth she still had.

Her hair was dyed a dull black, and the dark shapeless dress she wore hung loosely on her tiny body. Tiny, Jordon thought, like Bitsy Trotter. Rachel pulled a shawl around her bony shoulders and settled herself into her own chair, a cane-bottom rocker.

"What is it you want?" she asked.

"To talk about Bitsy Trotter," Jordon replied.

"You've come to the wrong place."

"I thought you might be able to help me. I'm trying to find out who killed her. You did know the girl, didn't you?"

Rachel eyed him coldly for a moment before answering. "What makes you think I did?"

"You don't live that far from the Trotters, through the woods. And I have information that you and Bitsy knew each other."

The cat arose from its throne across the room and made its way to Jordon, started rubbing against his shins. Why did cats always do that to him, he wondered. Every time he got near one it made a bee-line for his legs. Jordon was beginning to suspect that there was a secret network of some kind through which cats passed the message to one another: Berk Jordon hates to be rubbed against . . . make sure you do it. He didn't want to maybe rile the old woman up before he got started with her by pushing Princess away. So he let her rub. For the moment.

Rachel had not responded to his last comment, so he said, "Did you know Bitsy Trotter?"

She stared at him with an expression he took to be distaste. "I knowed her."

"What can you tell me about her?"

"Nothing." She fixed her attention on the open fire.

"Can't or won't?"

"It's all the same, ain't it?"

"The law says different. In a court of law you'd have to tell."

She looked at him and laughed. A dry cackle. "You believe that?" She studied him for a moment. "No, sir," she said, "you don't look that dumb." She beckoned for Princess, who came at once and jumped up into her lap.

"You don't care what the law says?" Jordon asked.

"Do you?"

"I do, yes."

"Sure you do," she said in a voice heavy with sarcasm. "They's people out there right this minute fighting and stealing, gambling and whoring and selling whiskey. All against the law. And others, crooked as a barrel of fish hooks, swindling people out of their last scrip nickel." Her voice cut through the room's quietness, filled it with venom. "Others working men in little dog-hole mines till they're ready to drop over, then using fancy figuring to take back ever nickel they make just to keep a roof over their head and a little something in their families' bellies. You think all them people care about the law? You're supposed to be upholding it. Why ain't you out arresting some of them?"

Not a bad question, Jordon had to admit. He said, "Right now I'm trying to catch the murderer of a young girl."

"What they tell me, you're running for high sheriff, too," Rachel went on. "If you get elected, you going to arrest everybody that breaks the law?"

Jordon parried. "You know me, then?"

"Knowed you when you first stepped up on my porch. Know a lot more about you than you might think. Ain't a lot goes on in Stanton County I don't know about, mister."

"But you won't talk to me about Bitsy Trotter. Why is that?"

"Maybe I don't know nothing to tell."

"My guess is you do."

She studied Jordon for a long time. "You know folks say I'm a witch?"

"I've heard that." Jordon looked around. His eyes had become more accustomed to the subdued light. The room was a jumble of odd pieces of furniture, tables with jars and dishes stacked on them, shelves filled with bric-a-brac, an old black dinner bell, a stuffed owl, a double-barreled shotgun in a corner near the door. Lined up on one table were a couple of dozen bottles of assorted sizes and shapes, all filled with liquids of varying colors. Jordon figured it must be the herb medicine he'd heard she made and sold.

"How about you?" Rachel asked. "You think I'm a witch?"

Jordon smiled and shook his head. "I don't much believe in witches. Or a hell of a lot of other things some folks do. So I guess I'd have to say, No, I don't think you're a witch."

Suddenly, she broke into a high, piercing laugh. Sitting there in her cane-bottom rocker, stroking her black cat, her head thrown back, shrieking laughter pouring from her, she looked the part. Jordon figured, by God, I might have spoke too soon. Maybe I should have said yes.

She stifled her laughter long enough to say, "But I remind you of a witch, huh? Is that what you're thinking?"

At this, Jordon began to laugh. "Now that you mention it. . . ."

As they roared in laughter at themselves and each other, Princess jumped from Rachel's lap and went to the edge of the fireplace where she sat regarding them both with a look that might well have been contempt.

When their laughter had run out, Jordon wiped his eyes and looked at his watch. He stood up. "I have to be going," he said. "There's a speaking at the courthouse at two." He started for the door. "Whatever you know about Bitsy might help me find out who killed her. But I reckon you'll have to be the judge of that. I'm not going to try to make you tell me."

"Like I said, you don't look that dumb. When it comes right down to it, can't nobody make me do nothing but die and pay taxes. Learned that a long time ago, Jordon."

He studied her a moment, then said, "I expect you did."

"Outlaws and sheriffs and soldiers and wars come and go,

and nothing don't change. Women generally pays the price."
She stood before him, looking up. No taller than a child.
"You know when I was born, mister?" she said.

He shook his head.

"Eighteen and fifty-two. I was just thirteen when the Civil
War was over. Living with my mother on No Business Creek.
Poppy had gone off to fight with the North. And before he
got home, two soldiers, blue boys from his own side, rode
through and stopped at our place looking for something to
eat. I went out to gather some eggs for them, and one of them
followed me. I was pretty then. He pulled me out of the hen
house. Dragged me around in back of it. And had his way
with me."

Jordon started to say something, but she silenced him
with her hand. "It was the first time any man had ever laid
a finger on me. Thirteen. I was afraid to holler out. He said
he'd kill me and Momma both if I did. So I let him. It was
over in a minute or two. After that, they made us cook them
some dinner. Then they left. But the memory of it never did.
Not to this day."

She hesitated, staring at him. Jordon reached out to her,
to hug her, but she stepped back a little.

"There ain't nothing I've seen since that time has changed
my mind much about men," she said. "Seen a few good ones,
but most ain't worth the salt it'd take to cure 'em."

After a moment, Jordon cleared his throat and said, "I
thank you for your time. And the warmth of your fire. I'll be
going."

She stood in his way. "They say you're a man who's got
no love for the coal companies," she said. "Is that so?"

"I reckon you could say that. I've never worked for them,
except for three weeks once in the mines. Enough to con-
vince me it wasn't for me."

She stepped close to him now and looked up into his eyes.
"If I was to think of something that might help you, I'll let
you know."

"Call the sheriff's office and I'll come out to see you."

"Got no telephone."

"I'll stop back by in a day or two."

"I could walk to the store and call from there. If I was to think of anything."

He smiled and reached for her again. This time she let him hug her. Her frail, bird-like body felt like little more than skin and bones.

As they stepped out onto the porch, they spotted a short, chunky middle-aged man wearing ragged overalls and with hair growing down over his collar ambling slowly up the road, singing some kind of off-key song to himself. He carried a small bundle wrapped in newspaper.

"There's Linwood Evermore, come to bring me some ginseng, I'll bet," Rachel said.

It surprised Jordon that she could see so well without glasses.

"I wish he'd quit poking along and come on before the day's plumb gone." She waited a moment, then added, with a twinkle in her eyes, "I've got bat wings and frog livers to see to. Halloween coming, don't you know?"

As Jordon stepped off the porch and Linwood Evermore came through the gate, Rachel started to laugh her high, dry cackle. Jordon wondered if it was directed at him or at the nature of things in general. Both, he figured.

"If you all vote for me . . . I'll . . . I'll . . ." The fellow trying to speak was a thin, rawboned man with long arms and huge hands which kept plucking at the collar of the white shirt he wore buttoned all the way to the top under his clean bib overalls. His hair was freshly clipped, showing the pale skin of his scalp all the way around, and his leathery face at the moment was a sickly yellow color.

He tried again. "If you all vote for me . . . " His voice was a croak and his adam's apple bobbed frantically as he swallowed and tried once more. "I'll be a. . . ." He was having obvious trouble getting his breath. "Oh, Lord," he said, looking desperately around at the other candidates sitting behind him, "I can't cut the mustard."

He sat down in a puddle of embarrassment as the large crowd of voters laughed and hooted. "Don't worry if you can't make a speech, Walt," somebody from the crowd yelled. "You make more goddamn sense than anybody I've heered during this whole damn election." The crowd roared and applauded.

Jordon said to the gray haired man seated next to him, a candidate for magistrate in one of the outlying districts, "Walt will probably get more votes than the rest of us put together."

"He'll get the 'pity vote,' that's for damn sure."

Sitting at the end of the row, Walt finally got his shirt collar unbuttoned and seemed to be breathing better. But he still looked as though he might throw up.

Jordon listened as Homer Sprague made a plea to the voters to reelect him coroner.

As the applause died down, the master of ceremonies, bald-headed old Judge Dabney, who hadn't sat on the bench for years but who still kept a fine hand in politics, took over, "And now, ladies and gentlemen, it is my pleasure to introduce one of the candidates for sheriff of Stanton County, Berkley Jordon."

Jordon got to his feet and looked out into the field of upturned faces. From their elevated position on the front steps of the courthouse the candidates could see all the way to the back of the crowd of several hundred.

"Friends and neighbors," Jordon shouted, trying to make his voice carry to the edge of the assembly, "most of you all know me or know something about me. So there's not a lot I can say here except to tell you that I'll try to make you a good sheriff, the best I know how."

A voice from the crowd yelled, "You know how to crack heads good enough, don't you, Jordon?"

A little wave of laughter rippled over the crowd.

"I've never hit a man didn't make me do it," Jordon said.

"What about when you was a deputy over in Perry County?" It was another voice this time.

Jordon scanned the crowd but couldn't tell who his hecklers were. "Like I said, I never hit a man that I didn't have to. Don't pay attention to lies you might hear about me in Perry County. Ask folks here in Stanton County. Or Mc-Creary County, right next to us. I was a deputy there once, too. If anybody can name one person I was rough on when I didn't have to be, I'd like to see him stand up here and say so, not holler lies from back in the crowd."

A wave of applause and whistles greeted his last statement.

"I don't have much to say," Jordon said. "You all will have to make up your own minds about me. But the best advice I can give you is to talk to folks who know me. I was born not a dozen miles from here. Been all over the world and back. This is my home. Lots of folks know me since I was a boy. Ask them."

"How about the ones you was in the penitentiary with? Had we ought to ask them?"

Jordon still couldn't make out where it was coming from. "I went to prison when I was a young man, that's true," he said. "I served my time till the governor pardoned me for helping put out a fire in the prison. I'm not bragging, but a lot of men probably would have died. I served in two wars in the service of this country. Discharged honorably both times. I've got the experience to be sheriff, and I ask you to vote for me. If that's not enough, well, then you'll have to decide that for yourself."

Somebody, one of the same men who had yelled before, shouted, "What about the dago Three-C boy that killed that girl? He going to pay for it?"

Jordon tried to spot who had asked it, but still was unable to. He couldn't be sure whether it was one of the previous yellers or not. "My job is to arrest them and bring them in.

The court will decide who's guilty and what to do with them." Jordon waved to the crowd and said, "Thank you all very much." He sat down to a respectable amount of applause, punctuated with a few boos.

One of the candidates for magistrate sitting next to Jordon whispered, "Some of John Bill Trumble's boys was laying for you." The man shifted a cud of tobacco from one cheek to the other, then spit off the side of the platform. "But you done all right." He grinned at Jordon. "At least as good as old Walt."

As Judge Dabney was introducing the next speaker, Jordon slipped off the platform and into the courthouse, down the hallway to the sheriff's office.

Willis glanced up from the desk at him, then heaved himself out of his chair and stood on his one leg, balancing himself against the desk. "The race must be pretty close. John Bill's boys are out to get you."

"That sonofabitch and his lies about Perry County. I notice he didn't show up to speak."

"He's busy rounding up votes out in the county while his buddies devil you here."

"You think it went all right out there just now? Could you hear all of it?"

"I heard it. And you didn't do too bad. All things considered."

Willis had never been one for flattery.

Chapter Nine

SUNDAY MORNING JORDON SLEPT late, then left Danny's while he and his family were at church. It was another cool bright day. At the bus station in King's Mill, Jordon picked up a copy of the Louisville *Courier-Journal* and went to a restaurant near the courthouse where he ordered coffee, eggs over easy, country ham, biscuits and red-eye gravy.

Most of the front page of the paper was devoted to stories about what the federal government was doing under Roosevelt's new leadership. "U.S. DEMANDS PRICE CUT ON STEEL RAILS," "NRA OUTLINES TRADE DEALS," "VETS BUREAU ACCEPTS BID OF FORD CO.," "U.S. SETS UP CORPORATION FOR HOUSING," "PROPOSED LIQUOR MARKETING PACT SUBMITTED TO FARM ADMINISTRATION."

Important as he figured such things were to the country, Jordon found it hard to get interested in them. His mind seemed to run more toward either things strictly local and personal, or the grand questions philosophers wrestled with. All the stuff in between he was happy to leave to others.

Jordon was interrupted several times by folks who stopped to shake hands, many of them pledging their support in the election. If all the people voted for him who said they would, he'd probably win. But Willis had assured him lots of people pledged their vote to all the candidates, making sure they'd be on the good side of whoever won.

A little story at the bottom of the front page of the paper caught Jordon's eye. "Mississippi Slayer Convicted," the headline read. The story was bizarre, maybe a sign of the times.

"Levee City, Miss.—Mrs. Viola Brown, 50, accused of killing her husband over a piece of pie that disappeared from a pantry shelf, was convicted of manslaughter today and tonight was awaiting pronouncement of sentence.

"Mrs. Brown contended she shot her husband when he threatened her with a pistol. The state charged she shot him in the back as the climax of a quarrel over the pie."

Jordon folded the paper and shook his head. He wondered, was the fellow running away with the pie when he was shot? Had he already eaten it? Did they both have pistols? The story didn't even say what kind of pie.

He paid for his breakfast and went to the phone and called Cassie. "I've got to drive out to Chambers Hilltop this afternoon," he told her. "Take some campaign flyers to a fellow. Since it's such a pretty day, I thought maybe you'd ride out there with me. I'd like to talk to you."

She was silent for a moment, then said, "Okay." They agreed he'd pick her up about one-thirty.

It was still a few minutes before noon now, and Jordon decided to go to the jail and talk to Sal Manochio. He found the young man sitting on his bunk reading a magazine he'd evidently borrowed from the jailer.

"How are you doing?" Jordon asked.

"I'd like to get out of here. When do you think that'll be?"

Jordon studied him for a bit. "Don't you understand? You're charged with murder. You're not likely to get out of here anytime soon." Jordon decided not to tell him about the threats on his life.

"I didn't have anything to do with Bitsy's death," Manochio said. "I already told you that." The anger was still in his voice.

"Have you been giving any thought to how you might help me prove that?"

"I didn't know people had to prove they're innocent."

"Don't get technical, son. Just try to help me if you know anything at all."

Manochio quelled his anger. "I did remember something Bitsy said the last time I saw her. I don't know if it means anything."

"What was it?"

"She said she thought she'd figured out a way to get out of Stanton County for good. She seemed excited about it."

"She mention how she might do that?"

"I asked her, but she wouldn't tell me."

Jordon watched Manochio's eyes closely as he asked the next question. "Did you know Bitsy was figuring on getting an abortion?"

Manochio's eyes widened and his nostrils flared. "No!" he shouted. "She wouldn't have done that. She knew how I felt about it."

Jordon wondered if his reaction was genuine. "Maybe she wouldn't have," Jordon said. "It was something I heard."

"It's a lie," the boy said, going back to his bunk where he crossed himself, then sat down and buried his face in his hands. "Oh, God," he muttered. "How did I end up in this mess."

"If you think of anything else I ought to know," Jordon said, "tell the jailer to get in touch with me. I'll come see you."

"Otherwise, I'm in here till..?"

"Till. . . ." Jordon shrugged and left.

With Cassie in the seat beside him, Jordon drove slowly across the "Narrows" toward Chambers Hilltop.

"It always scares me to death to come across here," Cassie said.

"Good reason to be scared along this road," Jordon responded.

The Narrows was where, just before you reached the Hilltop, the gravel road ran for nearly half a mile along the sharp crest of a ridge which fell off sharply on both sides to the valleys hundreds of feet below. Jordon steered the car carefully around a large pothole in the road. No protective rails of any kind were there to prevent a car or horse or wagon from plunging off the side of the road to certain destruction. And enough unfortunate souls had done so to persuade all but the most foolhardy to slow down and pay very special attention when they crossed the Narrows—or "Narrs" as Stanton Countians pronounced it.

On the other side, after he had taken a supply of his campaign literature to a worker who lived in one of the cluster of small houses at the top of the hill, Jordon said, "Let's go sit on the overlook for a while."

It was a huge flat rock from which you could look out over the bluff and see for miles down the holler, including the community of Chambers, one of Buxton's most productive mines and busiest coal camps.

Jordon and Cassie sat on the rock and gazed down at the small, gray, box-type frame houses lined up like soldiers marching to the front, two long rows on either side of the divide formed by the creek and the railroad. Maybe sixty or seventy dwellings in all, plus a huge wooden tipple where the coal was sorted and loaded into railroad gondolas. A commissary, a school, a church. A small cluster of slightly larger houses, originally painted white, but now a dull gray from the coal dust that clung to them. These houses, where the doctor and bosses lived, were built a little higher on the side of the mountain, away from the miners' houses.

"You never worked in the mines, did you?" Cassie asked.

"Three weeks once."

"In a Buxton mine?"

"No. In Harlan County."

"I never knew that. Which shows how little I really do know about you."

On the way out to the Hilltop, they had hardly talked at all, just small comments about how pretty the weather was, unusual for this late in the year, stuff like that.

A heavy curtain of distance hung between them, something Jordon had felt now for several days.

Last night when he'd stopped by Della's as he made his rounds through the county, he'd seen her busy at work, but they'd said nothing more than hello.

It had been an unusually quiet night, and he'd gone home to Danny's soon after midnight, early for a Saturday night, and gone to bed.

"What's going on between us, Cass?" he said to her now. "What's the problem?"

"Nothing new, I guess."

"Yes there is. Since I spent the night at your place, something more's come between us. I want to know what it is."

"What makes you think there's something?"

"Your warmth. It's gone. I'd like to know why."

It was a long time before she answered. "You haven't seemed too interested in me lately."

Her remark threw him off balance. "What does that mean? I don't have the slightest notion what you're talking about."

"How about at Della's the other night? You just barely spoke to me. Spent all your time outside talking with Della."

"Is that what it's about? Me talking to Della?"

"What about Friday night?" she said. "You came in, sat down at the counter, ate and left. Talked to her all the time you were there."

"I spoke to you. It felt like a blast of winter wind when you went by. Anyhow, that was after you'd already brushed me off the night before, when I called from your house. And besides you seemed all wrapped up in that guitar playing Hall boy."

"Don't you like him?"

"What I'm saying has nothing to do with him. He seems likable enough. It's you and me I'm talking about."

"Yes, it's you and me."

When she added nothing, Jordon just sat staring out over the holler. At last he spoke. "I don't understand you, Cassie."

"I guess you don't."

"The talk I had with Della outside, that was business. That's all."

"What business?"

"It's confidential. I can't tell you. Work."

"Work. She seemed happy enough when you all came in. All smiles."

"She most always seems happy. That's the way she is."

"Considering the men on her string, I can understand how she'd be happy."

He took her gently by the arm. "I'm not on her string. And not trying to be."

She pulled back a little. "I guess it's all the other stuff, too," she said. "The worry, your work, all of it."

Suddenly he was tired of it. "We've been over that before. Enough times."

She nodded. "We have." She started to get up.

He stood and helped her.

They got back in the car. She said, "Maybe we ought to just let things rest for a while. Talk later on."

"Not see one another, you mean?"

"I guess so," she said.

He took a deep breath and let it out slowly. "If that's what you want."

She sighed and looked away from him. "How about you?"

"Okay," he said. But it was not the way he felt. He just didn't know what else to say or do.

They rode back to Buxton hardly speaking. As they approached the Narrows, Cassie remarked about a flock of blackbirds winging off to the left toward Chambers.

He was looking at them when she screamed. He cut his eyes back toward where he was going, saw he was close to the edge and had to swerve sharply twice to get the car back in the middle and also miss the pothole. The car straightened out then and they made it to the other side of the Narrows.

Once there, Jordon heaved a sigh of relief. He didn't tell Cassie how close he had come to losing control of the car.

After they settled down, they rode on in cool silence.

When he let her out at her house, she said, "Let's be friends, Berk. Whatever else."

"We're friends. That's not the problem."

She stared at him for a long moment. "I guess not," she said, and went inside.

He drove to the sheriff's office. He had been neglecting some routine paperwork he had to do and decided to catch up on it during what was left of the afternoon. He knew he probably should be out campaigning, but his heart was not in it.

In the office, he had difficulty concentrating on paperwork. He found himself trying to sort things out in his mind. Nothing seemed to be going right.

At odds with Danny. I'm, by God, just not like my son, he thought. Or most of the other men I know. I'm not cut out to work in the mines or one of the other jobs Buxton offers. Lots of good men are miners, but I just can't do it.

He ran his hand through his hair and sighed. He thought about the sheriff being riled up at him for ruffling Young Harry Buxton's feathers.

And now, this split with Cassie. Not a complete split maybe, but things between them were definitely not in good shape.

Also, this business with Bitsy Trotter which was on his mind all the time. After all the people he'd talked to, he still didn't know where in hell he was going.

Sal Manochio was in jail. But that was mostly because

Noble wanted him there. Sal could have done it, sure. He was there with her. He ran away. He is high-tempered. He could have been crazy because she wouldn't marry him. Maybe jealous over Young Harry, if he knew about him.

Who else could have done it?

Abel Trotter, her stepfather? But why? What would have made him do it? Because she wanted to leave Buxton? Maybe something else between them? Possible. Milton Graham had the impression they hadn't gotten along. But Abel said he was home by a little after three the day Bitsy was killed. Wouldn't he have come in with blood on him?

Farrell Nilson. Why? Jealousy, maybe? Bitsy was a pretty girl he'd known for a long time, and according to Ike Sewell she was free with her favors. Maybe Bitsy's mother was wrong about them being more like friends.

Young Harry Buxton. He could have done it. He was out somewhere in the county the day Bitsy was killed, he said. But why? Jealousy, rage, fear of exposure? Maybe she was trying to blackmail him. She'd told Manochio she thought she had found a way to get away from the area.

Hell, maybe it wasn't any of them. Maybe it was someone else, someone he hadn't even considered. But who? And why?

He had to find out more about Bitsy Trotter. What had been going on inside her head. What kind of person she really had been.

He decided the best place to look for the answers he needed was with Lenarue Wooten. He'd talked to her twice already, but not as much as he wanted to either time.

Jordon looked at his watch. A little after four-thirty. He cranked the phone and when the operator came on he said, "Clyde Wooten's residence."

Chapter Ten

"I GUESS TO SOME people, Bitsy might have seemed to be satisfied. She had a job, that's more than a lot of folks got these days. She had enough boys and men interested in her. And she sure knew how to get them to do what she wanted. Most of them, anyway. But none of that means she was satisfied." Lenarue opened her purse and took out a pack of Avalons. She offered it to Jordon, who shook his head. She lit up and inhaled deeply, then blew the match out, leaving them in darkness again.

The two of them sat in his car near the Kady Creek Church watching the last of the congregation file out the door of the little white frame building and head back toward their homes. Jordon had brought Lenarue out to his car after the couple playing the guitar and mandolin had finished singing the last strains of "I'll Fly Away, Oh, Glory."

A little cluster of girls walked by the front of the car talking and laughing. Lenarue said, "I almost forgot. I have to talk to Gracie Gibbs about something. I'll be right back." She jumped out of the car and ran to one of the girls, taking her aside for a whispered conference as the others stopped to talk to a group of CCC boys.

Jordon had arrived after the church service was under way, having arranged to pick Lenarue up and drive her home after it was over. Although she had readily agreed, he knew it was something of a sacrifice for her because church was a favorite place for young men and women to pair up. "Can I walk you home?" was often a first opening for a bashful mountain boy in trying to get next to a pretty girl. By now Jordon was pretty sure Lenarue was well beyond hand-holding with bashful boys, but church was still a good place for socializing, especially after the service.

Jordon had gone inside and sat through the meeting. It was a good thing for his campaign for him to be seen at church, he knew, but he rarely went other than when he was called to take care of some disturbance outside. Sometimes young bucks would get too much to drink and create a ruckus in the churchyard. Somebody would call the law and he'd have to go settle them down.

Tonight's service had included a foot-washing. Jordon had watched quietly as the preacher placed a shallow pan of water on the floor in front of one of the seated deacons, knelt down and took off the deacon's shoes and washed his feet. Then, one by one, the other church elders repeated the ritual on each other. It was a ceremony performed in imitation of Christ and his disciples. An occasional public expression of humility that might be scheduled and then postponed at the last moment if outsiders were present who might find the activity amusing or odd. Mountain people were sensitive about being seen as odd.

After the closing song, the preacher had approached Jordon and shaken his hand, thanking him for coming. "If you are elected sheriff, I hope you won't be a stranger here," the preacher said. He was a small wiry man with rugged features and gentle eyes. Jordon knew the man was a coal miner, a lay preacher, one of the men who, out of a sense of reverence and duty, with no thought of personal gain, preached a strict, ascetic kind of fundamentalist salvation. "Even if you ain't elected," the preacher said, almost smiling, "come anyhow."

As he sat in the car watching the girls and boys walking

away into the darkness, Jordon could picture Bitsy Trotter
among them. He felt he was beginning to understand the
dead girl. In some ways, he could identify with her. Her
discontent with mountain life. There was some of it in him.
Some nagging, nameless dissatisfaction had always driven
him away, toward the big world outside.

He'd let it take him through two wars, to Cuba, the
Philippines, France, Germany, much of the American West,
and some of the great cities of the North. But always there
was that other something that tolled him back, calling him
home to the clear mountain streams, the fox hunts, the good
corn moonshine, even the simple little churches like this
one where strong, decent men washed one another's feet,
striving to subdue their pride as they believed God com-
manded them to.

Had Bitsy Trotter lived and realized her desire to leave the
mountains, would she, too, have been whipsawed between
the urge to run away and the compulsion to come back? And
was it this worm of discontent with her life that gnawed at
her until it somehow brought about her death?

Lenarue came back to the car and got in.

"Squared away?" Jordon asked.

"It was just girl talk," she replied. Then, looking him
directly in the eye, she added, "Can I ask you a question?"

"Sure."

"Why didn't you tell me when you drove me to the show
Friday night that you had Sal Manochio in jail?"

It surprised Jordon. "I don't know. I guess I didn't think
it was of any importance to you. Is it?"

She hesitated for a moment, then said, "I like Sal."

He sat watching her. The light on the front of the church-
house had been turned off, but the full moon's brightness
fell across her face as well as his.

Lenarue went on, saying softly, "To tell you the truth, it's
more than just liking. If it hadn't been for the way things
were between him and Bitsy, I'd have gone after Sal myself."

She gave Jordon an intense look and added, "You don't really believe he killed Bitsy, do you?"

"I don't know."

"But you don't *believe* he did it, do you?"

He shook his head. "I guess I don't. He could have, but I don't think he did." Jordon started the car. "Trouble is, I haven't been able to figure out who it was. Which is why I wanted to talk to you again. I want you to tell me anything else at all about Bitsy that you think will help me understand her. What was happening in her life."

"I don't know where to start."

"You mentioned the other day that she had some plans or ideas or something that was going to help her leave the mountains. What do you know about that?"

Lenarue was quiet for a long time, then said, "Not much, really. I just know that she was determined to do it."

Jordon steered the car along the road toward where Lenarue lived. "Then just tell me about her, what she was like."

"She was smart, I can tell you that. Any of her teachers in school could tell you the same thing. She made good grades. All the teachers told her she ought to try to go to college. She would have, too, but there was no way she could get the money."

"You think maybe her plan had something to do with Young Harry Buxton?"

Lenarue shrugged. "He didn't care anything about her."

"How do you know?"

"She told me. Said he'd never have anything to do with her in public, like he was ashamed of her or something."

"Ashamed? She was a very pretty girl." But he knew it wasn't a question of looks.

"He's from a different class," Lenarue said. "And Bitsy hated the way that stood between them. Another thing was, she hated that birthmark on her face and neck. You know about that?"

He nodded. "It bothered her a lot?"

"Something terrible. To her it was like a big rock tied around her neck, pulling her down. But even with it, she knew how pretty she was, her face, the way she was built. Not like me."

Jordon was surprised. "There's nothing wrong with the way you look."

"I think I'm too heavy. But anyway, Bitsy talked about the birthmark a lot. She thought it kept her from getting somebody like Harry."

"It never bothered Sal Manochio, did it?"

"He loved her. It didn't mean nothing to him. She made a big thing out of it in her mind, that's all. But thinking about it made her blue."

"Tell me, what was wrong between Bitsy and her stepdad?"

"You know about that?"

"I'd like for you to tell me."

"He was after her. You know."

"What?"

"Don't act like you don't know what I'm talking about. He tried to get into her pants."

Jordon was a little uncomfortable talking about these things with this young girl. But he plowed ahead. "How long ago was that?"

"I don't remember exactly. Four or five years ago, the first time. She got away from him. Then later, he tried again, and she threatened him. Said she'd tell the sheriff and everybody else in town if he tried it any more."

"Then what?"

"He said he'd kill her before he'd let her do that."

"What did she do?"

"Told him she'd as soon be dead as let him do it, and if he did, he'd have to kill her or she'd tell."

"How long ago was this, the last time?"

"Two or three years ago. I don't remember exactly."

"Had he tried it any more lately?"

"If he did, she never told me."

Jordon drove in silence for a little while, then asked, "Would you like to go to the drugstore and get a Coke? Or do you have to get home right away?"

"I don't have to get home yet. I can call and let my mom know where I am, that I'm with you. It'll be all right."

Jordon turned off the road at the next fork and drove toward Buxton. "Tell me what you know about Farrell Nilson," he said.

"I know he's not too smart."

"I noticed that."

"What do you mean?"

"We had a little disagreement Friday night at Stateline."

"What about?"

"I'm not sure."

Lenarue lit a cigarette. "Farrell's big, and strong. Sometimes he lets that get him in trouble."

"You and Farrell and Bitsy went to school together, didn't you? How old is he?"

"Older than me and Bitsy. Like I said, he's not that smart. He failed two or three years, and then he finally quit in high school. I never could figure out why he kept going, anyway. He couldn't learn anything."

"How did Bitsy feel about him?"

Lenarue smile at Jordon. "He was the first boy she ever let do it to her."

Clearly, Jordon thought, she enjoys being able to tell me all this. Thank God she does. "Was she serious about him?"

"At first she thought she was. Till she found out how dumb he is. Then she just, you know, strung him along."

"She kept on going out with him?"

"Off and on."

"Did she keep on . . . letting him . . . ?"

"Screwing him, you mean? Not for a long time, now. But he kept on trying. Kept taking her out when she'd let him."

They arrived at the Buxton Drugstore. It was crowded

with young people. When Jordon and Lenarue stepped inside, most of them stared openly. Jordon knew many of them, saw them on his rounds through the county.

He spotted a table in the corner where a couple was leaving, and Lenarue went to call her mother. When she came back they ordered Cokes.

She looked around the room, then smiled at him. "Everybody is just dying to know what's going on between us."

Jordon was caught completely off guard. When he recovered he said, "I'm at least as old as your daddy. Maybe older."

"So what? Lots of older men like young girls."

He smiled. "You know that for a fact, do you?"

"Sure do," she said.

He rolled his eyes. "Is it safe for me to ask how?"

Lenarue laughed. "No harm in asking," she said, but went no further.

For the first time, Jordon really noticed how pretty she was. Nice teeth, full mouth, bright eyes. A little plump, as she herself had pointed out, but not enough to keep her from getting her share of attention from men of whatever age, he felt certain.

"So tell me, how do you know so much about older men and young girls?" Jordon persisted.

"For one thing, I work around older men."

Jordon thought about that for a moment, then asked, "Which ones show the most interest in young girls, Lenarue?" His voice was quiet, serious.

"Most of them, I'd say." She was speaking quietly, too, but she smiled.

"How about Young Harry Buxton? He one of them? Or do you consider him older?"

She considered it for a moment. "He's older I guess. You already know about him and Bitsy. But, yeah, he made passes at me."

Jordon waited.

"If it hadn't been for Bitsy . . ." Her voice trailed off. Then she said, "Who wouldn't? HR Buxton's son."

After a moment, Jordon said, "What about the other men in the office?"

"Like who?"

"HR Buxton, for instance."

"Mr. Buxton himself? No. Never. At least not with me or anybody I know. I don't think he'd ever mess around with one of the girls who work for him."

"Milton Graham? What about him?"

"My boss? Sweet Miltie? Yeah, once when I first went to work in the office. He made a little pass. But I ignored it and he never did it again."

"What about with Bitsy?"

"He did the same thing with her. We talked about it and laughed. He was interested, all right. Just didn't want to take the chance to push it, I guess. Some men are like that." Her eyes caught Jordon's and held them. "Too careful for their own good."

Jordon looked at Lenarue with a growing sense of awe. How did young girls get so wise so soon, he wondered. He sometimes thought they must be born knowing more about men than a man, in a long lifetime, ever learned about them. More than he, at least, had ever learned.

"Bitsy and me," she said, "we figured Sweet Miltie might have a woman somewhere out of town, like when he traveled on business."

"Why'd you think that?"

"Just imagination, maybe. But he always seems to look forward to getting away."

"Why do you call him Sweet Miltie?"

"No reason. He's just kind of a sweet old thing, that's all." She drank the last of her Coke with a little slurp, then said, "Maybe you'd better take me home, now. I have to work tomorrow. I'll need my sleep. Monday morning the switchboard will be going crazy."

The rest of the Sunday night crowd was thinning out now

as Jordon and Lenarue made their way outside.

In front of the drugstore, lounging with several other young men, Farrell Nilson leaned against a parked car. His nose was red and swollen from Friday night. The dirty look he gave Jordon suggested Nilson would not soon forget the occasion.

Jordon stopped near Nilson and said, "I still need to talk to you. But it'll have to wait."

The young man's expression did not change. He said nothing, but his eyes burned with fury. Jordon opened the door and let Lenarue in his car, then went around to the other side and slid under the wheel. As he drove away, he saw Farrell Nilson still leaning against the car staring at him.

▽

Chapter Eleven

O<small>N</small> <small>MONDAY MORNING, JORDON</small> drove to the Buxton office building and rented the little three-room house near the mill pond that he'd heard about, paying for two months in advance. The place had some of the previous tenant's furniture in it which had been kept by the company for non-payment of rent. The rent was now a little higher since the place was "furnished," the woman in the rental office said, but she was sure he would agree that the convenience was more than worth the difference.

As he headed down the hall toward the front entrance of the Buxton building, planning to go to the courthouse, he passed the office of Young Harry Buxton. The door was open, and Harry was sitting with his feet up on the desk and a cup of coffee in his hand.

"Hey!" Harry said. "What the hell are you doing back in here?"

Jordon stopped. "Is the Buxton office building now off-limits to the law?"

"That all depends." Harry's voice was a sneer.

"But not on you, kid." Jordon walked on down the hall and outside onto the broad front steps of the Buxton building.

He stood looking out over the downtown square of Buxton. He decided he needed a cup of coffee and crossed over to the drugstore.

A few minutes later, as he was finishing his coffee and considering the possibility of another, a slender young man of maybe eighteen years entered the store, looked all around, then made his way to Jordon's table.

"Er . . . Mr. Jordon. I mean . . . Sheriff. . . ."

"What is it, son?" The boy was slim and blue-eyed, and his light brown hair was slicked down with brilliantine. He wore a clean white shirt and a little black tie under his jacket.

"Mr. HR Buxton," the boy said. "He said if I could find you, to tell you he'd like for you to come up to his office and see him."

Jordon nodded at the boy and said, "Well, son, you go back and tell Mr. HR Buxton that I'll be up to see him directly, soon as I finish what I'm doing."

"Yes, sir," the boy said, and left in a trot.

As Jordon had that second cup of coffee, he considered what HR Buxton might want with him. He had an idea, of course. He just wondered how HR would approach it. More than that, Jordon wondered how he might respond.

When Jordon reached HR's office a few minutes later, the secretary outside his door said, "Mr. Jordon? You can go in." She was a plain, severely dressed woman, somewhere in her forties, Jordon guessed. She got up, rapped gently on the door and opened it for him.

Jordon said thank you and stepped inside. The secretary closed the door quietly behind him.

HR Buxton was reading some kind of document. He didn't look up until he finished, signed it, and placed it in a wooden box at the corner of his desk.

It was the first time in his life that Jordon had ever been inside HR's office. It was impressive, no doubt about that. All dark wood with matched leather-bound volumes lining the shelves built in the walls. Shiny waxed hardwood floors. And the massive desk behind which sat the uncrowned king of Stanton County, Kentucky. Or at least duke of the

Cumberland River's Middle Fork.

Buxton looked at Jordon for a moment as if wondering what he might be doing there. Then HR indicated one of the leather chairs in front of the desk and said, "Sit down, sheriff."

"Deputy," Jordon said, taking a seat.

"Sheriff soon, though, huh?" HR smiled pleasantly.

"The voters will decide that, I reckon."

"That's the theory, isn't it."

"I figure it's more than a theory."

"Based on my observation, the voters are very often a minor factor in an election."

Jordon had no idea where this was leading, but he said, "You'd know more about that than I do."

"So I do," HR said. "So I do."

Jordon studied him carefully. Harrison Randolph Buxton, "HR" to everyone in the county, had to be near seventy, Jordon knew, but he projected the vitality of a much younger man. He was one of those men who somehow manage to seem bigger than they actually are. If you put a tape measure to him from scalp to sole, HR would measure barely more than five and a half feet. But you instinctively knew he was larger than that. Even out on the street, away from his imposing office, if he'd been dressed in work clothes instead of the navy blue suit and crisp white shirt he wore now, he would have seemed larger. His cool, intelligent gray eyes, his carefully combed sandy gray hair, his small, well-manicured hands, these and the other, non-physical, parts of him taken as a whole became something much greater than their sum.

"You wanted to see me about something in particular?" Jordon said.

"You in a hurry?"

"I do have work to do," Jordon said, then added, "as I'm sure you do."

"I'm working now," Buxton said with a little smile. "But I'll come to the point since you seem uncomfortable here."

The smile faded.

Jordon did not respond to what he took to be an insult.

HR leaned across the desk and stared at him. His voice was cold as he said, "Why are you so determined to try to implicate my son in the death of this poor unfortunate Trotter girl, Jordon?"

"Is that what he told you?"

"Never mind who told me what, just answer my question."

"All right. I'm not determined to implicate . . . Young Harry"—it pleased Jordon to say it—"in anything. But I *am* determined to find out who killed that girl and see that he's brought to justice for it." Pausing for a beat, he added, "*Whoever* he might be."

"I understand you've already arrested the killer. A Three-C boy."

"We've got a boy in jail. He hasn't been convicted of anything yet."

"Then why don't you spend your time collecting the evidence that will convict him? And leave innocent people alone?"

"Young Harry's innocent?"

"He's not guilty of murder. And you know it."

"What about the baby she was going to have? Is he innocent of that, too?"

"What's that got to do with you? Nobody knows whose baby it was. Nobody will ever know, in all probability. Have you appointed yourself the moral guardian of this county, running down every clue on who's getting screwed, and who knocked up who, and when and where and the rest of it?"

HR's unvarnished language surprised Jordon a little. "That's not what I'm doing." Jordon felt his anger rising, but tried to keep it in check. "I happen to believe that the girl's pregnancy might have had something to do with her death."

HR's face became flushed. "You're no goddamn paragon of virtue, yourself, Jordon. Oh, I know about you. One of the first stories I heard when I came here twenty years ago was about how you killed those two boys at Stateline. Over a bloody nose or a black eye or some such."

"It was a lot more than a black eye. And I paid for what I did. A long time ago."

"Well, by God, I'm not going to sit back and watch you try to make my son pay for something he *didn't* do. Understand that."

"Mr. Buxton, my job is to find who killed that girl, not try to pin it on somebody who didn't. If your son wasn't involved in it, he's got nothing to fear from me or the law."

"Except for his reputation. And mine." HR stood up and walked to the big plate glass window overlooking the town square. "I don't intend to see you or anybody else drag his name through the mud."

"Whatever his name is dragged through is his own doing, not mine." Jordon stood now.

HR came back to his chair and said, "Sit back down." Now his voice was conciliatory.

Jordon sat.

HR reached into a carved wooden box on his desk and took out a cigar. Then, as if it were an afterthought, he extended the box to Jordon. "Smoke? They're Cuban."

Jordon shook his head. "Never took it up."

HR bit the tip off his cigar and lit it, blowing a billow of fragrant smoke toward the ceiling. There was no outward sign now of the hot anger of a few moments ago. "Why is it you don't like me, Jordon? I've never done you harm or caused you trouble. Not that I know of. What is it?"

"What makes you think I don't like you?"

HR smiled. "Let's not indulge in pretense, shall we? It's my business to know men, gauge them, be able to assess their feelings. You don't like me. I'd like to know why."

"It's nothing personal."

"What, then?"

Jordon waited for a moment before he answered. "Let's just say I wish men like you had never come to the mountains."

HR seemed genuinely surprised. "Why, for God's sake? Look around you man, can you imagine what this place would be like without me and men like me? There'd still be nothing here but a goddamned wilderness. Like it was before we came."

Jordon eyed him coldly. "Exactly."

HR shook his head, as if he could not believe what he was hearing. "You mean, you think it was better then, when mountain people lived in ignorance and poverty, with no place to work, no electricity, no running water, no doctors, no telephones? You can't be serious."

"Mr. Buxton, through all the history of civilization until very recently, men have lived without electricity and telephones and such. Those things don't make living worthwhile. The people here had wells and springs for water, gardens for fresh vegetables, and streams and woods for fish and game. And there was a doctor or two here and there. And herbs growing in the woods for medicine. And granny women to deliver babies. I don't remember hearing that folks were crying out from this wilderness as you call it for somebody to come rescue them."

"What about poverty and ignorance? Don't you think we've done something about that?"

"Look out there on the square. Are you telling me you don't see ignorance and poverty? It's all around us still. Part of the human condition. You see it everywhere you go. Not just here. Everywhere. You haven't changed that."

"But we're making progress."

"If by progress you mean you're getting richer and richer every year while everybody else stays the same, okay. But trading a rifle and a trot line for a pick and shovel is not my idea of progress."

Buxton studied him for a long time before he spoke. "Well, whether you can understand what we're doing here or not, and whether you like me or not, is not what matters. You're entitled to your ideas as I am to mine." His voice had become persuasive, reasonable, almost seductive. "I've done plenty of business in my time with men who didn't like me." He paused. "And men I didn't like. But business is business. And in business, people can be friends without actually liking one another. Can you understand that? It's not necessary to like one another to find ground that is mutually beneficial to stand on. Right?"

Jordon shrugged. "I'm not at all sure what you are talking about."

"You seem like a reasonable man to me, Jordon."

"I like to think I am."

HR took a long puff on his cigar, expelled the smoke slowly. "You believe the election is still up in the air?"

"That's what most folks are saying. I'm not a very good politician, so it's hard for me to say."

"I know Sheriff Treadway wouldn't mind seeing you elected."

Jordon nodded.

"We have some influence in this county," HR said, waving his cigar in a casual gesture. "Me. The company."

"I reckon that must be what they call an understatement," Jordon said.

"If I wanted to, I could have our people put out the word that we'd like to see you win, become the next high sheriff of Stanton County." HR rolled his cigar between his lips, then dragged deeply on it. "If we did that, I am confident you'd be elected. We have lots of friends. And they have friends." A short pause. "Friends help friends. You know how that is." He puffed and shot a stream of smoke toward the window. "How would that sit with you?"

"What would you want?"

"Nothing. Not a thing."

Jordon watched him closely. "Nothing?"

"Only that we be friends. We'd want you to think of us—me, my son, our company—as friends."

Jordon chose his words carefully. "I'd appreciate your

support, Mr. Buxton. I'm sure it would make a lot of difference."

"It's settled, then? You're satisfied my son had nothing to do with this girl's problems, whatever they were?"

Jordon spoke very quietly. "Her main problem was that somebody cut her to pieces out there in the woods behind her house. And I'm not really satisfied just yet who it was that did it."

"So it's not settled. Is that what you're telling me?"

Jordon stared at him for a long while before he answered. "I told you I'd appreciate your support in the election. But I guess you'll have to make your own judgment on whether to give it." He paused a moment, then added, "And I'll have to make mine on how to run this investigation."

HR did not respond at once. When he did, his voice sounded almost sad. "You're not as smart as I thought you'd be. Either that, or you're just plain, goddamn stubborn."

"I've been told both of those things on occasion." As Jordon stood to go he said, "Was there anything else you wanted to talk to me about?"

"Just this little bit of philosophy. Call it advice, if you like: Obstinacy is a two-edged sword. It cuts both ways."

"I always listen to good advice."

"But you don't always follow it, right?" HR's lips were curled in a rueful smile.

Jordon smiled back at him and walked out.

It was mid-afternoon when the call came in to the sheriff's office. Jordon was going over some arrest warrants with Willis.

"I'll get it," Jordon said. "Take the heat off of you, if it's old lady Cross about bootlegging again."

It was Othel Marcum from the general store over near Buxton. "One of Rachel Blackwell's neighbors is here, says she wants to talk to the sheriff. Just a minute."

In a moment the quavery voice of an old woman came on

the line. "Sheriff? Is this here the sheriff I'm a'talkin to?" she said.

"No, ma'am. The sheriff's not here right now. I'm Deputy Sheriff Jordon. What is it you want?"

"I don't want nothin," the old woman said. "It's about Rachel."

Jordon waited. Finally he asked, "What is it you want to tell me about Rachel?"

"I found her a while ago."

"You found her?" He did not understand. "Where'd you find her?"

"Layin in her back yard."

"Is she hurt?"

"No, sir, she ain't hurt," the old woman said. "She's dead."

$\triangledown$

Chapter Twelve

"ACCIDENTAL DEATH, I'D SAY offhand," Coroner Homer Sprague announced as he and Jordon stared at Rachel's frail body. It lay on the ground in the steep yard behind the little back porch of her house. She had on the same clothes she'd worn when Jordon saw her Saturday. She was on her back, arms alongside, looking almost as if she were simply resting.

Jordon was silent as the coroner completed his preliminary examination. Homer did his work with an efficiency and detachment that almost made you forget that a dead body was the subject of his attention.

"Looks to me like she's been dead awhile," Homer added. The coroner was an elected county official holding an office that required no credentials, medical or otherwise, like other government offices, except for county attorney. Such offices were occupied by men who needed only to be expert at getting people to vote for them. But Homer, Jordon knew, was also good at his work.

"I saw her on Saturday, middle of the day," Jordon said.

"Then I figure she must have fell sometime Saturday night," the coroner said. "Doc Klein can maybe tell us better."

They looked up at the porch. It had no protective guard rail around it. But it really was not that long a drop to the steep backyard, five feet or so.

"So you figure she just sort of teetered off there and killed herself?" Jordon asked.

"Maybe," Homer said, scratching his head. "Could be the cold killed her. Maybe she just fell off and hurt herself, and then couldn't get up and get back in the house. Nights are getting colder than a witch's tit." He seemed to realize what he'd said and grinned sheepishly.

While they stood looking at the house, the heavyset old neighbor woman who'd found Rachel came to the back door and stepped out on the porch, staying well back from the edge. She wore a long dark dress and a tattered gray sweater.

"Will you all be wanting to talk to me any more?" she asked.

"No, ma'am," Jordon said. "You go on home. If I need to talk to you again later, I'll come by and see you."

The old woman nodded and went back into the house.

Jordon said to Homer, "I'll be back in a minute," and followed the old woman through the little house. By then she was already out in the front yard, working her way toward the gate, trying to fend off questions from several curious people who had gathered there, men, women and children.

"Folks," Jordon said in a loud voice. "I'd like to know if any of you all saw Rachel anytime after say, one o'clock Saturday?"

Nobody said anything. Several shook their heads.

"See anybody else around here anytime over the weekend? Or hear anything unusual?"

"I thought she fell," one woman said to Jordon. "You think somebody might have done something to her?"

"I don't think anything yet," Jordon replied. "I just wondered if any of you all might have seen or heard anything."

Again all he got were blank stares and a few head shakes.

"I want you all to go on home, now," Jordon said. "There's nothing you can do here. Rachel's dead. They'll be coming to take her body away in a little bit."

Some of them began to move slowly out of the yard. Others seemed reluctant to leave. "Go now. We'll take care of things here."

Jordon watched as the last of them left, then returned to the back porch. "I'm going to take a look around inside," he said to Homer. "Let me know when they come to get her."

Inside Jordon went through the kitchen and bedroom. Then the front room where he carefully surveyed everything in sight, trying to remember how it had looked when he sat there with Rachel on Saturday.

Someone had been through the place. He was sure of that. As much stuff as there was in the room, there nevertheless had been a kind of crazy order to it. Now it was different. Whether the person who had searched the room had found what he was looking for Jordon had no way of knowing. But he was sure someone had moved stuff around. Something seemed to be missing. But how in hell could he know what, considering all the junk?

One thing that certainly was absent was Rachel's cat. Jordon guessed it had gone some place looking for food. Just like a cat. A dog would have been there, hungry or not, waiting for Rachel to get up. But not a cat. Independent creatures. Did only what they damn well pleased.

Jordon sat down in the chair he'd used on Saturday and went over the few facts he had about Rachel's death. The neighbor woman had not seen Rachel anywhere Sunday, and had come by this morning to see about her. They did that for one another, the old folks, just to make sure everything was all right.

But, of course, it hadn't been all right.

The coroner had arrived first, found the front door locked, back door open and Rachel dead in the back yard.

It seemed simple enough. A frail old woman, out on the back porch in the dark, taking a misstep, going off the edge and ending up dead. Either from the fall, or as Homer said, from the night as cold as a witch's tit.

Jordon looked at the dead fireplace, went over and raked through the ashes with the poker, looking for nothing in particular. Which is what he found.

An hour later, sitting in the sheriff's office, Jordon had just finished filling Willis in on what he knew about Rachel's death when the phone rang. Willis answered it, listened for a moment, then said, "Hold on." He handed over the phone.

"Jordon here."

"It's Othel Marcum." The storekeeper, one of Jordon's political supporters. "I just wanted to remind you what I said about bringing me some more cards and flyers," Othel said. "And also, I wanted to tell you that Rachel Blackwell was in here Saturday night, before she died, trying to get ahold of you on the telephone."

"What did she want?"

"She never said. I just heard her tell the operator to give you a message to come see her."

"What time was this, when she called?"

Othel thought about it for a moment, then said, "I reckon it must've been about seven o'clock. Something like that."

"She seem upset or anything? Scared?"

Othel chuckled. "Rachel? Nah. Like always. Casting her special evil look around."

"I take it you don't believe in witches either," Jordon said.

"Just my old lady is all," the storekeeper replied.

"Listen, I appreciate you calling me. You think of anything else, let me know, will you?"

Jordon started to hang up, then had another thought. "Did Rachel make any other calls Saturday night?"

"It's possible. I didn't pay that much attention. Everybody uses my phone."

As soon as Othel was off the line, Jordon rang Lenarue Wooten at the switchboard. "Is there a message there for me?" he asked. "From Saturday night?" While officially the switchboard operators were only required to connect a caller with a specific number, in practice they did much more. They often knew where the doctors and law enforcement people were—and would track them down. Otherwise, they'd take a message. To Jordon this was further evidence of the telephone's intrusion in his life, an intrusion he nevertheless grudgingly appreciated.

"Let me check the bulletin board." In a moment she came back on and said, "No message. Is there supposed to be?"

"I understand Rachel Blackwell tried to call me about seven o'clock Saturday night. Who was working then?"

"Offhand, I don't know. There's seven of us qualified, you know, who—" She stopped suddenly, then said quietly, "Six now."

"You have a schedule you can look it up?"

She said she did and a minute later came back on and said, "Aileen Egan. She worked three to eleven Saturday."

"Will you ring her for me?"

Aileen's mother answered and called Aileen to the phone.

"This is Deputy Sheriff Jordon. Do you remember taking a message for me from Rachel Blackwell Saturday night about seven or so?"

Aileen responded immediately. "I did."

"What did she say?"

"Just that she needed to talk to you. It was important."

"Nothing more?"

"No. That's all. The call came in from Othel Marcum's store, I remember that."

"And what did you do with the message?"

"Pinned it to the bulletin board beside the switchboard. Like we always do."

"Tell me this: did Rachel make any calls to anybody else Saturday night?"

Aileen thought about it for a moment. "I don't think so. At least not right then. It was a pretty busy night. She might have done it before. Or after. The reason I remembered the call to you was she wanted me to write down the message for you."

Jordon thanked the girl and hung up.

"What's this all about, anyway?" Willis asked. "Connected with the Trotter girl, you reckon?"

"I wish I knew." Jordon sat for a moment thinking. "Listen, I'm going back over to Buxton to check out a couple of things. I'll call in after while."

Less than half an hour later, Jordon was hunkered down examining the tires of the line of cars parked at foot of the steps leading up to the Buxton office building. There were a dozen cars altogether, and Jordon took his time. He had the piece of paper from his notebook with the sketch of the tread, showing the half-moon cut mark he'd drawn from the impression in the dirt near where Bitsy Trotter's body was found.

Jordon glanced across the street and saw Chief Ike Sewell come out of the drugstore and head down the sidewalk, making his usual rounds at his usual leisurely pace.

Jordon went about his task deliberately, checking each tire on each of the three cars he'd found with tread similar to the one he'd seen in the woods. One of them, parked at the end, was a new Ford roadster, spotlessly clean. On the left rear tire of this one Jordon found what he was looking for. A half-moon cut like the one he'd found in the sand at the lover's lane. He held the paper with his pencil sketch alongside the cut. This was the car. There was no doubt in his mind. He wondered who it belonged to. He'd find out soon enough. Jordon wrote down the license number and glanced up at the Buxton building.

Someone, it looked like Young Harry Buxton, was standing in his office window looking at him. It was too far away for Jordon to be certain it was Young Harry or to be able to see the expression on his face, though he could imagine how it must look. For a moment, Jordon considered smiling and waving, but he resisted the impulse.

As he turned to leave, Jordon saw Chief Ike Sewell strolling back up the street. Jordon walked across so he'd intersect Ike's path.

Ike spotted Jordon and spoke first. "You learned who killed that little tramp yet, Sherlock?"

It was another of Ike Sewell's qualities, one that made it easier to dislike the sonofabitch. He loved to find something that irritated you, then use it as an abrasive to rub you raw whenever he could. He was good at it, had honed it to a fine art.

With an effort, Jordon let it pass. He had more important business to tend to. "You know who all those cars over there belong to?"

Ike pointed across the street. "Them? Right there by the steps?"

Jordon nodded.

"Sure do. That's where the company officials park their cars. Private."

"Tell me," Jordon said.

"What?"

"Which one belongs to who."

Ike pushed his hat back on his head. His curiosity was up. "What for?"

"No reason. I just wondered if you knew."

"Hell, yes, I know." Ike waited.

"Aah, hell." Jordon moved as if to walk on down the street.

"I can name them," Ike said defiantly.

"Do it, then."

"All of them?"

"Every one of them, if you know."

"If I know? By God, it's my job to know things like that." Ike started at the far end, naming each of the cars and its owner. "That Cadillac, looks like a million dollars? HR Buxton." "The Studebaker, that's Mort Saylor, in the book-keeping department." He went on. A.T. Chambers, Jr., Milton Graham, Seth Waterbury. Ike ran through the rest

of the list of Buxton Corporation officials. "At this end of
the line, see that new Ford roadster? Sporty looking? Rumble
seat? All shined up and ready for a spin?"

"Yeah. Whose is that?"

"Why hell, who do you think?"

Jordon shook his head. "I don't know. Who?"

"Young Harry Buxton, that's who." Ike said it with obvious envy. "Ain't that boy got the life?"

Jordon nodded. "It sure is a nice car, all right." He turned
to go.

"Hey, wait a minute," Ike Sewell said. "Tell me what
you've found out about the Trotter girl."

"Not much, I'm afraid. I'll talk to you about it later. By
the way, who was it you were telling me was mixed up with
her? Did you remember?"

Ike became sullen. "Maybe I'll tell you about it later. If I
remember." He turned away, muttering. "You and your
goddamned games. Naming cars."

Jordon walked down the block and mounted the stairs to
Doc Klein's office over the hardware store.

Inside, Doc's nurse was busy typing something. She was
an attractive, slender redhead, one of those extraordinarily
neat women whose hair and makeup looked as though she'd
just done them, even though it was nearly three in the
afternoon.

The woman looked up and recognized Jordon. "What can
we do for you?"

"Can I speak with Doc for a minute?"

"I'll see," she said, going back through a narrow hallway.
In a moment she returned and said. "Go on back. First door
on the right. He's with a patient right now, but he'll see you
as soon as he's finished."

Jordon thanked her and went into the small examining
room she'd directed him to. He sat down and waited.

In a few minutes the door opened and Doc came in,
looking natty as always, fidgeting with his glasses, straight-

ening his tie. "You're here to find out what I know about
Rachel Blackwell's death," he said.

"Right."

"I'm pushed for time. I'll give it to you short and sweet.
She died of a broken neck."

Jordon was surprised. He'd figured maybe the coroner was
right. The cold.

When Jordon didn't respond, Doc said, "You have any
questions? Or is that enough? I've got a baby to deliver this
evening down at Mine Number Three. At least I expect it to
be this evening. Woman's been ready for two days now."

"Rachel . . . was it the fall killed her?"

"I can't tell you that for sure. It's not like somebody stuck
a knife in her. Or shot her. But somebody just *might* have
broke her neck."

"You really think so?"

"Bruises on her neck suggest that to me. I couldn't swear
that's what happened. All her injuries *could* have been
caused by a fall off her porch, depending on how she fell."

"But . . . ?"

"They also could have been caused by someone who
wanted her dead. I just said that."

"Is that what you think?"

"All things taken into account, I guess I'd have to say yes,"
Doc said. "Come on with me while I get my coat and bag."
He led Jordon through the office and toward the front door.
"What do you think?"

"All of your things taken into account and all of my things
taken with them, I guess I'd have to say yes, too."

The two men walked outside together. "What's going on
around here, Jordon? Who the hell's doing this? And what
for?"

"Doc, that's what I keep asking myself."

"And what have you come up with?"

Jordon sighed and shook his head. "Just little bits and
pieces of stuff that don't prove a damn thing."

Doc said, "Well, you've got your job and I've got mine. I'm gone."

"Okay if I use your phone?"

"Help yourself," Doc said and headed out.

Jordon went back into Doc's office, cranked the telephone and asked the operator for the sheriff's office.

The girl at the switchboard said, "Jordon?"

"Yes."

"This is Lenarue. I'm glad it's you." Her voice was just above a whisper. "I've been thinking. I need to see you."

"About what?"

"Something else I need to talk to you about. But not now. Not on the phone."

"Where then?"

"Can you come to my house tonight? About seven-thirty?"

"I'll be there."

"You won't forget?" Her voice trembled as she whispered, "I . . . I'm scared."

"Go straight home after work and stay there until I come tonight."

She said she would and then put Jordon on through to the sheriff's office. Nothing special going on there, Willis said.

"I'll check in with you later," Jordon told him, then just sat there at Doc's desk, doodling on a piece of paper and wondering what it was that had Lenarue so afraid. And he wondered, too, about the cut he'd found on Young Harry's tire. What did it prove except that Harry had been out there? It could have been most any time. And with anybody. Jordon remembered the debris around the area. A place to drink and screw. Young Harry's natural habitat.

Jordon left Doc's office and drove to Danny's. On the way, he let himself think about Cassie, wonder what she was doing, how she was feeling. Was she as lonesome for him as he was for her? He felt an emptiness deep inside himself. His loneliness was bad enough now, he hated to think about how much he would miss her if he weren't run to death with

campaigning and investigating this case. Was it only yesterday he and Cassie had been out to Chambers Hilltop?

At Danny's Jordon picked up the trunk containing the
clothes, books, and mementoes which represented all his
earthly acquisitions. Somewhere he'd read that a man ought
not to get his life loaded down with a lot of possessions. Was
it that fellow Thoreau or somebody else? Well, it didn't
matter much, since Jordon didn't have that problem. The
accumulation of his whole life was in one trunk and the
clothes he wore on his back.

Mary Helen helped him carry the trunk to the car, with
Dan Jr. holding on to the handle with her. Jordon struggled
to keep from stumbling over the boy as he shoved the trunk
into the back seat.

"Will you ever come back, Granpa?" the boy said. His eyes
were about to overflow.

Jordon picked him up and hugged him, wishing he could
get his mind off the murder investigation, spend some time
with the boy, maybe take him into the woods and teach him
to hunt. He knew the boy needed it. And Jordon wanted to
do it. But it would have to wait. Bitsy Trotter and Rachel
Blackwell demanded his attention now.

Dan Jr. said it again. "Will you ever come back?"

"All the time," Jordon said. He kissed his grandson on the
cheek. "I'm just moving over by the mill pond. I'll be back
to see you real soon."

Little Cindy stood on the porch and watched in silence.

"Got a hug for your grandpa, honey?" Jordon called to her.

She trotted out to him, gave him a quick embrace, then
went back to her station on the porch.

Mary Helen said, "I still don't know why you have to
move. We'd love to have you stay on here with us."

He gave her a hug. "I need to have a place of my own. I
really do."

"Can I come see you at your new house?" Dan Jr. asked.
"And stay all night with you sometimes?"

"You sure can, if your mother and daddy say all right," Jordon told him.

The boy broke into a wide smile. "I can, can't I mom? Soon?"

"We'll see, son," his mother said.

Jordon waved to them as he drove away. He was relieved he'd been able to get there and get his stuff before Danny got in from work.

He found the house he'd rented sufficient for his needs. A front room, a bedroom and a kitchen. Little front and back porches. Its meager furnishings included a lumpy sofa and a straight-back cane-bottom chair in the front room.

Mounted on the wall near the door was an oak telephone. Its twin bells on the front stared at him like dead black eyes. Jordon picked up the receiver to see if it was hooked up. He heard a hum, pulled the lever down and turned the crank. Almost immediately, he got a "Number, please?" from the operator. It was a voice he didn't recognize. Lenarue had evidently gone for the day.

"It's just Deputy Sheriff Jordon, in my new place, checking to see if my phone is working."

"Oh, yes," the girl said. "We just leave them on and start billing you for it. Unless you don't want it."

"I want it," he said, and hung up.

He started unpacking his trunk, hanging his few clothes on a bar attached to the wall in the bedroom. He had sheets and quilts, including the one his Aunt Laurie had given him and Vera when they got married. It was now thirty years old or more, worn and thin, but he kept it.

He made the bed, spreading the quilt out carefully on it, seeing once again the patches of wool and cotton and denim and God knows what all pieced together in a random, pattern-less way that was etched in his mind forever. He inspected a threadbare place, rubbing his fingers over it, knowing one day soon the quilt would collapse, simply fall apart.

But maybe it would not come to its end before he did. Something told him this might be his time, if the white mare had anything to do with it. At the back of his mind, the damn thing had been hovering over him ever since his dream the other night.

Maybe it was just his frustration at being unable to get a handle of any kind on the Bitsy Trotter killing. And now, the Rachel Blackwell killing, if that's what it was. As he believed. Somehow he felt in his gut that it was related to Bitsy's death. Rachel didn't just walk off her own back porch and break her neck. Somebody helped her along, unless he was badly mistaken.

The question, again, was who? And why?

Jordon began to unpack the small personal library which, next to his .44 Colt, was his most valued possession. He ran his hand affectionately over the worn cover of *Collected Poems and Stories of Edgar Allen Poe* then laid it aside. He flipped through the pages of *The Epic of America* by James Truslow Adams. He took out the stack of Little Blue Books he'd accumulated in several orders from a man named E. Haldeman-Julius in Girard, Kansas. He glanced through them.

They were not made for endurance, these little paper-bound books no bigger than the palm of your hand and running only fifty or sixty pages, but they were cheap and fascinating to read. A nickel a piece, twenty for a dollar. And the subjects were a delight.

One was titled, *Controversy on Christianity* by Robert G. Ingersoll and William E. Gladstone; another, *On the Choice of Books* by Thomas Carlyle; and *Has Religion Made Useful Contributions to Civilization?* by Bertrand Russell. Jordon smiled as he opened this one and read again its first paragraph:

My own view on religion is that of Lucretius. I regard it as a disease born of fear and as a source of untold misery to the human race. I cannot, however, deny that it has made *some* contributions to civilization. It helped in early days to fix the calendar, and it caused Egyptian priests to chronicle eclipses with such care that in time they became able to predict them. These two services I am prepared to acknowledge, but I do not know of any others.

Jordon smiled again and shook his head. Well, Mr. Russell sure wrote like a smart man, but Jordon wasn't prepared to go quite that far in trying to figure out just where religion ought to fit in the overall picture. There'd been some terrible things done in the name of religion, Jordon knew. Some he'd read about and some he'd seen himself. But he thought it was going too far to make all of it out as bad as Mr. Russell did, smart as he was. Maybe it wasn't the fault of religion itself as much as it was some of the folks who pretended to be so all-fired religious. On the other hand, Jordon had known many men in his life who had been tamed by religion, men who'd fought and killed at the drop of a hat, and who became gentle and caring and productive men after they'd been converted. Maybe it was only because of the fear of hell fire. But Jordon thought there was probably more to it than that. Anyhow, who could really say that all religion was as bad as Mr. Russell thought?

Jordon wanted just to sit there and read, going back through the books he already knew, getting into some of the ones he hadn't even had a chance to open. It would be such a relief to sit back, relax and forget about the election, the murder—or murders—he was investigating, and read to his heart's content. "One of these days," he said out loud to himself, "maybe I'll get to do just that."

His telephone rang, startling him so he almost dropped the slender little book containing Mr. Russell's weighty thoughts.

He walked across the room and took the receiver off the hook. "Jordon," he said.

"It's me," Willis said. "You went ahead and moved, I see."

"I was just unpacking my trunk."

"Well, maybe you'll want to leave that till later, and come on over here to the sheriff's office."

"What's up?"

"Nothing much, I guess." Willis played it out. "Just a feller walked in a couple a minutes ago and confessed he killed Rachel Blackwell."

△

Chapter Thirteen

JORDON TURNED THE CANE-BOTTOM chair around, straddled it and eased his rump down on it, resting his arms on
the back. Willis reared back behind his desk and propped his
one leg up on it. He lit a Camel with a kitchen match and
shot a plume of smoke toward the ceiling.

Linwood Evermore sat near them, crying silently, watching his tears splatter in the dust on the floor. He knuckled
his eyes, then dried his hand on the bib of his overalls. "I
never meant to do her no real harm," he said. "I just wanted
my Beauty to get better."

Jordon glanced at Willis, then back at the ginseng man. "Just
take your time, Linwood, and tell us exactly what happened."

Except for telling Willis he'd killed Rachel Blackwell,
Linwood had refused to talk until now. Not until "the deputy
feller I seen at Rachel's Saturday gets here."

Linwood looked up at Jordon. "Everybody says I'm not all
there," he said, touching a finger to his temple. "I've heered
'em. And I reckon they're right. I knowed it since back when
they wouldn't take me in the service." He pointed to the
space between his eyes and said, "Army feller said I was too
narr' right through here."

"What happened, Linwood?" Jordon asked gently. "Just
tell us."

"All I wanted was for Beauty to get well."

"What's the matter with Beauty?" Jordon asked.

"Bad milk. Started to go bloody." He looked from Jordon to Willis for understanding. They cut wide-eyed glances at one another.

"Just who is Beauty?" Jordon asked.

"My cow," Linwood said. "Giving bloody milk."

Jordon took a deep breath and expelled it slowly, letting it puff his cheeks out. "She was giving bloody milk."

"Still is," Linwood said.

"So what happened. What did you do?"

"I got old man Spiers and we drenched her with epsom salts. She just got worse."

Jordon tried again. "All right. When she didn't get better, what did you do?"

"I decided it must be Rachel."

Jordon sighed. "How did you figure that out?"

"Everybody says she's a witch. And I been giving her things right along."

"What things?"

"A rabbit I killed. She fried it for supper. A mess of catfish I caught in Little Horse Creek. Once a flint arrowhead I found down by the Saltpeter Cave."

"So you gave her things."

Linwood nodded. "Everybody knows if you give a witch something of yours, that gives her the power to put a spell on you. But I never thought she'd do it to me. She liked me, I thought. I liked her." He started to sniff again. "It wasn't long after the arrowhead that Beauty took sick."

"And then you did what?"

"I killed Rachel. But I didn't aim to do it." Linwood started to weep again now, quietly. He stared at the floor and his body shook. "It wasn't what I aimed to do."

"Tell us how you did it," Jordon said.

Linwood again looked up, rubbed his eyes, and said, "First off, I stuck my finger with a needle and squeezed some blood

out in a saucer. Then I took a twig and drawed a picture of
Rachel on a piece of paper." He smiled at Jordon. "It didn't
look much like her, but I reckon it don't have to. Long as
you know who you aim for it to be, it works."

"Go on," Jordon said.

"I tacked the picture of Rachel up on the fence post, and
I got my .22 rifle, and I stepped off seven paces and turned
around and took aim at Rachel's picture and shot it. Hit it
in the neck."

"That's how you killed her?"

"That's how you break a witch's spell." Linwood nodded,
his face bright with a smile. Then, suddenly, as he apparently remembered Rachel was dead, his face darkened again.
He ran his hands through the shaggy gray-brown hair that
hung down over his ears and collar. "But I didn't mean to
kill her. I just wanted Beauty to stop giving bad milk."

Jordon glanced at Willis and rolled his eyes. "Did you ever
go anywhere near Rachel's house after you took the ginseng
to her on Saturday?"

"No. Just left it with her and went on home. That's when
I decided to make the picture and shoot it."

"She was all right then? And you never went back around
her house anymore? Never saw her anymore?"

Linwood shook his head vigorously. "She was fine when
I left. I heerd about her being dead. And I knowed I had to
come tell you I done it. Caused it. But I didn't mean to. If
Beauty had got better, I wouldn't a had to do it."

"Did Rachel say anything to you, did you all talk, when
you took her the ginseng?"

Linwood squinched one eye shut, trying to remember.
"She said Halloween was coming."

"Can you remember anything else she said?"

Linwood leaned his head back and stared at the ceiling,
his mouth open. Then he smiled at Jordon and said, "She
liked you. She said that."

"What else?"

"Said you was a good man. And she thought she was going to help you."

"Did she say how?"

Linwood studied the ceiling again. "No. That's all she said. I left then."

Jordon stood up and walked over to Linwood, put his hand on the man's shoulder. "How'd you get here to the courthouse?"

"Rode shank's mare."

"You walked from over past Buxton? Why didn't you go to somebody's telephone and call me?

"Don't know how," Linwood said.

Jordon took him by the arm. "Come on with me."

Linwood stood up. "You going to put me in jail?"

Jordon shook his head. "I'm going to take you outside and try to find somebody to drive you home."

"What about Rachel? What I done?" Linwood looked like he might start to cry again.

"You didn't do anything. It wasn't your picture and your shooting that killed Rachel. Stop worrying about it and go on home."

"My picture didn't make her die? Are you sure?"

"I'm sure," Jordon said.

Jordon found a man with a car who said he was going to Buxton anyway and would drop Linwood off. Jordon watched as the two of them walked toward the parking lot at the side of the courthouse.

Looking back over his shoulder at Jordon, Linwood smiled and waved. "Bye," he called.

Jordon waved back. "I hope Beauty gets all right," he said.

The two men sat in front of Sheriff Treadway's fireplace. Bonnie had let Jordon in, given him a wide-eyed look, and discreetly disappeared.

"No use beating around the bush," Noble said as soon as Jordon was seated. "I want you to stop this investigation into the Trotter girl's killing."

"What do you mean?"

"Goddamn it, don't you understand the English language no more? Stop it. Let it be!"

Jordon felt his anger begin to rise. He was still smarting from Noble's terse telephone summons a half-hour ago. "I want to see you. Now," is all he'd said.

Jordon stared at Noble for a long moment before he spoke. "You're not interested in finding out who did it?"

Noble spread his arms, palms up. "We already *know* who done it. We've got him in jail." His voice sounded like that of a parent trying to get through to a child who repeatedly tracked mud into the house.

"Manochio? I'm not sure he did it," Jordon said.

"Being sure's not your job. That's for the jury to decide."

"What about Rachel Blackwell's death? What if she was killed because somehow she was mixed up in this Trotter. . . ."

Noble stared at him. "So now you think Rachel was killed? The coroner figures maybe she fell off of her back porch."

"It's possible she was killed."

"What gives you that idea?"

"Her neck was broke. Doc Klein says it could have been somebody did it to her."

"But it could have been the fall, too. Right?"

"It could have been."

"Jesus Christ, Jordon. Take it easy on me. First you figure Rachel was killed, not fell. Then you want to mix it up with this other case. Can't you just let the law take its course? Let this boy stay in jail till his trial comes up, let the evidence come out in court?"

"There's no real evidence that he did it."

"How about this?" Noble held up his hands and began to tick off points on his fingers. "He was going out with the girl. Screwing her. Knocked her up. She didn't want to marry him. He sneaked off that day, met her in the woods, they argued, he killed her. Then he skipped out. And you're telling me he didn't do it. Who do you think *did* do it?"

Jordon looked at the floor. "I don't know."

"But you have to keep poking around the Buxton offices, pestering Young Harry and riling up old man HR. What is it with you anyhow?"

"I didn't go to the Buxton building today on account of Harry. I was there to rent a house. Anyhow, as I recollect, you're the one told me solving this murder would likely get me elected."

"You've solved it, man. Go out and tell folks how you done it. They'll vote for you."

"And HR Buxton will throw his influence behind me."

"He say that?"

Jordon nodded.

"Then he'll do it. He's a man of his word."

"And what if the Manochio boy didn't kill her?"

"He killed her."

"But what if he didn't?"

"Believe me, a jury will say he did."

"How can you be so sure?"

"It all points to him, like I said a minute ago. On top of that, he's an outsider. A foreigner. And Pete Creekwood over at the jail tells me the boy's hot tempered, boils over ever time Pete teases him a little bit. Trust me, boy, the commonwealth's attorney will make mince meat out of him in court. A jury will convict him."

Jordon sat quietly for a moment. Finally, he said, "But what if—just *what if*—it was somebody else killed her?"

Noble took a deep breath, as though he were ready to explode, then slowly let it out. He stared at Jordon a long time before he spoke. "I've talked about this all I aim to," he said quietly. "I'm satisfied the Three-C boy is the one. Now you find something else to do. Get out and electioneer a little bit. Do something. But forget about this case till it comes up in court."

"But just say—"

Noble held up his hand. "No more buts. That's all."

Jordon took a deep breath and heaved a long sigh. "You're telling me to stop right here, no matter what I might think or how I might feel?"

Noble rolled his eyes toward the ceiling. "By God, you've finally got it. I been trying to tell you that ever since you got here." Then, very slowly, with a hard straight look at Jordon, he added, "Leave it alone, boy."

Jordon took a deep breath and stood up. "I can't do that, Noble."

It was a long time before Noble spoke and when he did his voice was scarcely more than a whisper. "I'm the one was elected sheriff. I deputized you. As long as you work for me, you'll do what I tell you to do."

Jordon shook his head. His voice was as quiet as Noble's. "Not this."

Noble struggled to his feet. His bulk made Jordon look almost small. "I take it you know what you're doing?"

Jordon nodded. "I reckon I do."

Noble sighed. "Let me have your badge."

Jordon unpinned the badge from his coat and handed it to Noble.

"Too bad you can't understand things better," the sheriff said.

Jordon stared at him. "Maybe I understand all I need to."

Noble gave Jordon a straight look but did not speak for a moment. When he did, he said, "You can park the car behind the courthouse. Leave the keys with Willis. As of right now, your term as my deputy is over."

Chapter Fourteen

JORDON HANDED THE KEYS to Willis. "I'm out of a job."

"I heard. Noble called and said you'd be dropping the car off."

"It's out back."

Willis just looked at him for a minute, then said, "What are you going to do?"

"Try to campaign harder. See if I can win this election."

"What do you think your chances are?"

"Without Noble's support? And with HR Buxton now going to come out against me?" Jordon shook his head. "Whatever my chances are now, they're a lot less than they were a couple of days ago."

Willis said, "Well, you've got that figured right."

Jordon sighed and shook his head. "If I give it my best shot and still lose, I guess I'll go back to running a poker game. Seems to me that's a lot easier than trying to be sheriff. Less of a gamble, too."

Willis fussed around with some papers. "I'm about ready to close up here. You want a ride anywhere?"

"Give me a minute." Jordon opened his desk drawer and took out his meager belongings. A box of .44 cartridges, his hunting knife in its worn leather sheath, a half-empty bag of peanuts, half a dozen Little Blue Books, a pocket dictionary, a well-worn copy of *The Valley of the Moon* by Jack London.

When he and Willis got to the parking lot, Willis slid his crutches in the back seat of his car and handed the keys to Jordon. "You mind driving?"

Jordon took the keys, got in Willis's Model A and drove them toward Buxton.

"When the sheriff called," Willis said, "he told me he's coming by in the morning to swear Grover Jenkins in as his new deputy."

"Grover's a good man," Jordon said. "Not the smartest in the world, but steady. And he'd fight a buzz saw before he'd turn tail."

After a moment Willis said, "I hate to see you leave."

"I guess it's my fault. But, damn it, I think there's something more to this thing than that boy in jail getting mad and killing her."

"But you don't really have any evidence of that, do you?"

Jordon shook his head. "That's the problem. It's just a feeling, I guess. Maybe it's more than that, but I can't put my finger on it."

"And maybe you're wrong. You ever think about that? Maybe Manochio did it."

"Maybe I am wrong. But if he did do it, why is everybody so dead set on stopping me from poking around? What harm is there to anybody else if Manochio did it? You know what I think? I think HR Buxton is afraid of what I might turn up on Young Harry. I think that's the big problem."

"I don't know," Willis said. "Why would Harry want to kill that girl? What would he gain by that?"

"That's exactly what I'd like to find out. Maybe she was blackmailing him."

"About what? Gonna tell folks he's a pussy-hound? Screwing everything that wears a dress, her included?"

Jordon said nothing.

Willis went on. "Young Harry Buxton would frig a snake if somebody'd hold its head. Everybody already knows that."

"Something else, then."

"You sure you're not just after Harry's ass cause you don't like him and his daddy and his daddy's company?"

"Damn it, Willis, that's not all there is to it."

It was a while before Willis said, "Maybe you should have done what Noble said, just left it alone."

Jordon drove in silence for a while before he spoke. "Remember when we were talking the other day about how folks step over the big things and then get their bowels in an uproar about somebody taking a drink of liquor? Stuff like that?"

"Yeah."

"Well, this is one more of those things. They send me out to arrest Luke Purcell for stealing somebody's hog and slaughtering it to feed his family. We don't know if he's guilty or not, but there he is in jail. And nobody's troubled at all about that. But here Noble wants me to quit looking for whoever met that poor girl in the woods and slaughtered her. You see what I'm saying?"

"Big things and little things."

"Right. You understand why I couldn't go along with Noble?"

Willis sighed and nodded. After a moment, he said, "Well, it's out of your hands now. You've got nothing more to do with it."

Jordon was silent.

After a bit, Willis said, "Since you don't have a car, why don't you drop me off at home and take mine for a few days, just till you get one."

"I couldn't do that. Leave you on—"

Willis held up his hand. "I don't use it except to get to work and back. The old lady can't drive. And I don't do it anymore than I have to. You keep the car. Pick me up in the morning and take me to the courthouse, then use it till you get one."

Jordon started to thank him, but Willis interrupted. "Hell,

it'll be kind of nice to have a chauffeur drive me back and forth. Just like HR Buxton."

"He drives himself."

"But he don't have to."

"True."

"And now, neither do I."

Jordon grinned. "Also true."

After he let Willis out of the car in front of his house, Jordon looked at his watch. A little after six. He'd promised to meet Lenarue Wooten at her home at 7:30. But that was before he lost his job. Now, as Willis had said, it was out of his hands.

Or was it?

What difference did it make, when you got right down to it, whether he still wore a badge or not? He'd started this thing. Put Manochio in jail. Got Lenarue involved in something that had her half scared to death. At least he had a responsibility to talk to her, try to find out what she was afraid of and set her mind at ease.

And what about Rachel Blackwell? If her death was somehow connected to Bitsy Trotter's, to his investigation, then he couldn't just forget about that. What was he supposed to do? Let whoever killed her, maybe killed them both, just walk away from it all?

No, he'd go see Lenarue after supper. Find out what she was so scared of that she whispered when she called him on the phone.

After that he could decide what to do next.

Jordon read the letters over again but still couldn't make any real sense of them. "This is it?"

Lenarue nodded. "What's it about? Does it have something to do with who killed Bitsy?"

"I'm not sure," Jordon said. They sat in Jordon's car at the side of the road near where Lenarue lived.

"Hold the flashlight a little closer," he said. The brown

kraft envelope had once been sealed, but when Lenarue gave it to him, it had been opened. Nothing was written on the outside.

"Did you look at this stuff?" Jordon asked. "Is that what made you afraid?"

"I . . . I guess so. I mean, yes, I looked at it. Tonight. But I was scared when I heard about Rachel. I don't know what it is, but I got to thinking maybe . . . I don't know."

Jordon studied the three pieces of paper.

The first sheet was a letter to Milton Graham at the Buxton Corporation from a Mr. C. B. Morris, whose letterhead said he was a lumber broker in Cincinnati. The Buxton Corporation sold a lot of lumber up north, Jordon knew that. The letter, dated September 24, 1933, said,

> Dear Mr. Graham:
> By this letter I am ordering and authorizing you to ship to our firm a total of 100,000 board feet of No. 2 and better pine 2x4's, 8 feet long. Shipment to be made by rail to the Cincinnati freight yard as soon as feasable, but not later than October 15. The price, as agreed, is $76.00 per 1,000 board feet, F.O.B. Buxton. Payment will be made by us within 30 days.

It was signed by Mr. Morris.

Next was a ruled yellow sheet with handwriting on it. It was a draft of a letter in response to C.B. Morris, written by Milton Graham. Then there was the typewritten version of the same letter, on a Buxton Corporation letterhead, dated September 29.

Jordon read the typed version:

> Dear Mr. Morris:
> We are in receipt of your letter of the 24th, ordering 100,000 board feet of No. 2 and better pine 2x4x8's, to be shipped as soon as feasible, but not after October 15,

to Cincinnati. Price, $76.00 per 1,000 board feet, F.O.B. Buxton. Terms, 30 days net.

We thank you for this order and will proceed to fill it without delay. We value your patronage and look forward to continuing to serve you in any way we can. I also look forward to seeing you personally the next time I have an opportunity to be in Cincinnati.

Milton Graham

Jordon looked over the handwritten version, which appeared to be identical to the typed copy, except for a few minor corrections somebody had made with a fine-tip blue fountain pen. A couple of commas had been added, and a couple of words had been circled.

"Did Bitsy do all of Graham's letters?" Jordon asked.

Lenarue nodded. "He doesn't dictate, which is one thing she didn't like. She'd studied shorthand and didn't get to use it. He always wrote the stuff out longhand and she typed it up for him."

"Was she the one who made these corrections?" he asked, showing her the handwritten draft.

"Yeah. He's not the best speller in the world. And Bitsy was good at it, so he wanted her to catch his mistakes."

Jordon glanced back at the letters. "Why do you suppose Bitsy kept this stuff?"

"Maybe . . . ." She hesitated, then shook her head. "I don't know."

"Tell me, what made you so scared? What are you afraid of?"

"I don't know exactly. When I found out about Rachel, I just started getting scared."

Jordon stared at her for a moment before going on. "When did Bitsy give this to you?"

"Oh, she didn't."

"Then where did you get it?"

"From Rachel Blackwell, didn't I tell you that?"

Jordon shook his head.

"Rachel called Friday and asked me to stop by, said she wanted to tell me something. When I went, she gave me this envelope. Said she wanted me to keep it till she asked for it."

Jordon thought about it for a minute. "Was the envelope sealed then?"

"It was, but it looked like it had been opened and glued back shut. You know what I mean?"

Jordon nodded. "And you put the envelope away until you heard about Rachel. And got scared."

"Yes. Rachel seemed kind of scared herself when she gave it to me. Not scared exactly, just careful like." Jordon could hear the fear in Lenarue's voice as she said, "Did Rachel really fall? Or did something else happen to her, like some folks are saying?"

"I'm not sure yet." Jordon folded the letters and put them back into the envelope. "Who else knows about these?"

"I haven't told anybody."

"What I'd like you to do is, first, don't let on to anybody you know about these letters. Okay?"

She nodded.

"Next, I think you ought to stay close to home until this thing is cleared up."

"Not go to work?"

"Go to work, do everything just like you always do, except don't go out at night, don't go on any dates, anything like that. And I think I ought to talk to your dad about this."

Lenarue grabbed him by the arm. "Oh, please don't do that. He's so strict on me anyhow. He'd never let me out again. Don't worry. I'll be careful." After a moment she said, "You don't really think anybody would try to . . . hurt me, do you?"

"I think we shouldn't take any chances."

Tuesday morning Jordon picked Willis up at home and drove him to the courthouse, not mentioning last night's meeting with Lenarue. Or the envelope.

On the way back home, he stopped in the Buxton drugstore to pick up a copy of the Louisville *Courier-Journal*. As he stepped outside, he saw HR Buxton talking to one of his men on the steps leading up to the Buxton building. They finished their conversation, and HR came on down the steps as the other man went toward the office.

Jordon stood there thinking for a moment, then decided. He walked across the street and reached HR just as he was about to get into his car.

Jordon said, "Got a minute?"

Buxton stopped, waiting.

"You got me fired," Jordon said. "But it doesn't end here. I won't stop till I'm satisfied."

"What do you mean?" Buxton said.

"The sheriff asked for my badge, but I'm not finished."

"I'm afraid you're one of those men who never learn, Jordon. What goes on with you and the sheriff is between you and him. I've got other matters to tend to." HR wore a tight little smile as he got into his car and shut the door.

Jordon sat looking out the front window of the little house he'd rented near the mill pond. Home. How many places had he called home, and yet he'd never really felt he had one since he and Vera had set up housekeeping so long ago down by Stateline. That brief time before his temper had shifted the direction of their lives permanently like an earthquake shifts the course of a river.

Jordon got up and put on a pot of coffee to boil. He knew he ought to be out in the county trying to drum up votes for the election next week.

He took out the envelope he'd got from Lenarue last night and studied it again, trying to figure out what it meant.

He got up and went to the telephone. He gave the girl on the switchboard the number in Cincinnati which he read off the letterhead of C.B. Morris, Lumber Broker.

It took a little while for the call to go through. The woman who answered said Mr. Morris was not in. And she didn't know when to expect him. But she'd be happy to take a message.

"Is he out of town, or will he maybe be in sometime this week?" Jordon asked.

"I never know, sir. Mr. Morris doesn't operate on a regular schedule. He could be in any time, or he might not be in for weeks."

"Does he call in?"

"Sometimes, but I couldn't say when that might be. I'd be happy to take a message, sir."

Jordon said no, thanked her, and hung up.

He poured himself a cup of coffee and sat at the table sipping it, remembering the stuff he'd drunk at Black Cory's Saturday night.

He looked at the letters some more. Should he go see Milton Graham? Ask him? Something told him no.

What the hell, he thought. It's not that far to Cincinnati.

He got the small metal box in which he kept his few special possessions. His silver star from the war, a lock of Vera's hair tied with a faded red ribbon, a tintype of his father and mother, sitting on their front porch in their go-to-meeting clothes, holding a baby. He took out the small gold shield which said, "Deputy Sheriff, Perry County, Ky." The sheriff there had given it to Jordon when he'd left at the end of his term.

Then he packed his small leather grip and called Willis.

Jordon stepped aboard the train and found a seat in an almost empty coach. He stared out the window into the darkening evening. He'd be in Cincinnati well before daylight. The train jerked and began to crawl away from the depot. He leaned back in his seat and closed his eyes.

Riding a train always triggered a second trip for Jordon, back through his mind to when he was a boy becoming a man in the mountains.

Jordon's early memories were of the new communities that sprang to life along the railroad, a new river of steel with snorting, stinking vessels which roared through the mountains and connected them with the bustling commerce and industry of Cincinnati and Chattanooga, Louisville and Nashville.

When he was a little boy Jordon was taken by his father on a local passenger train which stopped every few miles to receive and disgorge men and women with their suitcases and bags and bundles. These images were lodged permanently among Jordon's early personal remembrances.

But even more potent were the pictures in his mind of the way it was before the railroad came. The pictures that illustrated stories told to Jordon by his father and his grandfather and his uncles. Stories about the old way of living in the mountains. The hunting and fishing. The isolation and quiet, broken only by natural occurrences: the seasons, storms, floods, fires, bloody confrontations between willful men over a property line, or a bet, or a woman, or plain mountain man-pride.

As a boy and young man, Jordon had watched the opening of the commercial coal mines and the building of the company camps. Watched the little box-like frame houses take shape under the hammers of company carpenters.

He had watched the mountain men and their families leave the woods and creeks and rivers and move into the camps to become lumber mill workers or coal miners. He had seen them put aside their long rifles and trot lines to accept picks and shovels and cross-cut saws and daily work orders from the company bosses.

Jordon had watched friends and uncles and cousins give up the ways of their fathers with little or no resistance. He had seen them spend their short lives of long days in a damp and dangerous underground world illuminated by flickering lamps. He had listened to their veiled references to the death angel that always lurked in the shadows, waiting to claim their souls from under a thousand tons of fallen coal and rock.

It was a world Jordon wanted no part of.

Something somewhere deep inside him refused to believe that working for a coal company was better than going his own way, uncertain though it had been.

Jordon had followed no orders save his own. Even in the army in two wars. He was a good soldier, up to a point. But when the orders seemed stupid to him, or motivated by something other than the best interests of his unit, he found a way to disregard them. Or delay their implementation. Most of the time.

It was no surprise to him when he never advanced beyond corporal. Or when he found he was liked much better by his fellow soldiers than by his officers. It was not a matter of performance under fire. He had done well in that respect. Had been decorated more than once. Wounded. But in his eyes, stupidity was stupidity even if it came from the lips of a captain or colonel. Or a sheriff.

He was dancing with Cassie at Della's, about to kiss her. And her face faded away to become the face of Bitsy Trotter, smiling at him. Then, once more, he was standing in the field, watching the white mare, waiting for her to look at him, then make her move.

He struggled to turn and run, then came awake with a start as the train lurched to a stop somewhere up the line toward Cincinnati. He glanced through the window into the night, watched people hurrying along the platform, then closed his eyes and found sleep again.

"I'm sorry, sir. You must know I can't let you look at someone else's files."

Jordon had already told her who he was. Now he pulled back his coat, showed her the impotent Perry County badge pinned inside. "I'm investigating a murder, miss."

The young woman looked at him for a moment, uncertainty showing in her eyes. She was an attractive, pleasant brunette, somewhere in her mid-thirties, Jordon guessed.

"I can get a court order, if that's what you want," he said, hoping she would believe the lie. She looked doubtful. "You're a sheriff?"

"That's right."

She hesitated again, looking at him, then apparently made up her mind. "If I get in trouble, you'll fix it, right?"

"Of course. But you won't get in any trouble. It's okay."

She took a folder out of a file cabinet. "This is all we have here," she said. "You understand we're just his secretarial service. We type correspondence for a lot of different people and businesses."

Jordon had not known that when he spoke to her on the phone. He opened the thin folder. He found a carbon copy of the letter from Morris to Milton Graham, the one Jordon had. Another copy of a letter to a Cincinnati bank, renewing the rental on a safe deposit box, and a carbon of a letter to a real estate company, stating Morris's intention to continue his lease on an office in downtown Cincinnati, not far from the secretarial service. Scanning the letters, Jordon could see this girl was not the speller Bitsy Trotter had been.

"This is it, then?" Jordon asked the girl.

"If that's what's in the file. We only keep these for a few months, in case there's some question comes up. Then we toss them out." The girl went back to her typing. "I have to get these letters out before noon."

Jordon wrote down the address and room number of the office mentioned in the letter, thanked the girl. "When Mr. Morris does come by again, maybe it would be best if you didn't mention this."

"Don't worry. I'm not stupid."

"I can tell that."

It was several blocks to the old building where Morris's office was. Past Fountain Square, up Vine Street, west on

Eighth. Past a Plymouth dealership advertising new sedans
starting at less than $600. Men with dirty clothes and bleak
faces walked the streets aimlessly, or huddled in small
groups inside doorways to cut the chill. Somehow to Jordon
the depression seemed worse in the city than in the mountains. At least in the mountains folks mostly knew one
another, could help out a little if things got too bad. Here, it
seemed to him, the aloneness at the bottom would be almost
as bad as the hunger.

Jordon had no trouble finding the building where Morris's
office was located. He'd played in some cut-throat high-
stakes poker games in Cincinnati more than once through
the years. And across the river in Newport.

He walked up to the third floor, down a dimly lit hall. The
door with the name C.B. Morris painted in small black
letters near the bottom of a frosted glass pane was locked.
He peered through the glass, but could make out only a few
dark shapes.

He went back out on the street, asked directions and after
walking several blocks, found a hardware store. He bought
a small crowbar and carried it back along the street in a paper
bag.

Inside the building where Morris's office was located,
Jordon passed a heavy woman in a long black coat who eyed
him with suspicion as he mounted the stairs.

When he reached Morris's office, he looked both ways,
making certain no one was in the hall, then tried the
crowbar. There was enough space to barely get the tip of it
in. He pressed his shoulder against the door, afraid if he
pushed too hard, the glass would break.

Suddenly, he heard a noise down the hall behind him. He
quickly slipped the crowbar inside his coat and under his
belt, walking away from the noise, toward the front of the
building, as he did it.

He looked back over his shoulder and saw a short thin
man wearing a shirt and tie and thick glasses coming up

behind him. The man glanced at Jordon, looked as though he was about to speak, then looked away. Jordon continued walking, as if he intended to go back down the stairs. The man turned left and pushed open a door marked "Men."

Jordon spun around and hurried back down the hall to Morris's office. He made sure no one was in the hall, then pushed the crowbar back into the space near the knob and gave it a hard shove. He threw enough weight behind it this time to break the lock. Looking up and down the hall, he saw no one and stepped inside, closing the door behind him. If anyone looked, it wouldn't be hard to see that the door had been forced. But maybe they wouldn't look.

He didn't know what he might find inside, but he hoped he'd turn up something that would shed some more light on Mr. C.B. Morris and why the letters Bitsy Trotter had taken were so important.

The office was furnished meagerly. An old wooden desk and chair, a battered file cabinet, a worn and spotted mohair sofa.

The file cabinet was empty except for a few office supplies. Pencils, a bottle of ink, paper clips, legal pads, stationery.

The desk had one large drawer which was locked, but it too responded easily to the crowbar.

Inside were only four folders. One marked "Buxton Corp.," another "Orders." the third, "Financial," and the fourth, "Sales."

In "Buxton Corp." Jordon found letters going back more than five years, all from Milton Graham, all confirming or otherwise dealing with lumber orders he had received from C.B. Morris. A lot of lumber.

In "Orders" were copies of Morris's letters ordering various substantial amounts of lumber. All addressed to Milton Graham at the Buxton Corporation.

In the "Financial" folder, Jordon found statements from the Third Queen City Bank and Trust Company. The statements showed that the account had little activity. Some months nothing had been deposited or withdrawn. Other times, a single deposit, followed by one or two withdrawals. The canceled checks were all made out to the Buxton Corporation, in payment for the lumber which had been received, to the real estate company for rent on the little office, and to the secretarial service.

That was it.

Except for the big ones made out to "Cash" and signed and endorsed on the back by C.B. Morris.

The folder marked "Sales" was empty. There was no record of who the lumber had been sold to. But it was clear from the deposits and the checks made out to the Buxton Corporation and to "Cash" that Mr. Morris was engaged in a successful brokerage business. A business in which he was able to mark up the lumber he bought from Buxton and sell it at a steady and worthwhile profit.

Glancing through the checks made out to "Cash," Jordon mentally totted up more than $14,000 since January 1933, which is as far back as the statements were available.

Jordon considered it for a moment. Maybe a total of $15,000 before this year was out. Times at least five years. $75,000 all told. Maybe a lot more.

A typical coal miner might make $600 a year, Jordon knew.

Mr. Morris was doing all right in the lumber brokerage business.

He apparently had just one source of supply, the Buxton Corporation. And from the bank statements it looked like he had just one customer whose deposited checks coincided with the orders of lumber from Buxton. A small check for the rent, another for the secretarial service, and a large one to "Cash," negotiated by Mr. Morris. That was the pattern.

A neat and simple—and profitable—business.

Back at the office of the secretarial service, the young woman was putting on her coat. "I can't talk to you any more. It's my lunch hour."

"I didn't notice it was that late," Jordon said, looking at
his watch. "If you don't have plans to eat with somebody
else, how about I take you to lunch?"

Jordon waited as she studied him for a minute. He looked
at her more closely than he had earlier. She was a slender
young woman, a little pale. He figured now she was no more
than thirty-two or three. She had put bright red lipstick on
her full lips. Her glasses and the straight dark hair she wore
pulled back into a severe bun made her appear school-marm-
ish. Take away her glasses and let her hair fall loose and she
would be more than pretty.

As she considered his offer, Jordon smiled. "I'm safe," he
said. "Just like to talk to you a little more." Then he added,
"And we both got to eat. Right?"

After a moment she smiled back, ready to trust him, at
least as far as lunch. "My name's Charlotte Braun," she said.
"And I remember, you said yours is Jordon."

"I usually get a bowl of soup in a little restaurant next to
the office and then walk around by Fountain Square and look
in the store windows. There are so many pretty things. But
everything is so expensive." She looked about the restaurant.
"This sure is a swell place."

The waiter brought menus and left. Jordon had insisted
on taking her somewhere she'd always wanted to eat but
never had. She'd chosen this restaurant on Fifth Street, near
the Square, an expensive looking place with clean white
tablecloths and well-dressed customers. Hartmann's, it said
on the door and the menus.

"Order whatever you like," Jordon said.

"I can take a little extra time," she said. "I just have to get
the afternoon work out, however long that takes."

"You work by yourself?"

She nodded. "There used to be four of us in our office, but
it's down to just me now. The man who owns the business

has three more offices in other locations around town, all small."

They ordered lunch. She wanted a steak, and they both decided on small sirloin strips, with salad and baked potato.

While they sipped coffee and waited, Jordon said, "Tell me what you can about C.B. Morris."

"Like what?"

"Like, do you have any idea how I might be able to get in touch with him? Where he lives, or a phone number?"

Charlotte shook her head. "The only phone number he has is ours, the one on his letterhead. And the only address we have for him is his office."

"On Eighth Street?" The one he'd just burglarized, he said to himself.

"Yes."

"How long did you say he's been doing business with you?"

"I've been there a little over five years. And he was with us when I came. I don't know how long before that."

Their food came and they busied themselves with it. Charlotte made an appreciative "Mmmm."

Jordon grinned, and she added, "This is such a change for me. A treat."

"Me, too. Where I'm from a good steak is hard to come by most of the time."

She smiled at him. "You seem like a nice man, Mr. Jordon," she said. "Or should I say 'Sheriff Jordon'?"

Thinking about it, he grinned. "Why don't we just make it plain 'Jordon.' " He forked a piece of steak and noticed she was smiling at him. "What is it?"

"Nothing really."

"What?" She seemed to be flirting with him.

"I was just noticing your voice. I like to listen to the way people talk. You know, the different people I meet. What their voices tell me about them."

"So," Jordon said, smiling at her now, "what does my voice

tell you about me?"

She tilted her head to one side and put her finger on her chin. "Well, not from your accent but more from the way you say things, you're a strong person, that much I can hear."

Jordon leaned back and looked at her. "Oh, you can, can you?" She *was* flirting, there was no doubt about it. But in a way that was very becoming to her. And very appealing to him.

She nodded. "Something else. Now don't be mad at me. But I think you're . . . gentle. You know what I mean?" She arched her eyebrows, as if to say, "Okay?"

"It's your guess, darlin, not mine. But I ought to warn you, not many people would describe me as gentle. Some other words I've had thrown at me lately, but not gentle."

"Well, the southern accent, along with the way you say things, I just think . . ."

"My accent's not southern," he said. "You're a little bit off there. I come from the mountains, a hundred and fifty miles or so from here. So maybe you're wrong about the rest, too."

"But you sound kind of southern."

It had always been a little puzzling to Jordon why people outside the mountains tended to roll mountain folks and southerners all together in the same ball of wax. From his experience in the army and his travels around the country over three decades, Jordon knew how much difference there really was between southern and mountain people. A good example was the difference in their attitudes toward colored folks. The typical southerner's feeling on the subject was pretty well known. But most mountain people didn't do much prejudging of anybody. A man had a chance to prove himself. If he measured up, he measured up, black or white. If he fell short, then he fell short. That's why mountain men mostly went to fight on the side of the North in the Civil War while the aristocrats from the Bluegrass mostly went with the South. And that's why colored men and Italians and Greeks and Polacks and mountaineers all worked in the mines together, digging coal and facing death side by side. What a man talked or looked like was not the main thing in the mountains. What he proved himself to be was something else again.

"I'm sorry," Charlotte Braun was saying to him. "Did I say something that offended you?"

He shook his head. "I was just thinking."

"About what?"

"How mountain people and southerners are different. It's too bad we don't have the time to go into it."

She looked at him and smiled warmly. "That would be a real pleasure. Someday when you have the time."

Jordon's smile was warm, too. The invitation in her voice was unmistakable. Not cheap or anything like that, but an invitation nevertheless, with the distinct possibility of more than just talk about accents and such. "Someday maybe we can." How bright and interesting this young woman was, he thought. And how much we all read into, not just what people say, but how they say it.

They both were silent for a while, eating and enjoying their food. Then Jordon said, "Tell me what Mr. C.B. Morris looks like."

She thought for a moment. "Well, he's about medium tall. A little on the heavy side."

"Like a lot of men," Jordon said.

"He's about forty or forty-five, I guess. Hair kind of light, what there is left. None here." Putting her hand on top of her head and sweeping it forward. "But he wears this funny looking wig to cover it up. It's so obvious. And he wears glasses, with gold frames." A little chuckle. "I don't have any idea what color his eyes are."

"That's very good. Helps me a lot." After a while, he said, "Anything else?"

"Let's see. He's always dressed up. In a suit and tie, and

a clean white shirt."

Jordon nodded. He had put his notebook on the table earlier and had been taking down the details of her description. He added suit, tie, clean white shirt. He looked up at her and raised his eyebrows. "More?"

"I can't think of anything else," she said.

The waiter came as she was getting to the last bite of her baked potato. Would they care for dessert?

"How about it?" Jordon asked her.

"Is it okay?" she asked. "Do you mind?"

"What about if we both do?"

She laughed and they ordered, both the same. The waiter brought them generous wedges of pecan pie with vanilla ice cream.

"Can you believe this?" she said. "I'm not only having lunch at Hartmann's, I'm eating like a little pig."

Jordon made a "V" with his fingers. "Two of us," he said. And they both laughed.

When they'd finished and the waiter had topped off their coffee cups, Charlotte said, "I wish I could think of something else to tell you. You say it's a murder investigation? You think maybe Mr. Morris might be involved in it?"

"It's hard to say right now. There's no evidence that he is. I just wanted to talk to him, see what he might know."

"He's kind of a funny man," she said. "Not that he tries to be. But some of the things he says." She laughed a little. "I listen to the way everybody talks, remember?"

"You say he's funny. How so?" Jordon asked.

"Things he says."

"Jokes, you mean?"

"No. Not *what* he says, how he talks. Pronounces words."

"Tell me."

"Like this: 'Will you "twy" to get these "wetters" out for me by the end of the day?' Not 'try,' and 'letters.' "

Jordon's whole body tensed. He tried to hold his excitement in check. "I'm going to try something, Charlotte," he said. "Let's see what happens."

She watched with fascination as he turned to a clean page in his notebook and started to sketch a man's face.

"Oh, you can draw," she said. "I wish I could."

"A hobby is all," he said. "I wish I'd studied it when I was young."

He sketched quickly from memory, trying to capture the essence of the round boyish face, the puffy lips, the balding head. He wished he had a photograph of Milton Graham.

In a few moments, when he'd remembered it the best he could and put it on paper, he sketched some hair on the bald head and turned the notebook around for her to look at.

She didn't take any time at all.

"That's Mr. Morris," she said, smiling and shaking her head in awe. "I'd give anything if I could draw like that."

Jordon sat on a bench near the center of Union Terminal in the late evening and watched the steady flow of people coming and going. Many were poor looking, shabby. Moving with resignation, as if away from a dreary past but toward some unknown new place, maybe worse. Some of them were clearly mountain people, fleeing hard times at home, seeking a place of refuge in Cincinnati, where times were also hard. It was the nearest big city. But it was a city that didn't need them. Or want them. Other people, better dressed, hurried through, carrying briefcases and bags, afraid, it seemed, that they might be too late for something of vital importance. Or worse, catch whatever malady the poor ones carried.

Jordon ran back over the afternoon's events in his mind. After Charlotte had identified his sketch of Milton Graham as C.B. Morris, he'd asked her if Mr. Morris dictated his letters to her. "Never," she'd said. "He always writes them out in draft on a yellow pad, then gets me to type them. I think maybe it's because of the way he pronounces his words. Maybe it embarrasses him." But he always took the handwritten drafts back with the typed letters, she said.

Then Jordon had shown her part of the handwriting on the draft letter he'd got from Lenarue. "That's Mr. Morris's writing," Charlotte had said. "I'm sure."

He'd walked back to her office and thanked her for being so helpful. "The pleasure was all mine," she said, patting her tummy as they'd strolled along once more past Fountain Square.

"And I don't just mean the food. It was very nice to spend the time with you." "I enjoyed it, too," he said. But as much as he'd enjoyed the long lunch with her, he couldn't help feeling a little uncomfortable as he looked at the hungry, empty faces of the men and women who drifted along the street. When he'd left her at her office, she said, "Come see me when you get back to Cincinnati again. Oh, and I hope you catch who you're looking for."

He gave her a little peck on the cheek and strolled about the city for awhile. He already knew the first through passenger train he could get would be almost midnight. And he had to do something to keep himself from setting off running toward Buxton.

He found a bookstore, new and used, and spent most of the afternoon browsing through it, resisting the impulse to buy more than a few. He didn't want to accumulate more of anything than he could easily move from place to place in his trunk.

But he did get a copy of *The Outline of Man's Knowledge* by Clement Wood, a book he figured he could read, a little bit at a time, and enjoy for years.

Also, he bought a detective novel, *The Glass Key*. It looked like it might be interesting.

Afterwards, he went to a picture show, saw "All Quiet on the Western Front." The actor who played the main part was a young man named Lew Ayres. He did such a good job that Jordon's own experiences of the war came rushing back in a flood. He was surprised how fresh they were as he watched the film play out on the screen.

Later, he wandered to the railroad station.

He was purposely avoiding dwelling on what he had learned from Charlotte and his burglary, wanting to let it all percolate through his mind for a little while before trying to sort out exactly what it meant.

Now, after he'd eaten a turkey sandwich at a restaurant at the station for supper, and paged through the Clement Wood book a little, he let himself think about what he knew.

C.B. Morris was Milton Graham. Or vice versa. Whichever.

And he looked mighty like an embezzler. Like he was buying shipments of lumber from himself at the Buxton Corporation, maybe at a discount, then selling it to somebody at a markup, and taking the difference out with checks made to "Cash" and endorsed by C.B. Morris.

A neat and simple business, just like Jordon had thought earlier. Also slightly felonious, which he'd not suspected at the time.

Jordon got out the letters Lenarue had given him.

He tried to piece it together. Bitsy had learned somehow, from working on the switchboard or doing Graham's correspondence, or both, what he was doing. She'd taken the letters out for leverage. Jordon read over them again. The word "feasable" jumped out this time in the letter from Morris to Graham, ordering the lumber. Charlotte Braun had not caught the misspelling, so it had come to Graham that way and Bitsy had noticed it.

It was also misspelled and circled by Bitsy on the hand-written draft of the reply that Graham had given her. But she'd corrected it on the typed version. She'd also changed "procede" to "proceed." And put in a couple of commas.

He was sure that Graham was embezzling thousands of dollars of Buxton money through the lumber brokerage scheme. And that Bitsy had stumbled onto it. Apparently she had planned to blackmail him, to get her passage to a new life.

But had he killed her? Embezzling—or maybe it was only

unfair competition with the company you worked for, say, fraud—was one thing. Murder another.

Graham had been out of town the day Bitsy was killed. Or said he was. Jordon cursed himself. Why hadn't he asked Charlotte if she'd seen Morris on the day Bitsy was murdered? Jordon went to a telephone booth and thumbed through a directory. There were a lot of Brauns in the Cincinnati area. But no Charlotte. Either she did not have a phone, or maybe lived with her parents.

He could call her at her office tomorrow when he was back in Buxton.

Chapter Fifteen

I T WAS WELL AFTER daylight when the train whistle pulled Jordon up out of a fitful sleep. He rubbed his eyes and looked out the window. He could see they were going around a sweeping curve, up a grade. It appeared to be the last stretch before coming into Buxton.

Half a dozen others were on the coach with him. An old woman with a young girl, mountain people who must have got on somewhere up the line. A man dressed in a suit. A couple of men in overalls.

Jordon stared out the window at the long curving body of the train as it crawled up the grade and around the long bend. He saw a man appear at the door of one of the coaches up ahead, stand there for a minute, then move down to the last step and hang on with one hand. In the other hand, the man carried a small grip, much like Jordon's. Jordon knew what the man was about to do. He'd done it himself more than once.

The man leaned away from the train, bent his knees a little, and let go. He hit the ground running, swinging his little bag, but easily maintaining his balance as he made an early departure from the slow-moving train.

Jordon watched as the man headed off down a path through the woods. Must be someone who lived nearby, Jordon figured, and just didn't want to ride on into the

Buxton depot, then have to walk back home.

Jordon leaned back and shut his eyes again, anxious to be home himself.

The station master at the Buxton depot remembered Milton Graham coming in on the evening train last Wednesday, the day Bitsy Trotter was killed. "Got off the 6:22." How could he be certain? "I was working the three-to-eleven shift last week. I know it was Wednesday, that's the evening my wife called, still haranguing me to get somebody to switch shifts with me on Thursday so I could be at my boy's birthday supper. While I was talking to her, listening to her actually, the train pulled in. And I looked up and there stood Mr. Graham. He wanted me to check to see if the railroad was planning any schedule changes. Said he liked riding the 6:22 when he comes back in from up north. It gets him home before too late."

"How was he dressed?" Jordon asked.

"Like always, spiffy."

"Suit and tie?"

The station master nodded. "Like always."

When he got home, Jordon immediately put through a call to Charlotte Braun. Lenarue was on the switchboard. Said she was all right. Then Charlotte came on the line. She checked her log. "Mr. Morris was here last Tuesday, getting some work done. But not on Wednesday." She was sure. It was in the book that way.

Jordon built a fire in the kitchen stove and put on a pot of coffee, trying to figure the best way to proceed.

Up to this point, the only thing he could actually prove was that Milton Graham had devised a scheme to siphon off money from Buxton's lumber business.

He poured himself a cup of coffee and sat down at the table to drink it and consider his options. It was important that whatever he did he think it through carefully. He had the distinct feeling he might only get one chance.

* * *

"I hear you're unemployed," Della said, offering one of her hundred dollar smiles as consolation.

Jordon smiled back at her and shrugged. "Life's a gamble. Lots of surprises if you play your hand right." After a moment he added, "Or if you don't."

"Maybe after next Tuesday, you'll be doing the hiring and firing."

"I could handle that."

Cassie came out of the back. "Oh," she said. "I didn't know you were here." Her voice was friendly.

"Man's got to eat," he said, standing up from the counter. "I think I'll sit over here," indicating a table near the window. "Bring me whatever you've got."

"It'll probably take a while," Della said. "We're mighty busy tonight." She swept her hand in a wide arc, taking in the almost empty room. "Thank God for Saturday nights."

In a couple of minutes, Cassie brought Jordon's dinner. A piece of fried rabbit, fried potatoes, pickled beets and a biscuit.

"I heard about you getting fired, Berk. I'm sorry. You're getting your share of trouble. I just wanted to say, if there's anything I can do . . . ."

"I don't know of anything. But thanks."

She was silent for a moment. "Well, if you think of something . . ."

"I'll let you know, Cass. Thanks again."

Since their day at the Overlook, he had been steering his mind away from thinking about her, not wanting to stare the loneliness in the eye. Letting himself get so close to her was not something he'd set out to do. Just the opposite. But it had happened anyway. Sometimes a man's life had a way of going where it wanted to, not where he said to go.

Cassie pulled out a chair. "You mind?"

"Of course not." He rose slightly.

She sat down. "Are you okay?"

"As you said, a few problems. But I reckon I'll manage."

After a moment she said, "I'm going home early. There's not that much to do here." Another pause, then, "Think I could hitch a ride with you?"

Jordon knew that sometimes Della drove her home, other times she took a taxi.

He wiped his mustache with a napkin, took a drink of coffee. "That'd be fine," he said.

Chapter Sixteen

JORDON OPENED THE DOOR for Cassie to get in, then went around and slid under the wheel. He pulled the car out of Della's parking lot, turned down the dirt road to the blacktop and headed for Cassie's. He drove in silence for a while, holding the car in close check as he rounded the curves on the road toward Buxton.

"You're mighty quiet," Cassie said.

"Just thinking," he said. "About this Trotter case. How in the last week it's gone from being my salvation to my damnation." He glanced in the rear-view mirror and saw the headlights of another car some distance back.

"You mean getting fired?" Cassie asked.

"Mostly. Noble's the one was elected high sheriff. That gives him the right to put me on whatever case he wants to. But the way he did a complete turnaround. First he said go to it, find out who killed her. By the way, he says, it ought to be good for your campaign when you solve it. Then he suddenly says move on to something else, leave it alone. When I said no, he said hand over your badge."

They arrived as Cassie's, and he parked in the little driveway by her house.

"What do you figure happened?"

He turned in the seat to face her. "Somebody leaned pretty

heavy on Noble. Somebody who wants me to drop this thing awful damned bad."

"You have any idea who?"

"Who has that kind of power? Noble is not exactly your average pussy cat. He's got power of his own. It's somebody big enough to make Noble sit up and pay attention."

"HR Buxton." There was no hint of uncertainty in Cassie's voice.

"And who would benefit most if I drop it?"

"Whoever killed Bitsy," she said without hesitation. "But you don't think HR Buxton would do anything like that, do you?"

"He might be trying to protect somebody else. Somebody important to him."

"Young Harry."

"Young Harry knew Bitsy Trotter. And it's pretty easy to imagine that HR would be highly distressed if his son and heir got caught with his britches down in a scandal involving the murdered pregnant daughter of a Buxton miner."

"So you think. . . ."

"I don't know what to think yet. I've found out some things in the last day or two that sure do complicate the picture."

"You're still digging around in it? Even though you're not working for the sheriff anymore?"

He took a deep breath, slowly exhaled, and leaned back in his seat. "I can't leave it the way it is. I just can't do that."

Cassie studied him for a minute. "Cup of coffee?" she asked.

He gave her a long, even look. "Sure. I'm getting so I can drink it all day and still sleep like a groundhog in January. I guess that ought to tell me something about how bone-tired I am. Or how old."

Inside Cassie's living room, Jordon leaned back on the sofa and stretched out his legs as she put coffee in the pot and set it on her little electric hot plate. She came out of the kitchen and sat beside him as they waited for the coffee to brew.

Jordon took her by the hand. "You remember that thing we were talking about a while back that I wrote down from Will Durant's book? Philosopher named Kant?"

"The part about the golden rule?" She smiled as she said it.

"Yeah, that."

She waited and when he said nothing, she asked, "What about it?"

"I've just been thinking how doing the right thing and doing what seems best for you don't always go hand-in-hand, do they?"

"Very often they don't."

"You come to a fork in the road."

She lifted his hand, put it to her face. "You've done what's right, Berk. And you'll keep on doing it."

He said nothing, just sat there staring into space. It still wasn't too late for him to talk to HR Buxton if that's what he wanted to do.

He turned toward Cassie, tilted her face to him and kissed her.

Outside, from the woods just behind the house, came the hoot of an owl. To a lot of old folks this was a sign that somebody close would die soon. Jordon felt a shiver run through Cassie's body. Even though you didn't believe in signs, and you'd heard hoot owls a thousand nights, you couldn't help remembering what folks said. Neither Jordon nor Cassie let on they'd noticed it, but it hung there in the air, a sign of death, whether you believed it or not.

A car door slammed out in the night, not far away.

"Coffee smells good," he said. He sat back and rubbed his legs, leaning his head on the back of the sofa. He closed his eyes. After a moment he said, "I've missed seeing you."

Cassie moved closer to him. "Me too."

He jumped a little when he heard it the first time.

"Jordon!" A man hollering for him. "Jordon!" Again,

louder. Outside somewhere. Near the front gate, it sounded like.

"Who could that be?" Cassie asked, her voice tight. "Who knows you're here?"

"It's not exactly a secret that I spend some time here. Till lately, that is." He stood up and walked toward the door. "Let's find out."

Cassie was up and at his side as he opened the door.

The light from inside the house silhouetted them in the doorway and streamed into the yard, reaching to the front gate and beyond.

Jordon couldn't see anybody.

"Who is it?" Jordon said, stepping out onto the porch. "What do you want?"

Cassie followed, her hand on his shoulder.

The first bullet struck the wall behind them at almost the same instant he heard the shot.

He turned halfway around, grabbed Cassie and jerked her to the floor. At the same time, he heard two more shots. Saw the muzzle blast from where the gunman was positioned across the road.

Another two shots rang out. He felt Cassie's body jerk. He was trying desperately to get her behind him and reach his pistol at the same time. His frantic fingers located the gun, clawed it out. He emptied it in the direction the shots were coming from.

He heard Cassie say, "Oh . . . Berk." Then, "Honey . . . I'm shot. Berk."

He looked at her and could see the widening stain on the front of her dress. Her right hand covered the place where the bullet had entered somewhere near her left breast. Blood oozed between her fingers. Her left arm dangled helplessly at her side. Her soft brown eyes were filled with terror.

"Berk . . . " she said in a thin, trembling voice, "am I hurt bad?"

He prayed he was telling her the truth when he said, "No,

baby. No." But he had no way of knowing.

He cradled her in his arms as his eyes scanned the area from which the shots had come. Whoever had been there was gone now, he figured. It wasn't the kind of person who'd want to stick around and shoot it out.

Anyway, getting help for Cassie was uppermost in his mind.

He let her down on the porch and grabbed the phone inside the door, giving the crank a jerk.

"Number, please."

He spoke sharply to the operator. "Get Doc Klein on the line!"

He listened for only a moment before interrupting to shout, "Goddammit, girl, get him up! This is an emergency. I don't give a damn if he delivered a hundred babies today. Cassie's been shot."

▽

Chapter Seventeen

JORDON SAT IN THE office of Milton Graham, who managed a thin smile from across the desk. "And what is it you wanted to see me about?" Graham asked.

"Why don't we get right down to it?" Jordon said.

Graham nodded, still holding his little smile.

"I know everything," Jordon said. "How you—"

Graham interrupted him. "Please keep your voice down."

Jordon lowered his voice. "I know how you've been feathering your nest with your C.B. Morris set-up. How the whole thing works. I can prove it in a court of law if I have to."

The telephone on Graham's desk rang and he answered it. He started talking to somebody about what sounded like some kind of emergency at the power plant.

Wondering how his plan was going to go, Jordon watched Graham and waited for him to finish. Jordon's head was a little foggy from lack of sleep, but his mind was clear about what he had to do. He'd decided on that as he sat up with Cassie through the night after Doc Klein had fixed her up.

"She's a lucky lady," Doc had said. "An inch or so more would have been a different story." But the bullet had gone clean through the fleshy part near her left armpit. Jordon dug it out of the wall, along with the others. From a high-powered 30-30 rifle.

Doc said she needed a lot of rest, and one of her cousins, a girl of seventeen or eighteen, had come this morning to stay with her.

Later, Jordon had gone home and sat at his own kitchen table and figured out what he was going to do.

He knew he would never be able to make a case in court that would stand up against Milton Graham for anything more than embezzling. Maybe not even that, considering everything. And he couldn't just sit and wait for Graham, or whoever he'd hired, to come for him again, or maybe Cassie, or Lenarue. That could happen at any time.

Jordon knew he had to play the hand he'd been dealt. And play it without delay.

Now, he watched Milton Graham talking on the phone, making business decisions. The round pudgy face, the fat lips, the sharp little eyes behind the thick glasses. Jordon was not sure of everything, but he knew he had to make a wager. Too much was at stake.

Graham finished his conversation and told his secretary not to put any more calls through except from Mr. Buxton himself. He looked at Jordon and said, "So if you know so much, Mr. Jordon, why did you come to me?"

"Because I don't want to see this thing go into court any more than you do."

It was only a moment until a flicker of understanding seemed to flash in Graham's eyes. He watched Jordon but said nothing.

Jordon continued. "I figure what you need, Mr. Graham, is a partner. Somebody who could help you handle all this extra business so it won't interfere with your many responsibilities here at the Buxton Corporation."

Graham continued to study him. "What do you have in mind?"

"A fifty-fifty partnership. All the way. I need you since you already have the operation going." Jordon waited a beat. "And Lord knows you need me. Lots of reasons. Right?"

At that moment, someone knocked on the door. "Yes?" Graham said. The door opened and Young Harry Buxton stuck his head inside. When he saw Jordon, his expression darkened. After a moment, he said to Graham, "It can wait. I'll talk to you later," and closed the door.

"I gather that Mr. Buxton Junior is no fwiend of yours," Graham said. "As a matter of fact, I'd say you don't have many fwiends awound here just now. You might be able to pwove wess in court than you think."

"It's not the number of friends that counts," Jordon replied. "It's the quality. Me, I have knowledge. Backed up by a certain set of documents stashed where absolutely nobody will ever find them but me. And that makes you my friend, right? Hell, with you as my friend, who else do I need?" He hoped he wasn't overplaying it.

Graham studied him for a moment. He seemed to make up his mind. "We can't talk any more here. It's too dangerous. We'll have to meet somewhere else."

"I'm easy to get along with," Jordon said. "Wherever you say."

Graham thought it over for a moment. "Some place where nobody is likely to see us together, maybe overhear us."

This was more than Jordon had hoped for. "You got such a place in mind?"

Again Graham took his time before answering. "How about the overlook at Chambers Hilltop? You know where I mean?"

"I do," Jordon said.

"Good. Tonight. Say eight o'clock? It'll be dark. We can talk it out then in pwivate."

Jordon said, "I'll be there."

"Alone, of course."

"Of course," Jordon said as he stood to leave. Then, in a stage whisper, "By the way, I'm a little short of cash right now. Campaign expenses. And I've been traveling some, too." He smiled at Graham. "Bring two thousand dollars with you tonight."

He could see the hatred in Graham's eyes as he nodded slowly and sat there behind his desk with his eyes narrowed to slits like a fat bald cat.

At the drugstore Jordon called to check on Cassie. The girl said she was resting okay.

Then he called Willis at the sheriff's office. "Thought I might drive by and see you after while."

"Ain't heard from you lately," Willis said. "Where you been? You wreck my car?"

"I'm real sorry about that," Jordon said, and hung up, just as Willis yelled, "What?"

The night was cold and clear, and you could see for miles down the holler in the moonlight. Jordon checked his watch again. 7:56. Unless he was wrong about Milton Graham, he would be punctual.

At just a minute before eight, Jordon saw the headlights of a car way down the road, coming across the Narrows. He leaned against Willis's car and waited.

Graham pulled in beside him and got out.

"Right on time," Jordon said.

"I believe in keeping commitments," Graham said. "You came alone, I see."

"Of course. I believe in keeping commitments, too."

"Are you carrying a gun?" Graham watched him closely.

"It's in the car," Jordon said. "I don't want to act like I'm suspicious of you. That'd be unseemly for business partners, wouldn't it?"

Graham took a step toward Jordon's car and glanced in the window. Jordon's .44 was lying on the front seat.

"You don't trust me?" Jordon said. "I'm kind of hurt."

"Just a pwecaution," Graham said, stepping back. "You're a man with a weputation."

"Well, hell, it's not all bad."

Graham started to speak, but held it. Then he said, "Now

exactly what is it you expect me to do?"

"What I said this morning. Fifty-fifty. Right down the middle." Jordon added, "By the way, what about the two thousand. Did you bring it?"

"We'll get to that in a minute. But first, tell me: what am I supposed to get out of this arrangement?"

"You get me as a partner. I'd never do anything to hurt my partner. You'd get my protection, so to speak."

"Protection from what?"

"Anything bad that could happen to you."

Graham said nothing.

Jordon watched him closely, but could see no sign of emotion. Graham was a cool sonofabitch. Maybe he didn't look like he was hard, but inside his pudgy body was a tough, clever man, playing his own hand. Jordon had learned long ago when he'd first started playing poker, sometimes the ones who looked the softest were the most ruthless of all. They'd rip you up one side and down the other without ever changing the expressions on their faces.

Finally, Graham spoke. "What kind of bad things are you thinking might happen to me, Jordon?"

"Let's say first of all, that your C.B. Morris scheme was to come out. That'd be a very bad thing for you. But with me as your partner, it'd be a bad thing for me too. So, I'd keep that from happening."

"How?"

"Well, I wouldn't say anything about it myself. Seeing that I do know about it." Jordon hesitated, then said evenly. "And, I'd be your insurance that nobody else would say anything about it, either."

"Just how would you go about that?"

Jordon looked at him steadily for a long moment, then said, "The same way you've done it."

"Which is?" Graham seemed compelled to know just how much Jordon had learned. Maybe he was afraid Jordon had talked to somebody else about the whole thing.

"Look, I'm tired of this," Jordon said. "I believe in saying what's on my mind. I know you killed Bitsy Trotter. And Rachel Blackwell. Let's don't stay here all night dancing around the mulberry bush."

"You're sure about all this?"

"I can prove you're C.B. Morris. Get your ass fired and sent to jail. As for Bitsy and Rachel, I know you killed them, and I may be able to prove it."

Graham laughed. "The sheriff believes Rachel's death was an accident. And I was out of town when Bitsy Trotter was killed, remember?"

"No, you went to a lot of trouble to make it look like you were out of town. Went to Cincinnati, stopped in the station after the 6:22 come in that day, made a point of talking to the station master. But that's not what really happened."

"Which was?"

"You took the late train out of Cincinnati on Tuesday night last week, wearing your C.B. Morris wig, dressed like a mountain man, I'd guess, with your suit in your grip. And you jumped off the train when it slowed down for the big bend and grade before it gets to Buxton. It's easy to do. I saw a man do it yesterday morning."

"And then?"

"You cut through the woods, waited till afternoon and met Bitsy Trotter at her little place behind where she lived. I don't know exactly how you got in touch with her, but that wouldn't have been too hard."

"And why would I have wanted to do that?"

"To get back the C.B. Morris letters, the stuff Bitsy took from your office that would have blown your scheme apart. My guess is you told her you'd pay her for them, quite a lot, so she could leave here. But instead, you killed her."

"Why would I have stabbed her and cut her up that way? That doesn't make sense."

"To make it look like a hot-blooded murder. Something that *wouldn't* make sense for somebody like you to do. But *would* look like something her high-tempered boyfriend Manochio would do. You knew about his temper, I figure, from hearing her and the other girls talk about him in the office."

"And Rachel?"

"You went there looking for the letters. Bitsy had left them with her because she was getting scared, I'd say. Maybe she told you Rachel had them, thinking it might keep you from hurting her there in the woods. Or maybe Rachel read them and decided to go in business for herself. Figured she could get some money out of you. People will do a lot of things for money these days. Look at Dillinger. Baby Face Nelson. Pretty Boy Floyd."

"Who else have you told all this to?"

"Just you. Up to now. I just got it all figured out. Everybody else seems satisfied to let the Three-C boy take the rap. And I didn't want to blow our partnership away."

In a casual, almost leisurely, movement, Graham reached inside his coat and pulled out a pistol. It looked like a .38 to Jordon.

Jordon said, "I see I'm right."

"You're very close, as a matter of fact," Graham said. "That's why I'm a wittle surpwised at you. You're smart enough to figure all this out, but not smart enough to know there's no way I could permit you to stay alive."

Jordon said nothing.

Graham went on. "When you told me this morning that you had the papers hidden someplace where nobody— 'absowutewy nobody,' you said—could ever find them, you made a big mistake. That's why I picked this pwace for us to meet. I knew you were twying to sucker me."

"How?"

Graham smiled. "I know more about you than you might expect. I know you wefused to go along with Mr. Buxton and Shewiff Tweadway and dwop your investigation of Bitsy's murder. And I knew you'd never go along with me, no matter

what you pwetended this morning. You're not as goddamn
smart as you think you are. I knew a 'partnership' as you
called it wasn't what you had in mind."

Jordon hesitated for a moment, then said, "My guess is,
you already have a partner, anyhow, don't you?"

For the first time, Graham's face showed surprise. "Why
do you say that?"

"I just don't think you could have pulled your lumber deal
off without somebody at the Buxton Corporation finding
out—or helping you out. And I think I know who it is."

Graham waited. "Well?"

"Young Harry Buxton," Jordon said. "He's the main lumber man in the company. The old man keeps him on a tight
leash financially. Pays him plenty by most folks's standards,
but I suspect it's never been enough for Young Harry and
his habits. So I kind of figure he either stumbled on to what
you were doing, or maybe even helped you set it up. Either
way, he gets a cut."

"Too bad you aren't smart enough to save your own ass."
Graham's voice was full of hatred.

"I'm sure Young Harry is smart enough to save his. I'll bet
he never put his name on anything, or took anything from
you except cash on the barrelhead. You'd do well to fix that
situation. Or someday, he'll hang your fat ass out to dry."

"Don't worry. I'll rearrange things after I'm finished with
you. I'll be leaving Stanton County soon, anyhow. I won't
need anybody then."

"Is that what made you set the whole thing up? You could
have left without that."

"I needed money. So I can live where I please, without my
whining wife, without ever having to come back here again.
Every time I go I hate to return. I should never have moved
here in the first place." Graham glanced around. "These
Godforsaken mountains."

"Some of us like it here," Jordon said.

"You're welcome to it."

"Another thing I was wondering about," Jordon said. "It was you, wasn't it, who put the screws to the sheriff to fire me. Not HR Buxton."

"It was me, for whatever good that does you now."

"There's just one other thing I would like to know," Jordon said. "Who tried to kill me last night? And shot Cassie? I don't think you have the balls to do it personally. Killing a girl or an old woman is one thing. But going up against a man with a gun is another."

For a moment Graham seemed about to lose control, but he relaxed and said, "Why should I take that kind of risk? The woods around here are full of men ready to do work like that. And some of them don't think too much of you. But that's another one of those things you don't need to trouble yourself over. Your string has just run out."

Jordon glanced toward the big rock off to the right. "How about it, Willis?" he said. "You reckon my string has run plumb out?"

Willis hopped from behind the rock, leaned on his crutches, and trained the double-barrel twelve gauge straight at Milton Graham's chest.

"I'd say you still got a little piece to go," Willis said.

Milton Graham looked dumbfounded.

At that moment, one of Willis's crutches lost its purchase on the ground and flew out from under him.

That's when the shooting started.

$$\bigtriangledown$$

Chapter Eighteen

WHEN WILLIS STARTED TO lose his balance after his crutch slipped, Graham saw him falling and looked back to Jordon. Graham fired a shot, but Jordon was already dodging for cover, and took the bullet in his arm.

At almost the same moment, Willis squeezed off a round from the shotgun, which was pointed up in the air as he fought against his fall.

Graham fired another shot in Jordon's direction, then spun around and ran for his car. From the ground, Jordon could see how fast he moved for a heavy man. Once in the automobile, Graham got it started, wheeled it around and spurted away, leaving a spray of dirt and loose gravel in his wake. Willis got off one shot at him with the twelve gauge. But Graham was on the road, speeding back toward the Narrows.

Jordon helped Willis get back up on his crutches. They headed after Graham in Willis's car.

Graham must have had it wide open as he reached the Narrows. They saw his car swerve, skid, hit the big pothole, then soar off the road in a graceful arc as it dropped from sight into the abyss.

They heard the crash and saw the flash of the explosion before they reached the place where he went over the side.

Jordon and Willis stood at the edge of the road on the Narrows and watched the ball of fire blazing in the hollow below.

Willis shook his head. "I reckon the sonofabitch must a had a hell of a ride down. To hell."

Turning to Jordon he said, "Come on, we better get you back into town and let Doc Klein fix your arm."

Jordon pulled on the tourniquet he'd made with his belt. The bullet had struck him in the left forearm. It was just now beginning to hurt like hell.

They got in the car with Willis under the wheel. "Some chauffeur you've turned out to be," he said. "First you run off for two or three days, and now you want me to drive. Just because your arm's shot up a little. Jesus."

"If you hadn't started dancing around on one crutch, I probably wouldn't have got shot," Jordon said. "Then I'd be driving and you wouldn't be bitching."

After a moment Willis said quietly, "I almost got both of us killed, didn't I?"

"Aah," Jordon said, tossing his head. "We're still here, aren't we?" He looked out the window into the night and ran back over the past few minutes in his mind. It was not exactly the way he had figured it would go.

It was better.

Doc Klein worked on the wound in Jordon's arm. "This late night stuff's wearing pretty thin," Doc said. "Is there some way you could arrange to have your shooting scrapes occur during the daytime?"

"I'll start planning them that way, Doc. Just so you can get your proper rest and concentrate on delivering babies and lancing boils."

"Lancing a boil is right important sometimes. Ask a man who's got one."

Willis sat nearby puffing on a Camel. "What I can't figure out is, how did you know it was Graham?"

"I didn't," Jordon said. "But I damn well knew I had to do
something. I went over everything in my mind sitting there
with Cassie all night after she was shot. The only thing I
was sure about was Graham's scheme to drain money off
through his phony company in Cincinnati. It finally came
down to betting that he was the killer, too. I didn't have a
good hand, but I had to play the cards I was holding."

"Be still," Doc said.

"Anyhow," Jordon continued, "I sat there with Cassie
going back over everything I'd done since I first went out to
where Bitsy's body was found. And I decided there were
several things that pointed to Graham."

"Like what?" Willis asked.

"The way Bitsy's and Rachel's bodies were found, for one
thing. Both of them were arranged too neat, almost like they
were on display or something. Not the way you'd expect
them to be, considering what had been done to them. I
remembered Graham's hobby of stuffing animals, posing
them, putting them on display."

"That's pretty thin stuff, seems to me," Willis said.

"True. But something else sort of tied into the same thing.
The day I went to Rachel's to talk to her, before she was
killed? I noticed a stuffed owl on her mantle. It looked like
it had just perched there for a spell. It didn't register on me
then that it might have been done by Graham. But when I
looked around after she was killed, I had the feeling something was missing. I just couldn't place what it was. Then,
setting up last night with Cassie, I thought it maybe was the
owl. I didn't remember it being there the second time."

"But you weren't sure."

"I was when I stopped back by Rachel's place this morning
and crawled in a window. It was gone."

"What did that prove?"

"Nothing. But it could have meant that Graham was there
and took it. Maybe not wanting anybody to connect him to
her."

"You think Graham give her the owl?"

Jordon shrugged. "More than likely she bought it from him to help her reputation for being a witch. She loved to put on her little show for everybody, make herself more interesting. Being an old woman is commonplace, but being an old witch is something else again. Good for her herb medicine business. Also, as far as I know, Graham was the only person around these parts doing taxidermy. It just kind of fit."

"I'll say one thing for you. You done a hell of a lot of far-fetched thinking last night."

"Cassie getting shot was far-fetched. The rest of it just came as I was sitting with her. I knew I had to do something."

"There must have been more in your mind than a stuffed owl," Doc said.

Jordon nodded. "Other little things. Like the message Rachel left for me at the switchboard. I figured Graham could have been the one that got it. He was over the telephone office. Had good reason to be around there. That could have tipped him off that Rachel was a threat. Same thing with my trip to Cincinnati. Graham could easily have found out about my long distance call to C.B. Morris and Company. That meant to him that I was getting close. So he had somebody take a shot at me when I got back."

Willis said, "Well anyhow, you put it all together enough to make Graham go for your sucker bet."

"None of the pieces by themselves meant a hell of a lot. But when I added them all up, it was the best I had. I figured that protecting his scheme for making money was reason enough for him to kill Bitsy and Rachel. And then when I thought back about watching a fellow jump off the train out there on the grade the other morning—was that just yesterday?—anyway, I saw how Graham could have done it, even though he was supposed to be out of town that day. My big problem was, I knew I'd never be able to prove it in court. I had to get him to make a move."

Willis scratched his head. "You told me Bitsy's body was found in one place in the woods, but that she was killed in another place. What was that all about?"

"I figure moving her body, plus the way he arranged her and Rachel, plus his deciding to take the owl back, these were all blunders made by a man who panicked when he got out of his depth."

"How do you mean?"

"Milton Graham was basically a man who was at home behind a desk. He could conjure up a scheme to build himself a small fortune buying and selling lumber through a phony company set-up. And he could put on a wig and play-act at being somebody else. But when he crossed over the line and committed murder, he was out of his element. I think he was trying to be clever, to throw suspicion on somebody else, like Abel Trotter, when he moved Bitsy's body to her little private place. Bitsy must have told him about it sometime or other, maybe just before she saw he was going to kill her. But, instead of putting distance between himself and the murders, he put himself closer to them. He was smart, and he made smart moves most of the time. But the mental burden of murdering somebody and trying to cover it up is often enough to muddle the thinking of an otherwise smart man. Desperate men do desperate things. And they often have unintended results." Jordon took a deep breath and expelled it slowly. He looked Willis in the eye. "At least that's the way I figure it. With Graham and Bitsy and Rachel all dead, some of it we'll never know about for sure."

"So you set your trap."

Jordon nodded. "I figured I'd make it impossible for him not to come after me. If he believed the letters would never be found after I was dead, he had no choice. I gambled that he was thinking straight enough to figure I'd never sell out to him. And he was desperate enough so that another murder didn't matter. He had to kill me. So when he picked the time and place, I felt pretty sure I was on target."

"You were the bait," Willis said.

"And you were the snare."

After a moment Willis said, "Deadfall is more like it." He shook his head. "I almost got us both killed. Me and my goddamned crutch. And Graham would have got away clean."

Jordon walked over to where Willis was sitting and put his hand on his shoulder. "What matters is that you *didn't* get us killed. That's twice you've pulled my chestnuts out of the fire now. And Milton Graham didn't get away."

"Because you played your cards right."

"And you backed me up. It was a good bet, that's all."

Doc spoke up. "Like all bets, there was an element of risk."

"Not just all bets. All of everything. You ought to know that better than the rest of us."

"I suppose I do."

"By the way, Doc," Jordon said. "A man gets his arm shot half off, don't you give him something to settle his nerves? This damn thing's starting to hurt."

"You've totally forgot about Prohibition?" Doc replied.

"Medicine, Doc, medicine. Anyhow, a fellow mentioned to me just the other day it's only a technicality or two before Prohibition's gone."

"So why worry about technicalities. Right?" Willis said.

"Exactly," Jordon said, watching Doc take a bottle and glasses from one of his cabinets.

"Get a glass for me, too, Doc," Willis said.

"What for?" Doc asked. "You weren't shot."

"Yeah, but I lost my leg. I know it's been a while, but . . . ."

Early the next morning, Jordon picked Willis up at home and the two of them drove, unannounced, to HR Buxton's office. HR's secretary kept eyeing the sling on Jordon's arm. From the way she sounded as she talked to HR on the interoffice phone, he was reluctant to see anybody. Finally

she said to Jordon, "You say it won't take long?" He nodded.
She said, "Go on in."

HR Buxton did not get up. "I've got a busy schedule
today," he said. "What is it?" He was making no effort at
cordiality.

Jordon and Willis stood in front of his desk. Jordon said,
"You know there was a car went off the Narrows last night?"

"What's that got to do with me?"

"You don't know who it was, then?"

"No. Do you?"

"Yes." Jordon said, and stopped.

HR waited, then said, "Well out with it, for Christ's sake.
I don't have time to waste on games."

"It was Milton Graham."

HR seemed stunned. When he spoke, his voice was less
impatient than before. "Are you sure?"

"We're sure," Willis said.

"How do you know?"

"We were there," Jordon said.

"You'd better sit down," HR said with a great sigh.

Willis let Jordon tell it. HR looked out the big picture
window at the square as Jordon laid it all out, everything
except his suspicions about Young Harry.

HR spoke to Willis. "What were you doing there?"

"I'm a deputy sheriff of this county," Willis said. "Jordon
asked me to go with him. He was a citizen with evidence
relating to embezzlement, two murders, assault with a
deadly weapon, attempted murder. It was my duty to go."
Willis smiled.

HR was silent for a while, then said, "So what now?
There's nobody to bring to trial. The man who did the killing
is dead. My thought is just let this thing be. Make nothing
more of it."

"I have to report it to the sheriff," Willis said.

"Of course," HR said. "I'm sure he'll see the wisdom of
keeping it quiet."

"I'm sure he will," Jordon said with a smile. "He has a lot of that kind of wisdom."

HR gave him a cold look, but let it pass. "Well, then, is that all?"

"Not quite," Jordon said. "There's the Three-C boy that's in jail."

"The sheriff will drop charges against him, no doubt."

"There's the matter of the embezzlement scheme."

"That was an offense against me, my company. As far as I'm concerned, justice has been done. It's a private matter."

"Embezzlement is a felony, a crime against the Commonwealth."

"Damn it, man, there's nobody to press charges against. I don't want any publicity about this."

"I don't feel like things ought to be swept under the rug," Jordon said. "Graham ought to be known for what he was, dead or alive. I expect the papers in Lexington and Louisville will most likely be interested in a story like this. You know, 'Those Primitive Mountaineers Killing One Another Again.' That kind of thing."

It was a while before HR spoke. "You still interested in winning the election?"

"That's why I'm running."

HR tried to smile, but it didn't come off. "My mind's not closed to helping you." After a moment he added, "Yet."

"With or without your help, Mr. Buxton, I aim to win. And I aim to see that folks know who killed Bitsy Trotter and Rachel Blackwell."

HR looked at him with distaste. "You are, by God, an obstinate man. You never quit, do you?"

"I seem to recollect you said something like that once before."

"Would you consider an arrangement of some kind where you did some, say, press agent type work for me? Maybe help me keep bad news out of the press?"

"You have a way with words," Jordon said. "No, I wouldn't

consider that."

"Then what if—"

Jordon shook his head and stood up.

HR said, "Then I guess we'll see who's right next Tuesday, won't we?" His voice was like frost on the side of the mountain.

Jordon and Willis turned toward the door. Just before he went out, Jordon looked back. HR Buxton's face was flushed and his lips were compressed in a tight line.

"One other thing," Jordon said. "You might want to think about giving Young Harry a raise. I'm sure he makes good money, working for his daddy and all. But just the same, I'm not sure it's enough."

Jordon followed Willis through the door and down the hall.

"Say what you will about him, that old bastard's got a lot of balls," Willis said.

Jordon nodded. "About twenty pounds apiece, I'd say."

$\triangledown$

Chapter Nineteen

ELECTION DAY DAWNED CLEAR and cool but soon clouded over. It looked like a period of cold rainy days might be about to begin. Jordon dreaded to think about it, though he knew it was a part of late fall and winter in the mountains. Such days always seemed to push his spirits right down into his socks.

He drove past a number of the polling places and could see the voter turnout was heavy. He had no idea whether this was good or bad for his campaign. But a number of people waved to him, and this gave him some basis for hope.

He went by Doc Klein's to get the dressing on his arm changed. "Cassie seems to be coming along, day by day, doesn't she?" Jordon said.

"She's healthy. She'll be all right if I can keep her from trying to do too much too soon. But, hell, that's a problem with all patients, including you."

"After today I may find myself with plenty of nothing to do, Doc."

"Politics is not my strong suit," Doc said as he finished with Jordon's arm. "But folks tell me the sheriff's race is close."

"Right down to the wire, it looks like."

That night when he got to the courthouse, he found cars

and wagons parked in every available space, horses and mules tethered to trees, posts and even cars.

He eased Willis's Model A into one of the spaces reserved for the sheriff and walked through the darkness to the back entrance.

Inside, the broad hallways were packed with people, mostly men, but a few women and children, all come to witness the counting of the ballots. Jordon made his way through the throng to the sheriff's office and found Willis sitting behind the desk in a fog of tobacco smoke.

"Any news?" Jordon asked.

"The northern precincts are coming in fast," Willis said, "and it don't look that good. Maybe the south of the county will bring it up."

Jordon sighed. "I guess I better dust off my Bicycles. I may have to start running a game down at Cory's."

"It ain't over yet," Willis said.

"I think I'll walk upstairs," Jordon said and went out into the hall. He made his way to the stairs and tried to push through. Somebody recognized him and shouted, "Sheriff coming through."

Another man looked and said, "Hell, Jordon. You ain't sheriff yet. Matter of fact, you ain't even a deputy right now."

Jordon laughed. "Sheriff or not, Harvey, move your ass over and let me through."

Harvey chuckled and pushed against the mass of bodies to clear a path. Jordon inched his way to the top of the stairs and into the courtroom where the election officials had set up their tables and charts to tally the votes as the ballot boxes were brought in from the precinct polling places.

Jordon had two of his own people in the room to observe the count, as did the other candidates. One of Jordon's people, Sally Duvall, spotted him and waved. He watched her for some sign of how the count was going. She stared at him for a moment, then frowned and shook her head.

Jordon felt a hand on his shoulder and turned to look into

the face of his opponent, John Bill Trumble. John Bill was a large, soft-looking, stoop-shouldered man who wore army khakis all the time. His oversize skull had always reminded Jordon of a great hound-dog's head. Big ears and sad, droopy eyes completed the picture. Underneath this exterior, Jordon knew, John Bill was needle sharp and as mean as a striped snake when he needed to be.

"Come to be present in person at the massacree?" John Bill said with a grin. His false teeth fit so poorly they clicked wildly and the uppers dropped down every time he spoke.

"Your breath stinks, John Bill," Jordon said. "Come to think of it, so does the rest of you."

John Bill never stopped grinning, but his sad eyes glittered. "That's no way to talk to the next sheriff of Stanton County," he said.

"The vote's not in yet," Jordon said.

"Might as well be. No way you can catch up with me without getting ninety percent of what's still out." John Bill hesitated a moment before adding, "And my people around the county promise me that ain't going to happen."

"Speaking of your people, I've been hearing some disturbing things some of them been saying about me," Jordon said.

"Like what?" John Bill acted surprised.

"Like when I was over in Hazard—" Jordon's voice was drowned out when a shout went up from the crowd as another precinct's results were handed from the table to be posted on the wall.

"Didn't catch what you was saying," John Bill said, cocking his ear and cupping his hand to it.

"I said some of your people have been telling folks I pistol-whipped some boys over at Hazard. And it's a goddamned lie—pure and simple. I never pistol-whipped a man in my life."

"You sure it was friends of mine said it?"

A couple of men nearby were leaning in closer. Jordon made no effort to prevent their hearing. "Well, I'm damned sure they weren't friends of mine," he said. "I'm also sure you already know about this and know it's a damned lie."

John Bill shook his head slowly, as if he were sorely grieved at Jordon's tale. "You still ain't learnt, have you?"

"Learned what?" Jordon asked.

"Lies and truth ain't what elections is about."

"What then?"

"Elections is about winning and losing, boy. Truth ain't got nothing to do with it. A feller ain't learnt that, he's better off staying home with the women and chillern. He don't know enough yet to be out in the world by his self."

Jordon felt the hotness inside his belly rising. "Lies are part of what I had to fight in this goddamned election," he said. "And I think you and your people had a lot to do with them."

John Bill shook his head again. "Well, it's all over but the shouting, now. Makes no difference what was said in the campaign."

"It makes a damn sight of difference to me," Jordon said. He felt he needed to get the hell out of here before he rammed his fist down John Bill's throat.

John Bill just stood there looking at him with his sad hound-dog eyes.

Not trusting his ability to control himself any further, Jordon set his jaw and pushed John Bill aside, making his way through the crowd and downstairs. If anybody said anything to him along the way, it was lost on him. Outside in the fresh night air on the porch, he inhaled deeply and tried to let the tightness in his body drain out.

But it would not go. He walked down the courthouse steps, past men lounging against cars and wagons, and on to where he'd parked, barely hearing the several greetings that met him.

He fired up the car and backed it out with a spurt, throwing gravel so a nearby couple had to leap out of the way.

He turned the car onto the road and headed for Della's. Later, before midnight, he went on home. By then the returns had dwindled down to a trickle. But it was nearly four in the morning when he finally got to sleep.

Chapter Twenty

Jordon STEERED HIS CAR into the drive at Cassie's and switched off the engine. For a minute he sat there, still torn between his need to see her and his uneasiness over things he knew they had to talk about. Today was a day different from yesterday, in ways that went beyond mere time.

He took out his watch and fingered its worn gold case, remembering the day he'd bought it in Knoxville more than twenty years before.

It was nearly one-thirty in the afternoon. Unable to delay any longer, he got out of the car and went to the door, giving his little tap . . . tap-tap trademark knock. The girl, Cassie's cousin, opened the door and let him in. "She's in her bedroom, Mr. Jordon. Said if you showed up, tell you to come on in."

Cassie was sitting up on top of the covers of the freshly made bed. Across her legs lay a patchwork quilt. It was a lot like the one his Aunt Laurie had given him and Vera when they were married. In another life, it seemed. So long ago.

"I heard already," Cassie said. "Della called and told me."

He nodded.

"How do you feel?" she asked.

He grinned a little. "As the fellow said, it hurts too much to laugh and I'm too old to cry." Then, seriously, "I'm okay.

I'm more interested in how you feel."

"Better. Doc Klein was by earlier. Changed the dressing. He keeps saying its going to heal fine. No serious effects. Except I'll have that nice dimple in my chest for the rest of my life."

"I like dimples." He swung his bandaged arm out of the way and leaned awkwardly over to kiss her. "We look like a couple of wounded birds." He found it hard to talk about her being shot. It had been so close. An inch or two. "You seem a little pale," he said. "You sure you're doing everything Doc says?"

"Of course. He says I can go outside for a little fresh air as long as it's not too cold. Which is exactly what I'd like to do right now."

"You certain it's all right?"

She smiled at him. "Here. Help me up." She reached to him for support.

He put his good arm around her waist and walked her outside. The sun warmed their faces as they made their way slowly to the bench in the corner of the yard by the rose bush. This lovely day was a rare gift so late in the year.

"Have you thought about what you're going to do now that it's over?" she asked.

"I keep putting it off. I'd hoped early on that I'd win. But toward the end I didn't have much hope it'd turn out that way. The money had already done its work. Nothing could have stopped it, I guess."

"You don't seem too disappointed."

"It's funny, but maybe I'm a little bit relieved. Not that I don't think I'd have made a good sheriff. Or that I'd have found it too much. But something else I now realize. Began to feel it when they really started to put the screws to me." He reached into his pocket, took out a peanut, and sat holding it. "Being sheriff's not what it was about."

A breeze carrying a little chill swept past them. Cassie drew her coat collar up around her neck. She smiled at him.

"I don't want to sound like I think I'm a saint," he said. "We both know that's not so. Lot's of other folks know it, too." He looked away from her, toward the woods now barren of leaves, the trees standing like hundreds of black sticks plunged into the earth.

"Some of us think you're not so bad," Cassie said, her voice very low. "You did what you had to do."

"I guess that's what I was trying to say. When it got right down to it, doing what I felt like I had to do was more important to me than the election. All my life I've watched working people live by rules they think they have to live by, doing things they don't like but think they've got to do. And all the time the Milton Grahams and HR Buxtons of this world ignore the rules, stretch the law a little here, pay no attention to it at all someplace else. And when they push it to the limit and cross the line, they get Tom William Knox or Marlow Clayton or one of the other slick-tongues around the courthouse to take care of it."

She held his arm and snuggled closer to him. They watched a small flock of birds rise from their perch in a gnarled old oak across the road, make a graceful dip and then swerve away south toward the river. "According to the signs we'll get an early snow," Cassie said. "That's what Momma says."

Jordon nodded. "Maybe this whole thing's just been more of my bullheadedness. Born in me, I guess. I can't stand to have something rammed down my throat. When they tried to make me stop, I knew I couldn't give it up. Not then, and not ever. Most of the time people with money and power buy whatever they want." He took a deep breath and let it out slowly. "For once, anyhow, it didn't turn out that way."

"Because of you."

He didn't say anything.

After a little bit Cassie said, "I saw the story the *Courier-Journal* ran."

He looked at her and nodded.

Cassie studied his face. When she spoke again, her voice was husky. "What you did is more important than being sheriff. You did what was right. I know that. And you know it. And other people know it, whether they voted for you or not." In a moment she added, "I'm proud of you. And you must be proud of yourself."

Jordon's reply was slow in coming. "Not proud, exactly. But satisfied."

Her eyes were misty. She squeezed his arm. "I'm glad you're not going to be high sheriff. I hope that doesn't make you mad."

"I still have to make a living, Cass. Gambling and being a lawman are all I know. They'll be needing some new deputies over in McCreary County. Whitley County, too. Maybe I'll look into that."

She smiled her weak smile and gazed out across the field and into the woods.

Jordon cleared his throat and coughed a little. "We talked about coming to some understanding about us once the election was over. I'm ready to take that up whenever you are."

She studied him for a moment before she spoke. "Is that what you want to do?"

"If it's what you want." It surprised him a little that he wasn't uneasy saying it.

She looked at him a long time. "Right now I'm happy enough just being alive," she said softly.

The birds had veered from their course toward the river and were swooping back for another turn around the big oak.

Cassie was a little unsteady as she got to her feet and gathered her coat about her. "There's a chill coming on out here." She put her arm around Jordon's waist and leaned against him. "Let's go to the house," she said. "It's warmer inside."

If you have enjoyed this book and would like to receive details of other Walker mystery titles, please write to

Mystery Editor
Walker and Company
720 Fifth Avenue
New York, NY 10019